Sound
the Retreat

Also by SIMON RAVEN

Novels
The Feathers of Death
Brother Cain
Doctors Wear Scarlet
Close of Play

Alms for Oblivion Sequence
The Rich Pay Late
Friends in Low Places
The Sabre Squadron
Fielding Gray
The Judas Boy
Places Where They Sing

Essays
The English Gentleman
Boys will be Boys

Plays
Royal Foundation and other Plays

Sound the Retreat

A NOVEL

SIMON RAVEN

BEAUFORT BOOKS
Publishers
New York

Copyright © 1971 by Simon Raven

Library of Congress Cataloging-in-Publication Data

Raven, Simon, 1927–
Sound the retreat.

Reprint. Originally published: London : Blond, 1971.
1. India—History—20th century—Fiction. I. Title.
(PR6068.A9S6 1986)   823'.914   85-26747
ISBN 0-8253-0343-5

Published in the United States by Beaufort Books Publishers, New York.

Printed in the U.S.A. First American Edition, 1986

10 9 8 7 6 5 4 3 2 1

CONTENTS

Sound the Retreat

PART ONE

THE ASPIRANTS

LATE IN NOVEMBER 1945, as His Majesty's Troop-Ship *Georgic* was approaching Port Said, the O.C. Troops said to the Captain:

"No shore leave for the Cadets, I think. They'd only go and get clap."

"Or worse," the Captain said.

"Precisely. But I think we ought to arrange some kind of treat for them. To make up."

"I know," said the Captain; "we'll have a conjurer on board."

"But we *always* have a conjurer on board at Port Said."

"The Cadets aren't to know that. They'll think that it is, as you say, a treat."

And so at Port Said the usual Egyptian mountebank was engaged to come on board and entertain the 300 Officer Cadets. This he did in the First Class Lounge, which would not be needed that day since all the Officers, and for that matter almost everybody else except the Cadets, had gone ashore, despite the risk of getting clap. All this, as the O.C. Troops had foretold, had made the Cadets feel left out and resentful, so that at first they were in no mood to pay attention to a smelly old Gyppo and his nursery magic. There were sullen and sceptical faces everywhere; much blowing of noses and shuffling of feet.

The Egyptian, being used to sullen audiences on Troop-Ships which were heading East, was not at all put out when his first offering – streams of coloured handkerchieves hauled out of his capacious sleeves – was received with something like a jeer. He simply went to the second item in his programme (an old routine of smashing eggs into a fez and pulling out live chickens in lieu), fully conscious that this too would be received with contempt, which at this stage was just what he wanted. And so with his third trick, his fourth and his fifth – the last being greeted with unrestrained booing, which fell sweetly on the magician's ears; for from this he knew that at last he had the spectators in exactly the frame of mind (mutinous and sceptical) which had always been most propitious to the illusion which he now proposed to work on them : an illusion which, by contrast with what had gone before, would so surprise and delight the Cadets that they would crowd round him with admiring smiles and liberal handfuls of coinage before waving him with honour on his way.

The trick which he was about to perform, though it was the pride of his repertoire, was in essence very simple. He would put one of his audience under an hypnotic spell and would order him to get into a coffin, which would then, with much ceremony, be closed, hammered down, weighted and thrown overboard by the magician and three apprentices. After the off-loading and sinking of the coffin and much keening by the Egyptians, the ship would be searched, and at length the victim would be found to have been 'resurrected' from the deep, usually in some faintly ridiculous posture, e.g. sitting on a lavatory seat. (As for the coffin, this was subsequently recovered by diving boys at nugatory expense.) Over the years, the conjuror had found that this combination of the macabre and the facetious had a particular appeal to British audiences, and since the mechanics had never once failed him, it was with absolute confidence that he now went into his preliminary stratagems.

"Gully, gully, gully," he articulated : "please will one gallant officer come forward as volunteer."

The Cadets were not put into better humour by his affecting to believe that they were officers. Nobody moved.

"Gully, gully," wailed the old charlatan, rather pathetically; "one gentleman . . . please . . . please."

It was at this stage that Peter Morrison arose, a large and slightly shambling Cadet with a huge round shining face. In fact Morrison was more bored than most by this performance, considering it to be not only inept in itself but of a kind suited only to the frivolous; yet at the same time, knowing that it was what his superiors had ordained for him, he felt it to be his duty to show an interest and try to keep the show going. He was also rather sorry for the conjurer, who seemed to be having a thin time. All of which being so, Morrison got up and approached the magician, who welcomed him with open arms and a low salaam, and at once began to hypnotise him.

Since Peter Morrison was a young man of intelligence and iron will-power, this might have been very difficult. But because he was keen to help, and also rather curious to find out what would happen, Morrison allowed himself to sink into an apparently trance-like state (while in truth keeping all his faculties) and was the better able to sustain his pretence as he had once seen a hypnotist at work on his victim in a music hall in Norwich during the war. When ordered into the coffin, he obeyed with sombre dignity; and even while the lid was being closed over him (an experience to perturb the most sanguine) he continued to simulate the repose which befitted his role.

There was now a hammering of nails and a wailing of neophytes for two full minutes, during which time the bottom of the coffin swung downwards and deposited Morrison in the cushioned interior of a hollow catafalque with a small thud which went unheard in the prevailing racket. The coffin bottom then swung upwards and clicked back into position, as did the false and velvet-covered top of the catafalque, which was similarly hinged and sprung. By this time Morrison had a pretty fair notion of what was to happen and was resigned, as he always had been, to letting the whole affair take its foolish but innocuous course.

And so, doubtless, it would have done, but for just one divergent factor. All went smoothly – the funeral procession down to 'C' deck, the sinking of the weighted coffin and the smuggling of Peter Morrison from the empty lounge – until the assistants so charged came to arrange Morrison for his 'resurrection'. Since their master had ordained that on this occasion the victim should be discovered supine on a dining room table and stripped down to his underpants, and since they had good reason to suppose that Morrison was still under trance, they started to undress him cap-à-pié. Nor would Morrison have resisted this, for it was respectfully done and he was a good-humoured boy who could take a joke at his own expense, had it not been that through some inadvertence of the ship's laundry he was without underpants on that particular day. When, therefore, the Egyptians began to remove his uniform trousers, he remonstrated firmly both with voice and gesture; whereupon the apprentices, startled by such sudden autonomy in one whom they had thought to be no more than a breathing corpse, fled screaming and cackling on to 'C' deck to find the sorcerer in chief.

He, meanwhile, was enjoying some esteem. As always happened, the contrast between the shabbiness of his earlier tricks and the impressive scope of this one had considerably enlivened his audience. A clever piece of ventriloquism had raised a scream from the coffin as it sank, and there were even those who hoped that Peter Morrison, whether through the malice or incompetence of the conjurer, had indeed been sent to the bottom. It would make something to write home about. All, therefore, were eagerly awaiting the next stage in events – when the assistants came gibbering along the deck and fell at the feet of their master.

The latter, when he understood what had happened, was perturbed. That Morrison should come out of the trance (as the magician saw it) before being woken by the person who had put him into it was unprecedented and might be dangerous. The worry and displeasure on the mountebank's face, being clearly genuine, at once communicated themselves to the Cadets . . . who correctly deduced that something had gone wrong, incorrectly concluded that this could only mean harm of some kind to Morrison, and then, in tones which variously conveyed dismay, indignation, fear, affection, racial hatred and pessimistic relish, demanded an explanation. Since none, in the circumstances, would have been audible, the magician was somewhat relieved when Peter himself now appeared to provide one with his presence. But as it turned out the explanation thus rendered was inopportune; for Peter, regretting his disruption of the assistants and wishing to provide an appropriate climax to the trick, had soaked himself in a sea-water shower, in order to give the impression that he had indeed returned *de profundis*. All of which would have been well enough, had it not been for the current mood of the audience. For the Cadets, having watched the magician become more nervous every moment and being convinced by now that something was badly amiss, remembering, also, the terrible scream from the coffin, instantly assumed that the dripping Peter had in truth been submerged in it and had only been saved by his own resource and exertion. This ridiculous notion would never, of course, have persisted for more than a few seconds; but before those seconds were up, a mass of Cadets, led by Peter's friend Alister Mortleman, had cruelly man-handled the luckless wizard to the gangway and thrown him headfirst into a lurking bumboat, which folded together, on the impact, like a closing penknife, and sank in ten seconds flat.

"Now then," said the O.C. Troops: "I am commanded to make an. enquiry into yesterday's little affair. Stand easy, gentlemen, please."

The O.C. Troops looked up reproachfully at the ten Cadets who were crowded into his day cabin, then screwed in his monocle and started to read the paper in front of him:

" 'It has been deposed before the British Consul in Port Said by Mustapha Duqaq, professional magician, that on the 25th day of November, 1945, being by official invitation on board His Majesty's Troop-Ship *Georgic* in the harbour of Port Said, he, Mustapha Duqaq, was flung by a party of Officer Cadets from the deck of the aforesaid vessel into a small boat, his own property, which was waiting to carry him off: that he himself sustained bodily injuries to the value of 73 pounds sterling and 14 shillings—' "

"—Sir," said Alister Mortleman, coming to attention like the clap of doom, "how could he possibly have worked that out so quickly?"

"Don't interrupt," said the O.C. Troops, blinking behind

his monocle. " '. . . That his boat, value 270 pounds sterling, was stove and sunk, that items of equipment pertaining to his profession and valued at 185 pounds sterling were lost or damaged beyond recovery—' "

"—But all his equipment was in the First Class Lounge, sir—"

"—Pray don't interrupt, sir. '. . . And that two of his servants, who were manning the boat, were drowned; estimated value one pound and ten shillings sterling *per caput*. It is desired that these allegations be investigated forthwith and that those responsible for the assault be placed under close arrest. An immediate report will then be rendered to both the Civil and the Military Authorities in Port Said, the latter of which will instruct you as to arrangements for handing over the culprits to the appropriate Egyptian authority. I am, Sir, di-da, di-da, J. Kershaw, Brigadier, B.M.C., Port Said.' You see," said the O.C. Troops petulantly, "what your little prank has ended up in?"

"But, sir, we didn't mean—"

"—For Christ's sake, man, shut up. Every time you open your mouth, you make things harder all round. . . . That's better," said the O.C. Troops, as apprehensive silence ensued. "Now, gentlemen: we are going to hear the principal witness of what occurred, Sergeant W. T. Pulcher of the Military Police. Listen to him carefully and do *not* interrupt."

"Can we cross-examine him later, sir?"

"If you want to"—this with an unexpected giggle: "S'arnt-Major, bring in Sergeant Pulcher."

". . . Leeft, right, leeft, right, halt."

". . . State your evidence, S'arnt Pulcher."

"SIR. On the 25th of November I was keeping the gangplank with the Ship's Officer of the Day. At approximately 1515 hours there was a yelling and a screaming like a load of banshees, and a crowd of Officer Cadets runs up with what looks like a bundle of manky washing, and chucks it past my lughole into the harbour. SIR."

"But in fact the bundle of washing was an Egyptian?"

"Sir."

"Didn't you recognise him?"

"No, sir. Just some thieving Gyppo – that's what I thought."

"But, Sergeant. The conjurer comes on board every time we drop anchor in Port Said, and you've been on this ship for over a year. You must know him by now."

"Sorry, sir. All them wogs are all the same to me."

"What about the Ship's Officer? Did he recognise him?"

"Ship's Officer, sir, had gone to drain his snake."

"Well then . . . could you recognise any of the Cadets responsible? Are there any here, for example?"

Sergeant Pulcher surveyed the Cadets with the courteous disdain of a reigning prince in a brothel. "Sorry, sir," he said at length, "but all them Cadets are all the same to me."

"So you can't help me any further?"

"No, sir."

"And do any of you gentlemen wish to cross-examine? No? Dismiss, please, S'arnt Pulcher. . . ."

"So," said the O.C. Troops a few minutes later, "no one saw properly what happened, and no one recognised the victim or any of his assailants. And yet those assailants, with perhaps one or two exceptions, are all in this cabin before me now. So someone, you deduce, must have recognised them after all. Ponder this mystery, gentlemen. An informer from your own ranks? Perish the thought. Myself? I was ashore. One of my staff? So were all of them – except, of course, for Sergeant Pulcher. Who has a wife and five children in Wolverhampton, gentlemen, and might appreciate a testimonial of how much you have enjoyed your voyage – when, that is, we arrive at Bombay in two weeks' time."

The O.C. Troops paused for this to sink in.

"Yet although evidence is so scanty, gentlemen, I can assure you that this would not be the end of the affair, were it not" – he glanced through a porthole – "that we are now safely out in the Red Sea. You may perhaps wonder why the ship was not detained at Port Said or Suez. The answer can only be that someone . . . someone or other . . . must have been dilatory. With the result that instead of a full scale police investigation, with the conjurer in person to assist, all we have to deal with is this radio message." He flourished the paper from which he had been reading earlier. "In short, the whole matter is now left to me."

The O.C. Troops lit a cheroot and glinted through his monocle.

"And since I can discover nothing, nothing can be done. No one can be sent back to Egypt, even if there were the means to send him. Although serious damage has been done, although two Egyptians have been drowned – and all because of a childish panic which in aspirant officers was a scandal and a degradation – yet nothing at all will be done. You know why not, gentlemen?"

"Because," Alister Mortleman began, "there aren't any witnesses to—"

"—For God's sake don't be a bigger fool than he made you."

The O.C. Troops inhaled a lungful of smoke and sent it back at the Cadets in a thin, hissing stream.

"There are just two reasons, gentlemen, why nothing will happen to any of you. First, because we – the British – are still in control. We may not be for long, we certainly shan't be for ever, but for the time being we are still able to arrange things to our liking at ports like Said and Suez and in countries like Egypt.

"And the second reason why you are being protected is that while on this ship you are my men. That you are also Officer Cadets makes no difference – I would do just the same for private soldiers. You are my men, I am charged to bring you safe to Bombay, and I *will not* leave any of you behind in Egypt or anywhere else. It is, you might say, a matter of honour; for the first and the last obligation which an Officer owes to those under him is *never*, in any circumstance whatsoever, to desert them. I give you good afternoon, gentlemen. Mr Morrison, you will be so good as to stay a moment. . . ."

When the rest had gone, Peter was invited to sit down.

"Now then," said the O.C. Troops; "none of this was really your fault, but I should like to give you a warning."

"Yes, sir?" said Peter, part smug and part resentful.

"Yes, sir. You see, once having embarked on a certain course – in this case, that of helping the conjurer by pretending to be hypnotised – you should have seen it through. Unless a grave emergency had arisen."

"It did arise, sir. I told you. Those Egyptians were going to uncover my private parts."

"Their intention was innocent."

"But everyone would have seen."

"Don't be such a baby," said the O.C. Troops. "Only the lower classes bother about that. And there's another thing. After you'd scared those Egyptians off, you decided to douse yourself in a shower. Why?"

"I *told* you, sir. Although I didn't care for being mucked about like that, I wanted to make the trick end well."

"Very commendable. But what you were doing, Morrison, was this. You were obtruding an additional factor into a situation of which you were totally ignorant. A very dangerous thing to do."

"I knew pretty well what was meant to happen."

"But you didn't know what was actually happening. You didn't know that out on deck that conjurer was in trouble. Or why. And so you did the one thing which was bound to make the trouble worse : you made a dramatic appearance that confirmed those boys in their wildest suspicions and turned them into a mob."

"I hadn't the slightest intention—"

"—My dear fellow, of course you hadn't. No one ever has. But all this fuss would have been avoided if only you'd obeyed the old rule : – never interfere. That was your crime, Morrison; you *interfered*; you did the wrong thing – the most calamitously wrong thing – for what you thought was the right reason. So be warned. It happens every day," said the O.C. Troops, "and every day it brings another promising military career to abrupt termination."

"That O.C. Troops," said Alister Mortleman : "a smooth performer."

"What they call a man of the world," said Barry Strange.

"Devious," said Peter Morrison.

The three of them were leaning over the rail and watching the flying fishes. These they found pretty sad entertainment after the first thirty seconds or so, and disillusionment had led to moroseness.

"He has simply taken advantage of his position," Peter went on, "to fix the whole thing."

"Just as well for me, I s'pose," said Mortleman, who was tall and very chunky in his jungle green shorts.

"And for me," said Barry, who looked like a radiant fourth former on Sports Day, his golden hair well matched by golden thighs.

"His example is a disgrace," said Peter, whose shorts hung down dismally below the knee. "How can one expect Cadets to treat Indians properly if they see a senior Officer behaving like that to Egyptians?"

"Behaving like what?"

"Ignoring their appeal for justice."

"I expect he thought it didn't really matter," said Barry very sincerely, "because Egyptians are so immoral and disgusting. But Indians are so much decenter – you know, loyal and clean – that we shall *want* to be nice to them."

"Shall we?" said Alister. " 'All them wogs are all the same to me,' " he quoted.

"You shouldn't use that word," said Peter primly. "It means that you consider them inferior, like Sergeant Pulcher or the O.C. Troops."

"I *do* consider them inferior. And for Christ's sake stop nagging on about the O.C. Troops. If it hadn't been for him, me and Barry and the rest might be rotting in a dungeon in Port Said."

"I suppose," said Barry, "that we really have heard the last of it? I mean, there won't be people waiting to arrest us at Bombay?"

"You heard what the gentleman said. They wouldn't know who to arrest."

"You're sure, Alister?"

"I'm sure, Barrikins."

"What do you think, Peter?"

"I think," said Peter, "that you've both been very lucky—"

"—We did it for you, for Christ's sake—"

"—And that it's up to you to redeem yourselves now that you've been given a second chance."

"Oh dear," said Alister. "I do see why you were head of your house at school. Heavy."

"Dependable," said Barry, and looked shyly at Peter.

"Bossing. It was the same at my place. If you went round all the boys and chose the ten longest faces with those spiteful sort of sticking out teeth, they'd be the ten heads of houses."

"Peter's teeth don't stick out. And his face is round."

"It gets a bit ovoid from time to time. He's bound to be made a J.U.O. when we reach Bangalore."

"J.U.O.?"

"Junior Under Officer. Responsible to the Platoon Commander for the conduct and turn-out of the Platoon."

"In which case," Peter said. "I'll have to do something about my own shorts."

He started to turn them up on the inside.

"Do you think I could do this and then sew them?"

"Don't you bother," said Alister. "We shall be refitted with new kit at the Transit Camp near Bombay, and then with still another lot when we get to Bangalore."

"How do you know?"

"Sergeant Pulcher told me. No one ever comes to the Far East, he said, without getting at least three different issues of tropical kit. Dhobi-man's shit, he called it."

"Dhobi-man?"

"Indian for washerman."

"But surely," said Barry, who had a careful mind, "it won't be worth issuing us with new stuff at the Transit Camp if they're going to change it again at Bangalore."

"We may be at the Transit Camp for months," Alister said.

"Nonsense," said Peter: "we are due at Bombay on December nine and at Bangalore not later than December sixteen."

"The official version, Peterkin. But people get lost in transit camps. They get forgotten. Every day," Alister said, "they go to the office for a movement order, and the Sergeant-Major says it hasn't come through yet, and then a new Sergeant-Major comes who doesn't know them, and *he* says he can't find them on *any* of the lists, not even on the ration strength, so they can't get any food or any pay, and they just totter round the camp like ghosts until they forget their own names and either die or go native."

"Oh no," said Barry, shocked.

"They can't lose 300 Officer Cadets," said Peter, reassuring.

"Why not? The war's over and nobody really wants us. I shall be very surprised," said Alister, "if we ever get commissioned at all."

"You've been too long on this ship," Peter said: "you need proper exercise."

"You can say that again. I haven't had a crap for a week. God, these flying fish are a bloody bore," Alister said: "whatever was Kipling on about?"

"Brahmin," announced a skinny and pallid Major in the uniform of the Madrasi Rifles, "are priests and teachers. Caste colour, red. Kshatriya are rulers, noblemen and warriors. Caste colour, white."

The 300 Cadets were assembled in the Main Lecture Hall of the Transit Camp at Khalyan, some forty miles from Bombay. They had already been there for ten days and had twice been issued with new sets of tropical kit, both of which had now been withdrawn, so that they were compelled to wear the thick shirts and battle-dress trousers in which they had left England six weeks before. However, they were told that they could expect yet another tropical issue any day now – as soon, in fact, as a train had been arranged to take them South to Bangalore. But here was the trouble. The Rail Transport Officer was not empowered to order a train until the Senior Quartermaster at Khalyan had fitted the Cadets with the correct Drill, Khaki, O/Cadets in Transit for the Wearing of;

and the Senior Quartermaster, for his part, was not empowered to fit out the Cadets until a definite date had been
fixed for the train. A little good will between the two Officers
concerned would soon have overcome this difficulty, but good
will was in short supply at Khalyan, and the affair had now
reached a draw by perpetual check. Meanwhile, the Cadets
idled sweatily through the days and were occasionally summoned to hear improvised lectures about the Empire which
they had come to inherit.

"Vaishya," said the skinny Major (who was in open arrest
while awaiting Court Martial and so, being relieved of all
other duties, was free for this one): "the common people,
tillers and traders. Caste colour, yellow. Sudra: servants,
slaves, what have you. Caste colour, black.

"Outside this structure of Hindu society, we also have other
people, who cannot come near the Hindu without polluting
him – the Untouchables, Pariahs or Outcastes. Some of them
are so degraded as to be Unseeable as well as Untouchable,
and may only emerge after nightfall."

There was a long pause, during which the Major, who considered that he had now exhausted his subject, tried to think
of some felicitous formula of conclusion. Before he could
accomplish this, however, his escort, a tubby red Captain of
Indian Ordnance, pointed reproachfully at the lecture hall
clock and murmured something about another thirty minutes
still to run. The Major sighed deeply, scraped into his
harassed mind for something more to say, and then went
grinding on:

"Between the castes or *Varna*, there were, and are, very
strict rules governing their relations. A Brahmin can kill a
Sudra for the cost of a cat. Or so they told me when I was a
Cadet, but that may have gone out now. On the other hand,
if a Sudra kills a Brahmin, he is ferociously punished right
there on the spot – quite how I'm not sure – and is also considered to have damned himself for eternity. This kind of thing
certainly makes a chap know his place."

The Major let out a despairing snort. He looked at the Captain, who shook his head gently but firmly.

"Hack on, old fellow," the Captain said.

"The point is, though," the Major whined, "that these wallahs here in India accept all this. They really believe in it. For these people, what we would call salvation is merely a matter of keeping in one's place. You don't have to *do* anything, you just have to stay in the right place and go through the motions.

"Suppose you're a Merchant. What you do is set up a notice saying, 'C. Hasri, Merchant', and then just sit underneath it. Going through the motions, you see. No one cares whether you actually buy or sell anything; just sit quiet under your notice, and you'll rake in tons of salvation marks, and the next time you're reborn you'll have gone up in the scale. You'll be a Kshatriya, say, a warrior. Now to be fair, the warriors are the one lot that do *do* what they're meant to. They're very good at fighting, as you'll find out."

For a moment the Major seemed to have been quite restored by this thought, but then he became glummer than ever.

"The only trouble is, they don't much care who they're fighting against, because they get their salvation marks just for fighting, you see, and it's all one to them whether they're bayoneting the Japs or scalping your mem-sahib. Provided, that is, they've been told to by their officer, because obeying your officer means you're staying in your right place, and it isn't your biswacks to bother whose windpipe you're splitting if once he's given you the say-so. So that's why we have to be so frightfully careful about what Indians we allow to be officers. There have always been Viceroy's Officers, of course, and now we're beginning to have King's Indian Officers, but it can be terribly tricky, because with these chappies you never know which way they're going to jump unless you're holding the whip yourself. So it's inconceivable that any of 'em should ever be given more than a very subordinate command. . . ."

"Was it true – what that Major was saying?" asked Barry Strange that evening.

"He made sense," said Alister Mortleman; "except that

some of the time he almost seemed to think that the war was still going on."

"I thought he was rather unhinged," said Peter Morrison. "He's going to be court-martialled, you know. Embezzling Mess funds."

They were walking in the cantonment fair ground. The Dive Bomber, unpatronised, hung athwart the sky. A few private soldiers, mostly young members of the Transit Camp's permanent staff, scuffed their way along the stalls.

"Of course," Peter said, "he was only talking about Hindus. Mohammedans are very different, I'm told."

Since none of them had ever met either, this remark passed without comment.

"Wall of Death," said Alister, pointing; "let's go in."

But the half-caste at the door said no, they couldn't. The motor-bicycle had gone wrong, he explained : could they come back next week? Whatever was wrong with the motor-bicycle, no one seemed very urgent to repair it; for it was standing a few yards away, its rear wheel propped in a bracket and its nose turned to the wall. Sitting on its saddle, the wrong way round, was a florid and seedy Englishman of about forty, smoking a thin, black cheroot.

"Sorry, chaps," he said.

"Is that the motor-bicycle?"

"Yes. We're waiting for the fair ground manager to stump up for a new back tyre."

"And are you the rider?"

"Yes. When there's any riding to be done."

"But surely," said Barry kindly, "when you get your new back tyre there'll be lots of people coming to watch."

The death rider took his cheroot from his mouth with thumb and finger.

"Don't you believe it," he said, pinching off the live end of the cheroot with his nails. "The old soldiers – the ones going home – they've seen too much to bother with me. And as for the boys who are coming through on the way out – this fair ground makes 'em home-sick and they stay away."

"Who does come here then?"

"The odd pen-pusher from the Camp. Hoping to pick up a girl." He put his half-cheroot in his breast pocket and lowered his voice. "There's a few blackie-white jobs about. Ten chips a throw and not too bad at the price. I can introduce you fellows if you like."

"No thanks."

They turned and walked away.

"Good luck with the bike," Barry called back.

"Sordid type," said Peter.

"It can't be much fun, being stuck in this dump with a burst tyre. . . . What did he mean – 'ten chips'?"

"Slang for rupees."

"Well," said Alister, "if we're here much longer I shall have ten chips' worth myself."

"Ten chips' worth of disease," said Peter. "We'll be off in a day or two, don't you worry."

"But if we're not," said Barry, "we must come back next week and see the Wall of Death. I'm sorry for that poor man."

"Barrikins wants an introduction to a blackie-white job," Alister teased.

"I think that's disgusting of him," Barry said, looking at Peter, "but I'm sorry for him all the same."

"We'll be off long before that tyre's mended," Peter insisted.

But despite this assurance, depression hung over the party as stark and ugly as the Dive Bomber.

"Come on," said Peter, feeling a duty to raise morale : "I'll stand us all a ticket for the Tattooed Rhinoceros."

The Tattooed Rhinoceros was stuffed.

Four days later they were still at Khalyan, so it looked as if Barry would be able to see the Wall of Death after all; and indeed Alister had promised to go with him the next day, which would be Christmas Eve. Meanwhile, there was some considerable excitement because an Officer had flown from Delhi especially to address them. He was called Lieutenant-Colonel Glastonbury, he looked like a taller and flabbier brother of Douglas Fairbanks Junior, and he was something

very important (Peter told them all) on Lord Wavell's staff.
The Officer Cadets thought he had come to explain the delay
in moving them to Bangalore; but so far from doing that, he
didn't even seem to know that there was a delay. He had come
to talk to them, he said, about their military careers.

"A good hundred of you," he drawled, "have come out here
as Indian Army Cadets of Infantry. But I must inform you
that it is most unlikely that more than a handful of you will
ever be officers in the Indian Army."

("What did I tell you?" whispered Alister fiercely to Peter.
"They don't want any of us. I can see by the look on his
face.")

"The probability is," Colonel Glastonbury droned on, "that
at least ninety-seven per cent of all of you will be commissioned
into British Infantry Regiments of the Line, and will join units
of those Regiments still in the Far East as soon as you leave
Bangalore."

He repeated this in a great many different ways for the next
twenty minutes, and then asked if there were any questions.

"Can you tell us, sir," asked Peter, "*why* so few of us will be
accepted for the Indian Army?"

"Because the new policy will be to commission native
Indians."

"Then why were we accepted as Indian Army Cadets?"

"Because no one had anticipated the new policy."

"Are we *still* Indian Army Cadets?" Peter persisted.

"As far as that goes, yes. It's no good getting all het-up with
me, my dear fellow. I'm just a messenger boy from Delhi. Anyhow, I'm a cavalry man myself" – this with tired complacency
– "and I don't really understand what the Infantry wallahs
are up to. With you or anyone else. But there's one thing I do
understand, and you'd better understand it too."

He looked down on the assembled Cadets like a benevolent
Jeremiah.

"It's all coming to an end, you know, out here. There's no
future in the Indian Army, even if you do get into it. Because
the show's over, chums. It may take a year or two to wind it
up, but the Durbar's done. So if you stay here long enough,

you can help put up the shutters and pull down the flag. And that's what's in it for you."

Before Lieutenant-Colonel Glastonbury left Khalyan, he went, on behalf of the Cadets, to the Commandant of the Transit Camp and asked how soon they could expect to be sent on to Bangalore. The short answer was that the Commandant didn't know and didn't care, and so he told Glastonbury, bidding him mind his own business for good measure.

"Pure nerves," as Glastonbury explained good-humouredly to the deputation of Cadets which accompanied him to the local air field. "He's not a bad little man really, he's just worried stiff about what's going to happen to him when the poor old Raj packs up."

"Even so, sir, he might have been more civil," Peter said.

"He didn't like the cut of my rig." Glastonbury's regiment, a British one, was the 49th Earl Hamilton's Light Dragoons, and his uniform, even in a tropical version, was distinctive. "And he don't care for visitors from Delhi. They seldom bring much comfort with 'em. . . . Thank you for seeing me off, gentlemen. When I've got any more news in your line, I'll look in on you all at Bangalore."

All of which was well enough but left the Cadets still mouldering in Khalyan, where, they must now presume, they would be spending the twelve days of Christmas. So the next day – Christmas Eve – Alister Mortleman and Barry Strange set off, late in the afternoon, to visit the Wall of Death and enquire whether it was now functioning. Peter, who was suffering acutely from the local variant of diarrhoea ('Khalyan squirt'), stayed behind in order to be near the lavatory.

"You know what," said Alister to Barry : "I think I'm going to have one of those blackie-white girls that chappie was telling us about."

"Do you know how?"

"Of course. You just – well – you know."

Barry, who didn't, nodded.

"What about you?"

"I wouldn't mind," said Barry, who liked to please and therefore adapted his moral tone to his company of the moment; "but I haven't got enough money."

"Ten chips? I've got enough for both of us."

They entered the fair ground. The Dive Bomber was still at precisely the same angle as when they had last seen it.

"Suggestive," Alister said.

"I don't want to catch anything."

"You won't – not if you use one of these."

Alister passed his friend a small envelope. They approached the Wall of Death, outside which the rider was sitting on the motor-bicycle; like the Dive Bomber, he did not appear to have moved since they last left him.

"I think," said Barry, "that we ought to be getting back. There's a carol service in the Garrison Church at six."

"Rubbish," said Alister. And then to the rider, "Hullo there."

"Hello again," the death rider said.

"We . . . we want you to introduce us to two of those girls you were talking about."

"Gladly. But you haven't got time."

"Plenty of time. Not even a muster parade till the day after Boxing Day."

"Your lot's packing up to go," the rider said.

"Nonsense. We only left them a few minutes ago."

"Have it your own way."

"But I mean to say . . . on Christmas Eve."

"It's all one to me," the rider said. "If you want two girls, you can have 'em. Ten chips each and five for me."

To Barry, as he looked across the twilight fair ground, down the rows of silent stalls and on to the hill which spiralled up behind them like a thin, malformed cone, there came some lines of verse from his childhood :

> True Thomas lay on Huntlie bank;
> A farlie he spied with his e'e;
> And there he saw a ladye bright
> Come riding down by the Eildon Tree.

True Thomas had taken the road to 'fair Elfland', and Barry, he now saw, had done the same. True Thomas had been doomed to wander for seven years – indeed, if Barry remembered aright, 'he never gat back to his ain countrie'. Barry must get back to his while there was still time. Already, perhaps, it might be too late, and he would find that he was cut off on an island in empty space, condemned to the fair ground for ever. Barry shivered, whirled about and bolted.

"Sensible young fellow," said the rider to Alister: "why don't you do the same?"

But Alister stood his ground. "Here's fifteen rupees," he said.

The rider took the money but didn't move.

"Through the entrance," he said to Alister, "first door on the left and up to the gallery."

"And then?"

"Take your pick. There's everything you need up there."

"Not very private."

"What did you expect for ten chips?"

Alister drew a deep breath and marched through the entrance.

When Barry got himself back to the Cadets' quarters in the Transit Camp, everything was in turmoil. An Emergency Movement Order had just come through (nobody quite knew whence, though the word 'Delhi' was in many mouths) and the 300 Cadets were to be entrained at midnight. Since most Cadets had scant belongings, packing presented few problems; but the formalities to be gone through were massive. Resentful Colour Sergeants clumped hither and thither with huge lists in triplicate; while groups of muttering officers, whom no one had ever seen before, stood around beating their calves urgently with canes.

"... Morrison, P."

"Here, Colour Sergeant."

"Mortleman, A."

"He's just gone for a walk. He'll be back soon."

"He'd better be, laddie."

"He couldn't know that this was going to happen."

"*Couldn't know*, laddie? No more could I, and I'm here shouting the odds, ain't I? On parade when I'm wanted, Christmas Eve or Doomsday, it's all one to me. Murphy, J. . . . Muscateer, Earl of . . . Zaccharias, W. Outside the lot of you, and get fell in."

"Please, Colour Sergeant. My diarrhoea."

"Follow the column to the stores at your own pace, and keep your cheeks together. What you lot need is a nanny."

"Please, Colour Sergeant?"

"Yes, my lord? Lost your coronet, my lord? No? . . . Only your Part One pay book? Is that all you've lost? Well, you'd better find it, Mr Lord Muscateer, sir, you had indeed, because if somebody asks you for it and you don't 'ave it, you'll be a man without a name – won't you, my lord? – and that means you'll be doubled away to a dungeon and never 'eard of again. OUTSIDE."

". . . Morrison, P."

"Colour."

"Bush jackets three, O/Cadets in Transit for the Wearing of, slacks three, shorts three. Sign there. Still keeping your cheeks together, I 'ope?"

"Only just, Colour."

"Mortleman, A. He's the one that's gone walkies. One of you young gentlemen had better find him, I promise you that, because if he's not on that train tonight they'll have him for desertion – absent when under warning to move. What's his size? . . . Big bastard, eh? Well, you take that lot for him, Mr Morrison, P., and hurry off out of here before you drop your tripes in my nice clean stores. Murphy, J. – bush-jackets, slacks, shorts – and here's 'is lordship again, I've got a special lot for you, my lord, in silk. . . ."

God, thought Peter, as he sat on the can with all Alister's tropical kit and his own piled about his ankles, it's like scalding water going through. Shall I go sick? *Go sick and miss the train?* It might be weeks before I got sent on; they might back-squad me to a later intake, they might say I'd lost my chance altogether – just send me home. Khalyan squirt – *ouuucchh* –

but there'll be a lavatory on the train, one must stay with one's friends in strange countries, one mustn't fall out for a small thing like Khalyan squirt – Phheeeuuwww, but that should do the trick for the next twenty minutes.

Someone came into a nearby cubicle and was violently sick. As there were no doors, Peter looked in as he passed. Alister, reeling and retching over the seat.

"Alister."

"Peterkin. I'm so *drunk*. Better now, but so tired. So tired. Help me to bed, Peterkin."

"No bed, Alister. You've got to get into this tropical dress, and fit up your equipment web, and get on parade at 2300 hours to get on to the truck to get on to the train at midnight."

"God, I feel awful. You look rotten too. Bed."

"No bed. Back to fit up our kit. But I think . . . I'll have to have another shit first. . . ."

So Peter had another shit and Alister was sick again for fellowship; and then they staggered to their basha (hut) and despite Peter's injunctions lay down on their charboys (beds), while Barry fussed about them fitting together their equipment web and asking prurient questions of Alister.

"She gave me this stuff," Alister said. "Not alcohol, I think, after all. Something to make me do it better, she said, very expensive, thirty chips extra, and it certainly worked and—"

"—And now it's made you ill," said Barry primly. "Lift your behind, please, Alister, or I shan't be able to get your slacks up. That's right. I'll just see how Peter's getting on, and then I'll come back to help you with your big pack and pouches. . . ."

". . . Morrison, P."

"Colour."

"Mortleman, A. . . . Glad to see you at last, Mr Mortleman. I hope you had a pleasant walk, sir, even if it has turned you bright green. Murphy, J. . . . Your lordship . . . Zaccharias, W. And now, all of you, up into that truck. Allow me, Mr Mortleman. (Jesus Christ, sonny, what have you been drinking? You stink like a Parsees' tower. Didn't they warn you never to take a drink from those girls?) And so up with the tail – thank you,

Mr Strange – my compliments, gentlemen, and a pleasant journey to Bangalore. You'll find it a nice place enough, but one last tip : never eat the orange meringue pie in Ley Wong's Chinese Restaurant."

When the Christmas sun rose on them, they were passing through Poona; their Christmas dinner they ate in a siding at Sholapur.

What with Peter's Khalyan squirt and Alister's repeated vomiting, the night had been a fitful one. Since there was only one W.C. for each coach, and since each coach contained two Platoons of Cadets, and since over-excitement had produced a strong propensity to evacuate even in those who didn't have Khalyan squirt, there were considerable problems of hygiene and logistics. However, Barry did what he could to mitigate his friends' discomfiture, and was stoutly assisted by the Earl of Muscateer, who devised an ingenious contraption, with an oil funnel and some mess tins, for the desperate Peter when the loo was occupied, and used most of his best eau de Cologne in cleaning up Alister. By the time they had passed through Poona, order of a kind had been achieved; and when 'dinner' was served at Sholapur (a thick stew, ladled into their mess tins from containers on the platform) both Alister and Peter were strong enough to dismount and queue up with the rest.

To make matters better, the late afternoon was mild and grateful where they were, and amusement was provided for them in the form of an Indian shanty village just below the embanked siding. Standing on the platform, they could observe the colourful and picturesque antics of a thousand-odd natives, whose total living space, it appeared, was just a little larger than a fair sized croquet lawn.

"Quarters for the Untouchables, do you think?"

"Like a nest of cockroaches," Alister said. "Thank God we live in a country which can never get as crowded as that."

"Can't it?" said Lord Muscateer.

"Can you imagine people in England ever living like that? Look at that squalid little girl – shitting on her own doorstep."

"After last night," said Peter, "one can hardly find fault with that. Where," he said to Muscateer, "did you get that oil funnel? Not the sort of thing one carries around."

"My governor told me to bring one. 'Whenever a man goes East of Calais,' he said to me, 'he should always take a large oil funnel. You've no idea how handy it can be.' It seems my governor was right."

"I'm very grateful to him – and you. It must be awkward to pack."

"At least it's not easy to lose. Not like a Part One Pay Book. I still can't find mine," said Muscateer miserably : "do you think they can make a row about it ?"

"A bit of a row, yes. It's rather the same as an Identity Card. I should own up."

"What did that Colour Sergeant mean, by the way ?"

"About doubling you away to a dungeon? That's rubbish, of course."

"No, not that. About not eating orange meringue pie in Ley Wong's Chinese Restaurant. Why on earth should he tell us that ?"

"I didn't hear that bit," said Peter. "How many Indians do you suppose actually sleep in one of those huts ?"

"I've just counted ten going into one," said Barry, "and no one's come out."

But oecological conjecture was now interrupted by a summons back to their wooden seats. The train pulled out of the siding and rattled away with them across the dusty Deccan towards Gulbarga. For a while they looked across the yellow, stony plain, until the sun sank behind the Western Ghats and all the ways were dark. Then they wrapped blankets round their thighs and stomachs, dozed and shivered, nodded off and nodded on, snored and dribbled and whimpered, while the distressful night crept by and slunk away at last before the kind old sun.

Not so kind, however, by twelve o'clock noon, when the train stopped at Kadur for lunch, which was thick slices of fibrous beef in a slimy gravy, garnished with undercooked potatoes. Now the sun was an enemy, an enemy who became more brutal with every minute of the slow afternoon, as they crawled across the flats towards the hills. These they reached at early evening and blessed the cool; until, as the sun sank and the train climbed, the cool turned to chill and the chill to bitter cold, which sent them to cringe in misery under their mean little blankets, like workhouse children waiting to be whipped.

At dawn, the coastal plain. By mid-morning, Madras. At Madras a breakfast of stewed tea and tiny pale yellow fried eggs (one each), and then a change of train.

"Last lap," said Peter to Muscateer.

For now they would ride due East to Mysore State and Bangalore; back over the coastal plain and then a slow ascent to the plateau, just high enough to temper the sun but not to reach the cold; and so into a promised land of blue days and whispering palm trees, an imperial land furnished with riches and tranquillity, a fabled land of chukkhas and barra pegs and tiger hunts, a comfortable land where Cadets were waited on by squads of bowing servants and Commissions were handed out like bright bouquets at a ball. With a lurch and a skip the train was out of Madras: Bangalore this evening, the cry went down the coaches; Bangalore for dinner – PASS THE WORD.

They arrived at Bangalore at 2.30 in the morning.

Once there, however, they found that they were very much expected. A motherly Sergeant-Major, overseen but not interfered with by a pug-faced Captain of Gurkhas, sorted them into Platoons and marshalled them into a fleet of open trucks, which carried them through a narrow bazaar and then through outskirts of shadowy, spacious houses, and stopped on a flat arena of sand, apparently in the middle of nowhere but in fact in the middle of the O.T.S. For out of the night on either side of the arena loomed long grey buildings with low verandahs, each of which, they were informed, was a Mess; and in one or other of these they were all swiftly and copiously fed.

Indian bearers had meanwhile assembled in strength and were now dished out, by the motherly Sergeant-Major and two placid assistants, at the rate of one bearer to four Cadets. Each bearer promptly gathered up the kit-bags of his four young sahibs and then, having first excused himself courteously for being unable to carry their valises as well, led them off at a short-arsed trot (no quicker than the Englishmen's walk) to their quarters in the Cadets' Lines, which consisted of parallel and single-storeyed bashas, each basha containing fifteen separate rooms and thus housing a Platoon of thirty Cadets in companionable pairs. The beds were made up with clean sheets and mosquito nets; there was hot water in the adjacent showers; there was a tumbler and a carafe by each pillow : but also by each pillow, and less for their comfort, was a polite note welcoming Mr —— (as the case might be) to the O.T.S. and requesting him to be on parade in the arena between the two Messes at 6.15 the following morning. It was already 4.45.

So at 6.15 they mustered (having been woken by their bearers with tea and green bananas at 5.45) and now everything was made very plain. They were to be formed into three Companies, two of three Platoons and one of four; A and B Coys would use one of the two Messes ('Clive'), while C Coy with its four Platoons would use the second and slightly smaller Mess ('Wellesley'). Each Platoon would be commanded and in large part instructed by a Captain of the Indian Army with the disciplinary assistance of a Cadet Junior Under Officer; each Company would be commanded by a Major of the Indian Army, who would be assisted by a Sergeant-Major (British) and a Cadet Senior Under Officer. There were six other Companies of Cadets at present in the O.T.S., all at various stages of the normal training, and also an Indian Company (Experimental), whose status was uncertain and whose members, should they chance to meet any, they must treat with polite indifference. The whole shooting match (as the motherly Sergeant-Major explained) was commanded by the Commandant, Brigadier Percy de Glanville Manwood, O.B.E., formerly of the Chota Nagpur Lancers – "and don't ask me why an Officer of Horse is training Officers of Foot, because I'm a simple man, gentlemen, who minds his business. Which is now to invite you to proceed in order of Platoons to the Contractor's Store, where you will be issued with the correct kit and lovely black tin trunks to put it in."

Whereupon 1 Pl. of A Coy was marched off by the Cadet considered the most likely candidate for the office of J.U.O. (a quondam Corporal of Military Police) and the rest settled down on the verandahs to wait.

"They needn't have got us up this early just to hang around here," said Alister crossly.

"Everyone," said Peter, "has to get up early in the East. It isn't healthy to stay in bed."

"And at least," said Barry, "we can hang around together."

For so it had luckily turned out. Cadets had been allotted to Platoons on a basis which was partly alphabetical and partly snobbish, those from the public schools and the better regiments being firmly segregated from their less fortunate comrades, since it was felt by Brigadier P. de G. Manwood (official policy to the contrary notwithstanding) that people were happier with others from their own social background. However, it was also felt that lip service must be paid to official doctrine in the matter; and so a judicious compromise had been reached whereby each Platoon was socially cohesive but each Company, taken as a whole, presented a social mixture – there being in A Coy, for example, one Platoon of upper-class boys, one of minor public school boys and one of what Alister called oiks. (This was the one which had just marched off under the ex-policeman.) Now, Peter Morrison, Alister Mortleman, the Lord Muscateer and Barry Strange all belonged to an upper/upper-middle alphabetical block which was to constitute No. 2 Pl. of C Coy; and so, while they indeed had the pleasure of hanging around, as Barry said, together, they also had to hang around for a very long time, since 2 Pl. C Coy was low in its numerical if not in its social order. They were still hanging around, in fact, some two hours after lunch (or, more properly, tiffin).

"I thought," said Barry, "that in India everyone had siestas."

"They gave that up in 1941," Peter told him: "it wasted too much time which might have been devoted to valuable training."

"But surely, that's why we get up so early – to do the valuable training before it gets too hot."

"Up here it never gets too hot. This is a Grade I Weather Station."

"So they think they can have it both ways," grumbled Alister: "drag us out at vulture-fart *and* keep grinding us the whole afternoon."

"Officers," Peter reminded him, "must be prepared to work long hours. This is no place for the shop steward mentality."

"Anyhow," said Muscateer, who liked hanging about, "you can't say they're exactly grinding us just now."

"It's surprising they haven't found something useful for us to do," said Peter. "I haven't seen an Officer since that one at the station last night."

(But what Peter didn't know was that all Officers of the O.T.S. were attending a special conference, convened by Brigadier Manwood on receipt of urgent orders from Delhi, in order to discuss the modernisation of the curriculum – e.g. whether or not the Cadets should still be instructed in stick drill.)

"I wonder," said Barry, "what sort of Officer we'll have for our Platoon."

"Indian Army in any case," said Alister.

"Does that make a difference?"

"I had a great-grandfather in the Coldstream," said Muscateer, "who had to transfer to the Indian Army after a row about some other fellow's wife. Usually, after that sort of row, they just sent you to a line regiment to get you out of London. But my great-grandpapa was so awful that they sent him all the way out here. Do you suppose *that's* any guide to the form?"

"What happened to him then?"

"He got mixed up in a duel with a Rajah. On elephants. But the next day they heard that he'd inherited, so they hushed it all up. He always said afterwards that Indian Army Officers were the most frightful tuft-hunters. —But some of you chaps are for the Indian Army, aren't you? Sorry and all that."

"I've got an Indian Army Cadetship," Peter said, "but that man who came to Khalyan didn't fancy my chances."

"I'm hoping for the Rifle Brigade," said Alister, pointing to his cap badge with some insistence.

"And I'm for the Wessex Fusiliers," said Barry proudly; "my brothers were with them, you see."

"Yes," said Muscateer : "I do see."

"What regiment are you going into, Muscateer?" – this from Alister.

"I've been with my county mob so far – the Wiltshires."

"I'd have thought you'd have gone into the Guards."

"They haven't been too keen on us since great-grandpapa's little affair. Anyway, my old governor says a man ought to join his local lot. He says that's what the best chaps always did, and that your smart London regiments are just a load of shit-stabbing grocers."

"Rather strong?"

"My old governor always puts things strong," said Muscateer with a lazy smile of love. "Here's that nice Sergeant-Major. I think it's our turn at last."

At the Contractor's Store, each of them was issued with and required to sign for : five new suits of khaki drill, these being of rather poorer material than any of the several previous issues : a fly whisk; a bicycle; three pairs of lumpy flannel pyjamas (whether they wanted them or not); ten pairs of brief white drawers, of a kind difficult to manipulate when one was peeing and guaranteed to cause and exacerbate tinia cruris; a jungle hat; a tent; a camp bed; a camp wash-stand;

a leather hip-flask; a bible and a prayer-book (for conducting burial services when no Minister of the Church was available); and a split swagger cane. They were also given, as the motherly Sergeant-Major had foretold, one black tin trunk apiece, in which to put everything except the bicycle. For some reason that was not very clear they must pay for all this themselves, the Contractor told them, in instalments which would be deducted from their emolument (henceforth equivalent to that of a junior Sergeant) over the next six months. When everything had been checked and stowed, their bearers came trotting up from the Lines to collect the loaded trunks, while they themselves rode off to tea on their new bicycles, all of them, that is, except Lord Muscateer, who had never learned to ride a bicycle and had to wheel his instead.

The next day they started their training in earnest. From 6.15 a.m. to 7.45 they had stick drill with their new split swagger canes. After breakfast they had Urdu, which was taught to them in groups of four by grave and white-robed Munshis, who addressed them as 'Sahib' and expected the courtesy to be returned. Peter Morrison was glad they were learning Urdu, because he thought this meant that he had a better chance of getting into the Indian Army: after all, as he said to Barry, why should the authorities make them learn Urdu unless some of them at least were going to need it? Barry, who liked people to be happy, agreed with Peter about this; but Alister, who was fast developing a nose for Indian proceedings, said that Urdu lessons were simply an old habit which the authorities were either too lethargic or sentimental to abandon.

Later on in the morning, they were introduced to the Officers of their Company. C Coy was to be commanded by a man called Major Baxter, a cheerful and loud-mouthed little chap from an Indian regiment so unsmart that it was quite famous for it. Major Baxter had a head the size of an elk's and wore shorts which came down to about a foot below his knees; which was just as well, perhaps, because his legs resembled those of a spider with stockings and shoes on. As for the Platoon Commanders, there was one called Captain Better-edge (handsome and morose) for No. 1 Pl., and another called Captain Lafone, who had a voice even commoner than Major Baxter's, for No. 3 Pl., and yet another for No. 4 Pl.; but for some reason No. 2 Pl. hadn't yet got a Commander, which made them feel rather left out. However, Major Baxter said that an Officer would be coming to them very shortly and that meanwhile Peter Morrison, who had already been appointed J.U.O. on account of his large and reliable face, would be responsible for their welfare and deportment.

The C.S.M. of C Coy was a disappointment. They had all been hoping that they would get the motherly Sergeant-Major, who had so far been controlling everybody and everything single-handed; but it now turned out that he was to be C.S.M. of A Coy, while C Coy was to have a man called Sergeant-Major Cruxtable. This Warrant Officer, who came from the Wiltshire Regiment, was prematurely obese and had a sideways look like that of a pi-dog who was afraid lest someone might kick it out of the way before it had finished crapping. Although Muscateer, loyal as ever to his own 'mob' and his own county, pretended to find Cruxtable satisfactory ('the sort of man who's been about a bit'), everyone else disliked and mistrusted him on sight. In truth, however, and as they later found out, they might have happened on much worse; for Cruxtable was simply a slut and like most sluts was happy to leave all men in peace providing only that they served him similar.

Having been introduced to their superiors, the Cadets were then lectured by Major Baxter on the conduct and esprit which would be expected of them. In the main, exhortation was negative: the Cadets were *not* to get drunk, borrow money from native money-lenders or frequent native women (in which category, for all practical purposes, Eurasians were included); they were not to interest themselves in Indian politics or walk about with bare feet (in case they picked up hook-worm); and in no circumstances whatever were they to complain about anything that had to do with the O.T.S. Let them only observe these simple and sensible conditions, Major Baxter said, and they would all have a pleasurable six months'

course with Commissions thrown in at the end of it. Failure
was unheard of at Bangalore (since it cost the Government so
much to send people out there) except in case of insanity,
death or thrice-repeated venereal infection, which was why
they were requested not to sleep with natives. If they had any
personal problems, they might always come to him, but frankly,
gentlemen, potential officers were expected to keep their
troubles to themselves and not go whining round for pity like
a shower of illiterate conscripts. And so good morning to them
all, and a very pleasant week-end . . . oh, and just one thing
more. Although there was no formal Church Parade at the
O.T.S., it was held to be desirable that some thirty per cent of
the Cadets should attend Matins at the Garrison Church each
Sunday. Sergeant-Major Cruxtable would therefore select one
man in three by lot, regardless of individual creeds, as future
Officers must learn to subordinate private belief to public duty.
The only Cadets who would be exempt when the lot was
drawn were those who had been selected to take part in the
O.T.S. Cricket Trials, which would start on Sunday at 11 a.m.
and were to be honoured by the presence of H.H. the Maharajah of Dharaparam. Should His Highness approach any
Cadet in a familiar manner, such Cadet was warned to be
cautious but very polite.

Several Cadets from the new intake had been chosen, on
account of their school records, to take part in the O.T.S.
Cricket Trials that Sunday. Two of these were Peter and
Alister. Peter, who had just failed to get into his School XI in
a good year, bowled slow off-breaks all so exactly similar in
flight and pace that they soon bored even the most wary
opponent into some contemptuous and fatal error; while
Alister was a flashy batsman who used too much right hand
but had played for Winchester.

The proceedings were undistinguished but pleasant; for the
O.T.S. Cricket Ground was agreeably sited and had one of the
few grass wickets in all India. 'Napier' (Peter's and Alister's
team) was first in the field and dismissed 'Curzon' (three of
whom had been bored out by Peter's off-breaks) for 194 runs.
Batting after tea, 'Napier' swiftly put on 97 for 2 (with the

help of an aggressive 34 by Alister at first wicket) and then settled down to plod slowly and without risk towards a very probable victory. When the score was 150 for 3, Peter, who was to bat No. 10 and did not expect to be called upon, suggested to Alister that they should take a turn round the ground, if only to avoid the succulent giggles with which H.H. the Maharajah of Dharaparam was favouring Alister from his box in the pavilion.

Taking a turn round the ground in the opposite direction were two men in light civilian suits and panama hats. Although one of them was large and loose and the other was stringy and sparse, they kept perfect step as they walked together and made a model of easeful and elegant progression.

"That's Colonel Glastonbury," said Alister: "the chap who came to Khalyan."

"And the smaller one's called Captain Detterling," said Peter. "I've met him once or twice in England – down at my school. He's the only man who ever made a double century in a school match. Before my time, of course."

As Glastonbury and Detterling approached the two Cadets, they lifted their hats in effortless unison. Detterling sported the Butterfly 'riband, Peter noticed, and Glastonbury the Eton Ramblers'. After the introduction of Alister to Captain Detterling and the shaking of hands in all other required permutations, the two Officers replaced their hats and turned about as if to accompany their juniors.

"But we," said Peter politely, "will walk your way."

"No," said Detterling. "You two are players; we're only spectators."

"So we walk *your* way," Glastonbury said.

Before Peter had time to consider the full implications of this courtesy, Glastonbury launched into an explanation of their presence. He himself had come from Delhi to impress upon the Commandant of the O.T.S. that certain rather radical changes were now necessary in the Syllabus of Instruction.

"We asked them to fix it up themselves," Glastonbury said. "and let us know what they'd done. In fact they've done precisely nothing, so I've been sent to chivvy them along. They're still teaching you Urdu, I hear?"

"Yes," said Alister; "*and* stick drill. That's about all they have taught us so far."

"Well, Urdu will certainly go," said Glastonbury, "but stick drill will probably stay."

"Why, sir?" said Alister petulantly.

Glastonbury simply opened his eyes slightly wider at Alister, as if the answer should have been obvious to any sane person, and changed the subject.

"Captain Detterling has come here as an instructor," Glastonbury said, nodding across at his companion.

"For our Platoon? We haven't got one yet?"

For no evident reason, Detterling and Glastonbury exchanged guilty glances.

"I'm afraid not," said Detterling. "I'm to teach Military Law and Infantry/Tank Co-operation to the whole O.T.S. I'm cavalry, you see. The same regiment as Giles here."

It occurred to Peter that if these two were friends and near-contemporaries, as seemed to be the case, then there was a marked contrast in their comparative rank; no doubt Glastonbury's Colonelcy was only temporary, but there was no reason why Detterling, after nearly six years of war, should not have achieved some similar brevet. It also occurred to Peter that the last time he had seen Detterling, which was at their old school in England only three months before, Detterling had been newly appointed to the job of sifting recruits at the various Primary Training Corps in order to find suitable candidates for the Cavalry. Since posts like this required long experience, they also carried long tenure; which being the case, Detterling's arrival at Bangalore required elucidation.

"I dare say," said Detterling, anticipating the question which Peter would have been too well mannered to ask, "that you wonder what happened to that job of mine in England. Cavalry (Armoured Corps) Selection Officer. The thing was, my dear fellow, that I wasn't getting any recruits for them. On the contrary, I simply put everyone off."

"Why was that?"

"I could never get up any enthusiasm about tanks. I kept on telling them how nice it would have been if we'd still had horses but how horrible it was having tanks."

"Are you going to tell us that? When you teach us Infantry/ Tank Co-operation?"

"I don't suppose we shall do much of that when it comes to the point – eh, Giles?"

"It will be in the new syllabus," said Glastonbury in tones of mild rebuke.

"But since there are so few tanks in India," said Detterling happily, "we shan't have any to practise with."

"You can always do the theory."

"The theory's all right," said Detterling; "it's the tanks themselves I can't stand. Nasty lumps of metal, making such a bloody awful smell. . . . I think I'm going to like India," he said, looking across the Cricket Ground to where two old ladies, attended by turbaned syces, sat in an open landau. "There's rather the sort of atmosphere there used to be in Malta, when I first joined the Regiment in '37. You know, a guard of lancers for the G.O.C. and all those randy wives in long white dresses."

"It may not last," Giles Glastonbury said.

"That's part of its charm. Incidentally," said Detterling, "there's a sort of cousin of mine here somewhere. Muscateer, he's called. Does anyone know him?"

"Yes, sir," said Alister quickly.

"Well, rustle him up, there's a good chap, and we'll all go out to dinner . . . if you're free, that is."

Peter and Alister said they were free and Wellesley Mess was appointed as the initial rendezvous for the evening. A few minutes later 'Napier' made the winning hit, which they all four applauded, though Detterling grumbled bitterly about the quality of the stroke. Then there was much flurry of puggrees and cummerbunds; the two old ladies in the landau sailed serenely off the grass; His Highness, still giggling, was driven away in his 1924 Lagonda, which was painted in the Old Harrovian colours; and Peter and Alister rode in rickshaws through the sweet, gritty Indian dusk, to find Muscateer (who had spent all day learning to mount his bicycle) and change for Detterling's dinner.

Since Glastonbury and Detterling were too fastidious about their food to risk dining in the Bangalore Officers' Club ('Brown Windsor Soup and boarding house curry, I expect'), it was decided that they should go to Ley Wong's Chinese Restaurant, where the cuisine was versatile, Giles Glastonbury told them, and credit was as long as anywhere in the East. Not that Detterling would need credit for this dinner; but it might prove useful to the three Cadets to have Glastonbury's personal introduction to Ley Wong, who would then let them cash cheques whenever they wanted to and would also avail them of his superior services as a procurer at special rates.

"He always lets me off twenty-five per cent," Glastonbury said in the horse-drawn gharri that took them there, "and he makes the girls do the same."

"How do you know him so well?" asked Detterling. "You were never stationed here that I'd heard of."

"I did him a good turn some years back. It was when I first came out here – you remember" – this to Detterling only – "just after that spot of bother I had in Tunisia."

Detterling remembered and nodded. Alister opened his mouth to ask what 'the spot of bother' had been, but was silenced by a look from Peter.

"Well, when I first appeared in Bombay," Glastonbury said, "no one really knew what to do with me – my arrival being rather sudden, you see – so they put me in charge of what they called the Hygiene and Amenity Board (South India). I had to go round with a Medical Officer and a Padre inspecting all the cinemas and restaurants and bars, and then report back about whether or not they were suitable for clean-limbed British soldiers. You get the idea?"

They got the idea, and Muscateer remarked that his old governor had done much the same sort of thing in France in 1944.

"And a proper pantomime he made of it," said Detterling; "your old governor dished out Army Licences to every cathouse between Calvados and the Ardennes, just to annoy

Montgomery. They had to send someone round after him to close them all down again."

"Well, in course of time," Glastonbury continued after this parenthesis, "the Hygiene and Amenity Board passed through Bangalore, and the first place we had to inspect was Ley Wong's Chinese Restaurant. Before we even started, an Indian informer came to see us, and said that Ley Wong had been cashing cheques drawn on a Japanese Bank, i.e. trafficking with the enemies of the King Emperor. Needless to say, this informer was the owner of a rival restaurant, but the charge still had to be investigated. In fact it was my plain duty to go straight to the police.

"But there was something so outlandish about the idea of a chap cashing Japanese cheques that I thought I'd have a word with him myself. And a very nice little man he turned out to be. His story was that he had a good client, a British Officer, who'd left some money in a Japanese Bank before the war and didn't see why he shouldn't get the benefit now. Nor did Ley Wong – especially as his client was prepared to have his cheques discounted at fifty per cent. And anyway, Ley Wong told me, it was an interesting challenge."

"And he managed to get the cheques cleared?"

"Yes, bless his oriental heart. He simply passed them through neutral territory. Not that this was as easy as it sounds of course. But Ley Wong got up some sort of pipeline, and fed the cheques through to Japan, and had the ready money fed back again. He had to pay the agents a small fortune, and he lost heavily over exchange rates en route, but the end of it was he made twenty per cent on the deal and everyone concerned was quite happy. And so, now I came to think of it, was I. After all, if the Japanese were fools enough to pay out on cheques drawn by an Englishman, who was any the worse off?"

"Unless," said Muscateer apologetically, "there were coded messages or something on the cheques?"

"There was no question of that game," said Glastonbury, "because the Officer who issued them was in the Grenadiers. So of course it must have been all right, Ley Wong told me, and naturally I agreed."

Detterling sighed very gently.

"So what did you decide to do?" he asked.

"Well, the Grenadier had moved on by that time, and no harm had been done, as I saw it, and it seemed to be a very pleasant sort of restaurant, so I told Ley Wong I'd forget it. The informer wouldn't make any more trouble, Ley Wong said, because he was in such bad odour with the police about something or other himself that he wouldn't dare go near them. Which was why he'd come to me instead."

"But he'd also told the Doctor and the Padre on your Board," said Detterling: "how did you keep them quiet?"

"Took 'em for a slap up dinner at Ley Wong's and told 'em the whole story was rubbish. It seemed simpler than going into detail."

"And they were happy with that?"

"I suppose so. As it happens, I never saw them again. They both had killing hangovers the next morning and had to stay in bed; and meanwhile some cousin of mine had found out I'd got to India and where I was, and wired me to come to Delhi juldi juldi to take up a post on his staff. So to Delhi juldi juldi I went. But whenever I've been here at the odd time since, Ley Wong has always shown himself most grateful."

"Those girls at cut rates?"

"Not only that. He once gave me an ivory casket with a collection of gold coins inside it minted by the Mogul Jehangir."

"Rather . . . valuable?"

"I dare say," said Glastonbury with superb indifference; "a very touching present, I thought. Apparently Ley Wong had somehow got into his head that my hobby was collecting coins. Of course I've never cared anything about that, but I didn't want to hurt the poor fellow's feelings."

"So what did you do with the coins?" said Detterling casually.

"They're knocking around somewhere in my bungalow up in Delhi. . . . And there's Ley Wong now. Grinning all over his face."

But to Peter it seemed, as Ley Wong bowed them through

the entrance and on into a private room, that the little China-
man's grin was not wholly amiable. There was a lack of elasti-
city about it. Perhaps, thought Peter, Ley Wong was getting
tired of accommodating the Glastonbury Sahib with cut-price
girls and Mongol gold. But if so, there was no further sign of
his resentment. Long chains of waiters, under the personal
supervision of Ley Wong, came and went with course after
course of classical Chinese delicacies and bottle after bottle of
rare White Burgundy. The waiters came ever faster, and Ley
Wong bowed ever deeper with the presentation of each new
dish; while Alister grew ever more loud-mouthed, Muscateer
more agreeable, Detterling more laconic, and Glastonbury
more confidential. It seemed to Peter that all the inner mys-
teries of Delhi were being revealed to him and that these made
a truly Byzantine spectacle of levity, betrayal and decay.

"You know what's happened?" Giles Glastonbury said.
"They've lost their confidence. Everyone from His Excellency
downward. They've been told so long and so often that they've
no right to be here that they've begun to believe it. Which
means they've stopped believing in themselves and their function. When that happens, everything starts running down –
no, not just running down, but *falling apart*."

"You don't appear to be falling apart, sir."

"It's different with me. You see, I never really believed in it
much; I just took it as it came from day to day, because I only
ever came here by accident. I'm just someone who's passing
through, Morrison. But the old hands out here . . . the men
who are the core of it all . . . they *loved* what they were doing,
they even loved the Indians in their way, and they did their
damnedest to get it right. They got a lot wrong, of course, they
were nagging and self-satisfied and they couldn't understand
that to most Indians custom matters much more than cleanli-
ness – all that kind of thing; but at the same time they really
did try to bring in justice and sound administration, to stop
people starving or selling their eight-year-old bodies, to increase
wealth and knowledge. Up to a point they succeeded, and up
to a point they were thanked, and so they thought they could
stay for ever. They made this their country, and even stayed on

when they had to retire, some of them, because their *lives* were here.

"But now what's happened? They're being told they're not wanted and never really were. The Government in England is embarrassed by them, the Americans mock at them, the educated Indians are screaming for their jobs, and the very cows in the street seem to hate their guts. So not unnaturally, they're rather hurt. Hurt . . . and dispossessed. Soldiers and civil service – it's the same with them all."

"And so they've turned vicious, you say?"

"Not exactly that. When things fall apart," said Glastonbury, "you get a feeling that nothing matters any more . . . that you can just let yourself go. All those things you've wanted to do for so long and haven't dared to because of your career – well, you can ahead with the lot now, and what the devil? Girls, boys, booze, hashish, telling the boss upstairs to piss in his own navel – you can do it all when the barbarians are banging at the gate and the world's about to go up in flames. What's to stop you?"

"Decency?"

"Well, yes. And that's what's keeping the show going. If we've got to hand over, some of them are saying, let's do the pukka thing and see that everything's in good order first. That's the best chaps, of course. But the middling sort – they've just ceased to care and started shouting for the belly dancers. They've not turned vicious . . . but irresponsible."

"Not here," said Peter; "not yet."

"You wait and see. You're the last lot of British Cadets which will come to Bangalore. From now on it's going to be Indians only. With Indian instructors for the most part. So as far as the white Officers are concerned – whether they're Indian Army or British Army – this is the last term at the old school. And when that comes round," said Glastonbury, "when people are doing the old things for the last time, they're too depressed to trouble very much how well or how badly they do them. Irresponsibility again, you see; a more honourable kind than the other, but it comes to much the same in the end."

The waiters set a final dish before each of the diners: a

creamy confection topped by a light crust of sugar and flavoured (so Peter thought as he tasted it) with grapefruit or sweet citron.

"Anyhow," said Glastonbury, "there's one way in which all this is certainly going to affect you here. Would you like to tell them" – this to Detterling – "or shall I?"

"You seem in a teaching vein, Giles," said Detterling languidly: "you do it."

Glastonbury nodded. He pushed his untasted sweet away from him and beckoned to a servant to remove it. But since Ley Wong was out of the room the servant was dilatory, and before he could collect the bowl from in front of Glastonbury it had been seized by Muscateer.

"Sorry and all that," said Muscateer, "but waste not, want not. Fascinating taste this stuff has."

Detterling, as host, signalled to the servant to return to his place against the wall.

"Your grandmother always had a sweet tooth," said Detterling in extenuation of Muscateer's conduct. "All right, Giles, you tell 'em the form."

"It's like this. As I've been saying to Morrison here, from next month onwards the O.T.S. is going to take in Indian Cadets only, with Indian instructors. But there aren't many Indian Officers who've had experience at that, so they're going to let 'em have a practice go on your lot. Or rather, they're thinking of it – and Delhi's in favour as it'll be a sop to Indian nationalists to see Indian Officers training white Cadets. But before the final decision's taken, they're going to run a test to see how it works. And they're going to run this test on your Platoon. 'No. 2 Pl., C Coy,' the bumf says." Glastonbury turned to Peter. " 'J.U.O.: O/Cdt. Morrison, P.' "

"So that's why we haven't had an Officer yet."

"You'll have one at 6.15 tomorrow morning. Captain Gilzai Khan of the 43rd Khaipur Light Infantry."

"A Moslem?"

"Yes. There was a bit of feeling about that. The Hindus only came round when we reminded them that if the test flopped the Moslems would get all the blame and if it succeeded they'd both share the benefit. I should tell you that Gilzai Khan has been chosen as an Officer of forceful character who is fully expected to succeed."

"I don't understand," said Muscateer: "my old governor said that native Officers were called Jemadars and Rissaldars – things like that."

"Jemadars and Rissaldars only hold the *Viceroy's* Commission. Gilzai Khan has his from the King."

"Your governor was always a bit behind the times," Captain Detterling remarked.

"A wog," said Alister bitterly: "a wog Officer for *us*."

"There are wogs *and* wogs," said Detterling blandly. "I'd drop the word if I were you. Gilzai Khan might not care for it much."

"You're on their side, sir?"

"We're on nobody's side," said Glastonbury. "We're just warning you what's going to happen. Morrison here may have a tricky time as J.U.O. As his friends you'll want to help him."

"Why didn't Major Baxter warn us?" said Alister shrilly. "He's the Company Commander. It was his job, not yours."

"You have a point, Mr Mortleman," Colonel Glastonbury said, "though I cannot applaud your manner of making it." He drummed a little tattoo with his fingers on the table, glanced at Muscateer, who was sweating rather a lot, sucked his lips in and resumed. "Major Baxter," he said, "is a wartime Officer of good record, but he is not by nature a diplomat. He himself is well aware of this defect; and when I told him that I knew some of you, he asked me to take on this task for him."

"We're most grateful, sir," said Peter. "But in a day or two you'll be going back to Delhi. If there should be trouble, we shall need a diplomat to represent us. Since Major Baxter, on your showing and his, is hardly the man to apply to . . ."

". . . You may apply," said Detterling, "to me. I can manage Major Baxter for you."

There was a heaving and a choking and then another heaving, and Muscateer was very, very sick.

"Why is it," said Glastonbury crossly, "that whenever I dine here with people they get ill?"

"Too much of that pudding . . ."

"What was it?"

"Orange meringue pie," said Glastonbury; "Ley Wong's famous for it."

"Funny. I thought it tasted of grapefruit."

Muscateer went on being sick.

"If you ask me," said Alister, "it's the idea of being ordered about by a bloody wog."

Detterling looked at Alister coolly but said nothing. Many waiters appeared with buckets and mops. Soon afterwards, when Detterling had paid the bill, they all took Muscateer home to his basha. He retched desperately all the way but managed to say one thing, this to Detterling: "You won't tell my governor, will you, sir? He'd feel so dreadfully let down."

PART TWO

THE KHAN

AT 6.15 on the morning after the Cricket Trials and Captain Detterling's dinner, the Cadets of C Coy paraded for P.T.

Muscateer, who was looking very wan and feeble, had mustered with the rest of them. Although he survived the initial routine of 'deep breathing' and 'knees bend', when invited to vault the horse he collapsed along the top of it like a rag doll. The British Sergeant Instructor who was taking No. 2 Pl. scraped him off, shook him out and set him on his feet.

"Try again, laddie," the Sergeant said : "take your time."

So Muscateer walked ten paces away from the horse and tottered back at it once more. When he was only a yard or two short, his knees sagged under him and he fell flat on his face, smacking his nose against one leg of the horse as he went. This time, when the Sergeant picked him up, he was streaming with blood and staring into nowhere with a fixed smile which reminded Peter Morrison, oddly enough, he thought, of Ley Wong's grin when he had welcomed them to his restaurant the evening before.

"Go and sit in the shade, laddie," the Sergeant said.

Muscateer didn't move. The Sergeant beckoned to Peter and Barry, who helped Muscateer into the shade of a large banyan tree on the edge of the Physical Training Area. While they were making him comfortable and trying to arrange his long legs in a more or less dignified position, a short, thin man, who had a large, bald head like that of a chess pawn, walked round from the other side of the tree. He was wearing Khaki Drill with shorts, boots and puttees wound up to the knee; his two thumbs were tucked into the twin shoulder straps of a black Sam Browne belt, from the left side of which hung an empty sword-frog.

"I," he said, "am Captain Gilzai Khan. Who are you?"

"Cadet Morrison, sir. J.U.O."

"Cadet Strange, sir . . . and this is Cadet—"

"—Let him answer for himself."

"Muscateer," mumbled Muscateer from the roots of the banyan tree.

"You are Officer Cadet the Earl of Muscateer," Gilzai Khan stated flatly. He squatted down on his hunkers. "Listen to me, bahadur. You are my man now, and my men do not fall out of the ranks unless they are dead or unconscious."

"But he's ill, sir," Barry said.

"Hold your tongue, little boy, until I ask you to use it."

"Sir."

"Not 'sir'."

"Sahib?"

Gilzai Khan spat like a cobra.

" 'Sahib'," he said, "is for a box-wallah or a munshi. My men call me . . . Gilzai Khan."

He looked carefully at the limp and ashen Muscateer. "Muscateer bahadur," he said, "you will get up and follow me and vault over that horse."

Still squatting, he put a hand in Muscateer's left armpit, then slowly flexed himself upright, dragging Muscateer up with him.

"Come," said Gilzai Khan.

Keeping his hand in Muscateer's armpit, he stepped out on to the Physical Training Area. He released Muscateer (who staggered but remained standing), ran towards the horse, clapped his hands twice before his face, and vaulted neatly over on both hands, while his black sword-frog lifted from his rump and fell back just as he landed. He turned to Muscateer and beckoned.

"Bahadur," he called.

Muscateer took two painful steps and stopped. His throat was working and the sweat was rolling down his face in drops the size of cherries.

"Bahadur," called Gilzai Khan.

Muscateer lurched forward. His head went down and he

ran straight at the horse. His absurd legs looked like flapping rope's ends and his arms were stiff along his body. When he was about four feet from the horse, he skipped crazily and then hurled himself into the air, arched over the horse like a length of hose-pipe, and was caught by Gilzai Khan, who held him, bottom upwards, in an inverted 'U'.

"Good, bahadur. Very good. But now you are unconscious," remarked Gilzai Khan, "and now, therefore, you may fall out."

He hung Muscateer over the horse, saluted the gawping Cadets, and strode fiercely away.

"Tactics, gentlemen," said Gilzai Khan: "Lesson Number One, The Frontal Attack. But first . . . where is the Bahadur Muscateer?"

"They took him to hospital, Gilzai Khan. After P.T., while we were having breakfast. The M.O. thinks he's got jaundice."

"Thank you, Morrison huzoor. This evening we shall visit him. All of us, gentlemen; together. And now, the Frontal Attack. When . . . Cadet Mortleman . . . do you think that we use the Frontal Attack?"

"When the enemy is in front of us," Alister said off-handedly.

"That, Cadet Mortleman, is usually the case. But we do not usually employ the Frontal Attack. In what special circumstances do we do so?"

"When we're late for lunch or in a hurry to get home."

"I have a name, Cadet Mortleman, and a title. Kindly use them when you address me."

"A title?"

"Khan."

"I thought that was part of your name."

"No, Cadet Mortleman. It means that I am descended of a princely house of the tribe of the Gilzai."

"And who are they, when they're at home?"

"Frontier men. Warriors. As you would say, real bastards," said Gilzai Khan, laughing lightly, "who do not take insolence from schoolboys. You will write out five hundred times, Cadet Mortleman, 'Officer Cadets must learn the manners of gentlemen', and you will deliver your work to me at first parade tomorrow."

"Like all these wogs," muttered Alister to his neighbour; "can't take a joke."

"What was that, Cadet Mortleman? I did not quite hear you."

"You weren't meant to . . . Genghis Khan."

Whatever the Cadets might have expected by way of retribution for this silly remark, they were disappointed. For Gilzai Khan merely threw his head back and laughed.

"Haw, haw, haw," he chortled, "how I love your British humour. Genghis Khan – that is good, very good, Cadet Mortleman – such powers of thought, such clever play with words. Haw, haw, haw – we have a jester in our midst, brothers, we must show our appreciation. All together now: haw, haw, haw."

"Haw, haw, haw," went the Cadets, swept along by Gilzai Khan's irresistible example: "haw, haw, haw," they went, while Alister sat glowering and champing in humiliation: "haw, haw, haw, haw, HAW."

"Enough, gentlemen; enough, my children. The days will go faster for us now we have one among us to make jokes . . . one – how do you say it? – buffoon. But we must not neglect our work. Life is not all jokes. The Frontal Attack, my Cadets, is no joke at all. Now when . . . Mr Zaccharias . . . do we use the Frontal Attack?"

"I suppose," said Zaccharias, who was a tubby boy with a bland face and a mean mouth, "that we use it when there is no safer way . . . Gilzai Khan," he added hurriedly, as the huge pawn's head made a sudden thrust towards him.

"You are right, Mr Zaccharias." Gilzai Khan pronounced 'Zaccharias' with the stress on the second syllable. "You are right, and yet you are wrong. We use the Frontal Attack when there is no cover, because when there is no cover we must go the shortest way."

"That's what I meant, Gilzai Khan."

"That I know, and so far you are right. But you are also wrong. Why is he wrong ... Mr Murphy?"

"He hasn't mentioned fire-power," said Murphy, a glum, spotty youth, who was even fatter than Zaccharias and was reputed to masturbate four times a day. "If you have superior fire-power, Gilzai Khan, you can blast the enemy to bits and then walk straight on to his position."

"No, you cannot, Mr Murphy. That is what the Yankees thought. They thought they could destroy the enemy with bombs and shells from a distance, while they sat on their bottoms drinking Coca-Cola and reading comic papers. Afterwards, they thought, they could just drive through the enemy lines in their jeeps without fear of opposition. Time after time they made the same mistake – and time after time they and their jeeps were wiped out when they reached their objective. And then they thought they had been heroic, whereas in truth they were simply lazy. They refused to realise that if the enemy is properly entrenched he will survive almost any bombardment; and that in order to take ground, you must engage those who hold it hand to hand and kill them man by man."

"What about the Atom Bomb, Gilzai Khan? No enemy could survive that."

"We are discussing Tactics, Cadet Mortleman, not Grand Strategy. They do not issue Platoon Commanders with Atom Bombs. Platoons must attack their enemy over the ground. If there is no cover, they must attack the shortest way – from the front. So much was correctly implied by Mr Zaccharias. But he said something that was wrong, and I am still waiting for somebody to tell me what. Morrison huzoor, cannot you tell me?"

"Zaccharias lacked confidence, Gilzai Khan. He seemed to think that a Frontal Attack is a last resort."

"So it is. It is much better to advance close to your enemy under cover and then pounce from the flank than to run into the muzzle of his rifles over open ground. Believe one who knows, huzoor: charging over open ground is not enjoyable. No. Mr Zaccharias was wrong in something else. What was it?"

Gilzai Khan moved his black eyes from Cadet to Cadet and then let them rest on Barry Strange.

"Officer Cadet Strange," he said. "They say you had brothers who were soldiers. So tell me, little Officer Cadet: what would *they* have said in this matter?"

"Zaccharias used the word 'safe'," said Barry. " 'When there is no safer way,' he said. My brothers, Gilzai Khan, would have told him that when a man starts thinking of what is safe, he starts thinking of the quickest way home."

Barry, who had surprised himself and everyone else, sat back and blushed.

"Good," said the Khan.

He walked round behind Barry, rested his hands on his shoulders and started to massage the top of his spine with his thumbs.

"Listen, my Cadets," he said. "Officer Cadet Strange has spoken what I wished to hear. In battle there is a right way and a wrong way, a near way and a long way, a fast way and a slow way; but a *safe way* there can never be except for the way home, and that way, my children, we do not take."

That evening the whole of No. 2 Platoon went to the Garrison Hospital to see Muscateer. They marched there in column of threes, commanded by Gilzai Khan, who marched at their head; not behind them, or off to one side of them, or slopping along at his own pace as many Officers would have done, but right there bang in front. This pleased the Cadets very much, though they would have found it hard to say quite why.

But it did not please Alister.

"Why couldn't he let us walk over in our own time?" he said to Peter, as they all crowded into the hospital.

"I think . . . that he sees it as a ceremony."

"Since when was visiting a chap in hospital a ceremony?"

"Gilzai Khan," said Barry, "is not just visiting a chap in hospital but doing honour to a comrade."

"Fiddle di rum-tum-bum," said Alister. "And talking of

bums, you'd better watch yours, little Officer Cadet. All those Moslems are buggers, and this one fancies you."

Barry flushed like a pillar box. "Don't be foul," he said. Then they all followed Gilzai Khan, who himself followed the Matron, who, having seen the Platoon arrive, had recognised the quality of the occasion and turned out in person to conduct them all to Muscateer's bed.

Captain Detterling, who was there before them, sitting by Muscateer and looking worried, rose to bow to the Matron and greet Gilzai Khan.

"He seems rather low," Detterling muttered, and then took the Matron on one side. Peter, who watched them walk slowly down the ward together, caught the words, 'Father in Wiltshire . . . cousin . . . what shall I write to him?', as they went.

Meanwhile the Khan was rallying his man.

"We have come to see you, bahadur," he said rather unnecessarily : "we wish to know when you will return."

"I feel rather low just now," said Muscateer, echoing Detterling.

The Cadets gathered round the bed in a half circle. Gilzai Khan pushed aside Detterling's vacant chair and crouched over Muscateer like a lion over a carcass.

"You must not feel low," he said. "You did well. Muscateer bahadur, *you will come back to us soon* ?"

"All this fuss," muttered Alister to no one in particular, "about someone he hardly knows. But he knows he's an Earl all right, and that's why he's making the fuss."

"If you fellows don't mind," said Muscateer to the Cadets, "I would like a little more air. It's awfully kind of you all to come and see me like this – please don't think I don't appreciate it – but I do feel a tiny bit shut in."

The Cadets moved back a little. Muscateer smiled his thanks and closed his eyes. Even the Khan, crouching silently over the bed, seemed at a loss what to do next. Muscateer opened his eyes again.

"Near our house," he said, "there is a river which flows through a wood. When the spring came and the summer, my

governor and I used to row down the river in a little boat,
through a long tunnel of green trees – until suddenly we'd
come out into the open, into a meadow which there was.
Although I loved the trees, it was a wonderful feeling when we
came out into the open, into the blue sky and the sun. I was
reminded of it just now, when you fellows moved back. Just for
a moment, it was like coming out of the trees into the sun."

His voice, hitherto precise, now wandered slightly.

"Into the sun . . . into the meadow. A meadow by the river
it was, the sort you see in those old pictures, with coloured
flowers, each one by itself . . . all alone . . . as though it had
been specially painted into its place. And there were always
grasshoppers singing. Do they sing, do you think? Anyway,
making that chirruping noise of theirs. And I used to imagine
a knight riding through that meadow, in a long robe, carrying
one of those guitar things, with his 'squire riding behind him
and two dogs with those kind of greyhound faces, leaping
about round the flowers. Not far away was the spire of Salis-
bury Cathedral – *really* was, I mean, not like the knight, who
was imaginary . . . except that he wasn't *only* imaginary
because I knew he had been there once, hundreds of years
before, because my governor used to tell me about him. He was
a sort of ancestor of ours, you see, and one day he'd ridden out
to visit his lady-love – just as I've told you, the robe and the
lute – but he was murdered on the way by six black knights in
armour, who'd been sent by the lady's husband. 'Bloody
shame,' my old governor used to say, 'what a rotten mean lot
of spoilsports.' So they struck him down in this meadow, six
to one, soon after he came out of the wood. You'd think they'd
have killed him in the wood, wouldn't you, where no one could
see them, but there was only a narrow path by the river and
the trees were very thick, so perhaps there wasn't room for all
their horses. That was how the 'squire escaped : he rode back
into the wood, leaving the poor knight dead in the meadow
and the silly dogs whimpering in the flowers."

Muscateer closed his eyes and fell asleep. Gilzai Khan, who
was still crouching close over the bed, straightened up and
shook his head briskly.

"We shall come again soon," he said, half to Muscateer and half to the Cadets. "You may return to your quarters in your own time, gentlemen. Officer Cadet Strange, you will come with me."

"Was he delirious, do you think?" said Alister.

"Jaundice doesn't make you delirious."

"Perhaps they'd given him some drug that made him peculiar."

"He was certainly rather odd," Peter said. "We'd better step out a bit, Alister. You've got those lines to do tonight."

"Lines?"

"Five hundred lines for the Platoon Commander. By first parade tomorrow, he said."

"You don't suppose I'm going to take any notice of that."

Peter heaved a deep sigh.

"I don't yet know much about Gilzai Khan," he said, "but I do know that if you set yourself up against him you're going to come off worst."

"Supporting him, are you?"

"I'm his J.U.O."

"And you're my friend."

"As your friend," said Peter, "I am advising you to write those lines."

"You make it sound like an order."

"You already have your order. From the Platoon Commander."

"A conceited, pushy wog. And what's he doing with Barry, I'd like to know?"

But even as Alister spoke Barry came running up behind them.

"Gilzai Khan," he said breathlessly to Alister, "says you needn't do those lines."

"Mighty big of him. And why not?"

"He says that you must have been upset this morning because of Muscateer and didn't mean what you said."

"Damn his eyes. I meant every word of it. Who does he think he is to start reading my mind?"

"He's let you off," said Peter. "Just leave it at that."

"Then why couldn't he tell me himself? Why use *me* as an excuse for hob-nobbing with Barry?"

"*You* were only an afterthought," said Barry, rather cuttingly for him. "He wanted to talk to me because he thought I'd be able to explain that story of Muscateer's. About the knight in the meadow."

"Simple enough, I should have thought. Horny chap goes riding out to shaft another chap's wife, so the second chap has him ambushed and done in on the way."

"Gil' Khan didn't find it simple."

Barry paused. All round them in the dark was a whirring and a chirruping (grasshoppers? or did they have some special Indian name?) and in the distance was the slow, dull clank of cow-bells. Under their feet the dust of the path on which they were walking squeaked very lightly with every step they took.

"Gilzai Khan," Barry said, "was worried about the 'squire. I had to explain just what a 'squire was in those days, and then he asked me if the knight and the 'squire would have been . . . you know . . . keen on each other."

"How very embarrassing."

"Funnily enough, it wasn't. The idea seemed so ordinary to him that I found it seeming ordinary to me too. But I told him I didn't think they could have been, because the knight was so obviously keen on ladies. So then Gilzai Khan said that that needn't make any difference: the knight could have been keen on ladies *and* on his 'squire too. Is that right?" said Barry to Peter.

"Yes," said Peter unhappily; "I think it is."

"But what really worried him was this. Whether or not they were keen on each other, he said, the 'squire should never have run away. He should have stayed and died with his master. I suggested that perhaps the knight had *told* the 'squire to run away (especially if they *were* keen on each other) but Gil' Khan said that even then the 'squire should have stayed and died. 'From 'squire to knight,' he said, 'or from boy to lover, the duty is clear. If it were you and I, huzoor, you would not leave me.' "

"What did you say to *that*?"

"Nothing. What could I say? But then he pressed me. '*Would* you leave me, huzoor?' he said. 'Would you?' 'I should obey your orders, Gil' Khan,' I said, 'because you are my Platoon Commander.' 'I am your *Captain*,' he said: 'say it.' 'You are my Captain, Gil' Khan,' I said. 'That is true, huzoor. Now good-night and go well. You know how to answer? Stay well, you must say.' 'Good-night, Gil' Khan,' I said: 'stay well.' "

Barry came out of this narration with a flushed look on his face; flushed and excited.

"What's that you called him?" Alister said.

"But just as I was going," Barry went on, ignoring Alister's question, "he called me back to tell me that you needn't do those lines because you had been upset. Then, 'Good-night, huzoor,' he said again: 'go well.' 'Stay well, Gil' Khan,' I said, 'stay well.' "

Something about this ancient formula had evidently caught Barry's imagination. For as he repeated it now his eyes shone and his lips quivered with pleasure.

"What's this new name you've got for him?" Alister insisted.

"New name?" said Barry, puzzled.

"His name is Gilzai Khan."

"That's what I called him."

"No, you didn't. Gil' Khan, you've been calling him. Several times."

"Oh," said Barry; "I hadn't noticed."

"Now, my Cadets," said the Khan: "this is the Assault Course. While you are going over it, live ammunition will be fired over your heads. The regulations state that the Bren Guns from which it is fired must be firmly secured on tripods, having first been so aimed as to fire twelve feet above your heads. And so they will be – except for the gun from which I myself will fire.

Morrison huzoor, assemble the Platoon by sections on the start line. . . ."

As they jumped the first obstacle (a pit with barbed wire at the bottom) Gilzai Khan fired quick bursts which seemed almost to scrape the soles of their leaping feet. As they climbed the hundred-foot net, the bullets cut the strands a bare six inches above their scrabbling fingers. When they emerged from the long crawl through the underground tunnel, it was to find puffs of sand spurting right up their noses. By the time they reached the finishing post, limp, tottering and drenched in sweat, they had a very lively idea of what it was like to be under fire, as distinct from what it was like merely to go over an artificial Assault Course while careful instructors fired on a fixed line many feet above them.

"Now," said the Khan: "I see that some of you have soiled your trousers. Do not be ashamed, gentlemen. The first time I was so close to real bullets I stank of fear for the next week."

"Please, Gil' Khan, can we fall out and change?"

"Indeed you cannot. Where on a battle field could you fall out to change your breeches? You are stuck with it, my brothers, until the end of the morning."

"Now, gentlemen," said Captain Detterling: "Military Law. What you have to understand is this. Whereas there is a lot of ill-informed chatter about the harshness and injustice of the Military Code, in fact this is simply a faithful reproduction of the Civil Code as adapted to military circumstances. The same rules of evidence are insisted upon, the same safeguards are applied, the same rights, in all essentials, are guaranteed. Indeed I have heard it said that the Military Code is often more fair to an accused person than the Civil, in that far greater freedom is in practice allowed to the defence in the style and method of presenting its case . . .

". . . And so, gentlemen," Captain Detterling concluded at the end of the period, "we are confronted with the paradox inherent in all systems of discipline: the most powerful sanctions are those which are never applied. For every time a sanction is applied there is a risk that it may fail of its object and so appear less formidable. Or to put it another way, any overt exercise of authority is apt to cheapen authority, because it reveals that authority must first have been questioned. *The ideal authority is one that is never questioned and is therefore never invoked.* So a final rule of thumb, gentlemen: to prefer charges is a sign of failure; but if you must prefer them, make absolutely sure that they stick."

Captain Detterling gave the class a Machiavellian look.

"Did anyone go to see Muscateer yesterday?" he asked. "I was tied up."

"I did, sir," said Alister. "He seemed in much better shape. He says he's much happier now he's got a room to himself."

"Hmmm," said Detterling. "Nasty business, jaundice. It drags on for ever, and even when it's over I'm told you can't drink for months. I'll pop up and take a look at him tonight."

"On the word of command 'one'," said C.S.M. Cruxtable, not very briskly, "Cadets will place their canes under the left armpit in a horizontal position. Cadets will then remain motionless during the intervening chant of 'two, three', and at the next word of command 'one' they will release their canes with the right hand and bring the right arm smartly down to the side. Now then:—

"ONE – two, three – *One*. Horrible," said C.S.M. Cruxtable good-naturedly, "perfectly horrible. Like a lot of old women waving to their fancy boys in the park. So we'll try it again, gentlemen. Kindly remove your canes from under the left armpit and hold them in a vertical position, flush with the right forearm and down the right side. . . ."

"Map Reading," said the Khan: "Lesson Six. Last week, my friends, we were discussing contours. Today I will show you how to use those contours to draw a cross-section of the terrain as between one point and another. Pencil, paper and instruments, gentlemen, please. And where, Cadet Mortleman, is your ruler?"

"I forgot it, Gilzai Khan."

"I have told you : when we have map reading, bring pencil, paper, compasses, divider, protractor, set square, and *ruler.*"

"And I've told you : I forgot it."

"Then go and get it."

"Oh, I say," said Alister. "It's a good half mile back to the basha."

"I know, Cadet Mortleman. And you will not take your bicycle. You will run all the way there and all the way back. And if you are not back in seven minutes, you will do it again."

And then, as Alister did not stir, "Juldi, juldi," he rasped, seizing the chair from under Alister's bottom and brandishing it with one arm above his head; "juldi, juldi, *pi-Cadet.*"

Alister turned pale and then puce. He clenched his fists and he ground his teeth. Then he slouched from the classroom and was back with his ruler in seven minutes flat.

"I am glad that you have come, huzoor. There is one thing I must know."

"Yes, Gil' Khan?"

"Your friend, Cadet Mortleman. Why does he hate me so much?"

"That is something you should ask Peter Morrison," said Barry. "He's the J.U.O., Gil' Khan, and he understands it all much better than me."

"Come, huzoor; truth between friends."

"All right. It's because you're an Indian. What he would call a native. He doesn't like having to obey you."

"Why is that? I know my trade. The others all obey me. You too, huzoor : you obey me, do you not?"

"Yes, Gil' Khan. . . . You are my Captain."

"Come here, then, and sit. Is it my colour that Cadet Mortleman dislikes?"

"It could be."

"So. . . . And you, little Officer Cadet? Do you dislike my colour?"

"No, Gil' Khan. I like your colour."

"Do you, huzoor? But I have scars, big, white scars. Do you think that you would like those too?"

"I . . . I don't know."

"Then I shall show you and you will see. Do not be shy, huzoor. I am your Captain, and it is a great honour to be shown your Captain's scars."

"Where's Barry?" said Alister.

"The Khan sent for him," said Peter.

"To go to his quarters?"

"I think so."

"Why?"

"Does it matter?"

"It matters very much. If that beastly wog thinks he can start playing games with Barry . . ."

"There is no reason to suppose anything of the kind. Gil' Khan likes Barry and he wants to talk to him. And Barry's not the first to go there; I've been several times."

"You're the J.U.O. And he doesn't fancy your ring."

"Gilzai Khan is an Officer of the King. Barry is one of his Cadets – and old enough to take care of himself."

"Is he? *Is* he, Peter?"

"Look, Alister," said Peter uneasily, "why not drop all this about the Khan? I like him, we all like him except you. And as for Barry – it'll be time enough to start complaining about that if Barry starts complaining himself. He's got a tongue in his head and he's got good friends to come to if he needs them."

"He might be afraid."

"Afraid? He half worships the Khan."

"That's just it. The Khan might take advantage."

"Listen," said Peter. "If I see Barry looking unhappy, I'll take it up with him, I promise you that. But meanwhile, Alister, just stop making trouble. I've had some experience with this sort of thing, and *believe me*, it's fatal to interfere unless and until there is very clear reason. For the rest, you'd make life a lot easier for me and for everybody else including yourself if you'd stop flaunting your ridiculous pride and trying to bate up Gilzai Khan."

"Now this," said Captain Detterling, "is what they call good tank country. Nice and flat, you see, for the beastly things to roll over."

They were standing on a low ridge and looking out over a dreary plain of sand which was unbroken except by occasional dried-up nullahs. Formerly fertile country, all this had been appropriated by the O.T.S. as a training area at the beginning of the war; but beyond the desert which the military had made over the years, and still within the Cadets' field of vision, were kinder sights – small patches of green, scattered wooden shanties, and, just discernible, a yoked bullock plodding interminably about a well.

"You may be hoping," said Detterling, "that those nullahs would put a stop to any nonsense with tanks, but not a bit of it. They're not deep enough. The tanks would just crash in, nose first, and then heave themselves out the other side. It's astonishing what purchase they can get with modern tracks. No, gentlemen; there's nothing to stop tanks for as far as we can see from here, unless some of those fields in the distance turn out to be paddy fields. But as it happens, they're not paddy fields. Can any of you," said Detterling with a self-satisfied air as of one who had been in India thirty years instead of barely thirty days, "explain how I know that?"

Since he was obviously itching to tell them himself, the Cadets maintained a tactful silence.

"Paddy fields," said Detterling, "are always below the level of the surrounding countryside because they have to be flooded. And since they're flooded, they sometimes bog down tanks. However, none of these fields appears to be lower than the rest of the land, *ergo* they're not flooded, *ergo* they wouldn't bog down tanks, *ergo* we've got the whole damned area to play with.

"Now, gentlemen. Let us imagine that we have at our disposal one Sabre Squadron, with which to support one Rifle Battalion of Infantry."

"*Sabre* Squadron, sir?" said Cadet Zaccharias.

"It's what we call a fighting squadron of Cavalry," Detterling said, "even though we now have bloody tanks. In battle, my Sabre Squadron would consist of a Headquarters Group and three Sabre Troops of four tanks each. Each Troop would support a Company of Riflemen and each tank would support a Platoon. You infantry chappies would use the tanks as carriers and cover and sources of supporting fire. To illustrate how it all works, and at the risk of boring us all to death, I have devised a theoretical manœuvre which we shall now carry out on this charming plain."

They spent the rest of the morning wandering over the plain, some of them pretending to be tanks and the rest of them being the infantry. In fact Captain Detterling's manœuvre was quite interesting, because it had been clearly thought out, it progressed by definite stages and it proposed a number of dramatic problems. It was rather difficult, however, to connect such very sedate proceedings with actual warfare, especially when they remembered what it had felt like, on the Assault Course, to have real live bullets spitting dust up their nostrils. Indeed Detterling himself felt bound to point out how artificial it all was.

"I've not seen much action myself," he told them, "because I kept out of it whenever possible; but I've seen a bit, and of course it's not at all like this. On this exercise we have a plan and we're following it. In action the plan has to be changed every five minutes, and anyhow everyone's too frightened to remember what it is, even supposing they ever knew in the first place. So you just muddle on and hope for the best."

After hearing this, they executed several more precisely ordained movements, until Captain Detterling announced that the enemy was defeated and that it was time for lunch. By now they had arrived at the far end of the sandy plain, where they were gratified to see a large marquee which had just been erected by the mess servants. They could not, of course, eat their lunch in the open because the kite-hawks would have spoilt it by swooping at their food.

"It's this sort of thing," said Detterling as he sat down next to Peter, "which did for the Italians in the desert. The Officers insisted on a proper lunch, so every day at noon everything else had to stop while a marquee was put up by the men and their Officers were served with the whole damn rigmarole from antipasta to zabaglione."

"You were in the desert long, sir?" Peter asked.

"No longer than I could help. It was perfectly foul," said Detterling crossly, "what with the heat and the cold and nothing to drink and that bloody man Montgomery sucking up to the troops, it made one despair of the human race. The only sensible people there were the Italians, who did nothing but surrender, so *they* didn't last long, and when they'd gone the British and the Germans got so enthusiastic that it positively turned your stomach. Even Giles Glastonbury got enthusiastic and took it all seriously, so much so that he shot a sentry because he found him asleep on guard duty. Of course that was going too far, and so they told him, but it was the *kind* of thing everyone was doing, otherwise Giles wouldn't have got away with it so easily."

"Was that why he was sent on to India?"

"Yes. Mind you, there's good precedent for shooting a sentry who goes to sleep – I think it counts as desertion in the face of the enemy – but it's not what one expects of one's friends. Giles ought to have been more tolerant. And while we're on the subject of Giles, he ought to have known better than to talk like he did the other night. All that stuff about getting his whores from Ley Wong on the cheap. He's very rich, and he's a sort of cousin of the King's, and a man in that position jolly well ought to pay full price. How can one respect one's sovereign if his cousin's being stingy in knocking shops?"

This question being quite unanswerable, Peter turned the conversation to Gilzai Khan.

"I hear he's rather a success," Detterling said. "He wanted to come on this affair today – said he was jealous of other people taking his Platoon without him – but I persuaded him to go and spend the morning cheering up Muscateer."

"He'll like that. They both will."

"Yes. . . . He says there's only one thing which really bothers him, and that's your chum Mortleman. I was afraid there might be trouble there."

"Alister's been very silly, but I think I've made him see sense."

"Good. You see, they're an odd lot where Gilzai Khan comes from and they've got a funny streak. If Mortleman goes on taking the piss, the Khan might turn up nasty – and I mean nasty – and that," said Captain Detterling, "would be rather a pity for all concerned."

"I have to tell you, sahibs," said the Munshi, "that today has been our last lesson. Your study of Urdu is to be discontinued. For myself, I am sorry, as I shall no longer be employed; for my country, I am glad, as it means that the British will soon be departing."

"Why are you so keen to get rid of us, Munshi sahib?"

"Because, Morrison sahib, we wish to order our own affairs. We shall not order them as efficaciously as you do, my God, no, but then efficacy is not important to us, you understand."

"No, Munshi sahib; I don't understand."

"We do not set the same values on the same things. And that is all."

"But you aspire to be a modern nation?"

"Politicians' talk, Murphy sahib. We merely aspire to be left in peace."

"And if you starve?"

"We have always starved. Many of us are starving at this minute."

"Not nearly as many as will starve when once we're gone."

"You are right, Mortleman sahib, but there is no need to sound so pleased about it."

"It's your fault. You will insist on the British leaving."

"Partly because we do not like being spoken to in that tone of voice. But let us not quarrel on our last morning together.

It is important that we should part in amity. And so : salaam, Morrison sahib, it has been a pleasure knowing you and you have done well. Salaam, Murphy sahib, you have been idle but in no way offensive. Salaam, Mortleman sahib, and may God lend you gentleness. And the last of our little group, my Lord Muscateer, he is still in hospital, poor boy?''

"Yes, Munshi sahib."

"You will take him my salaams, then, and say that I am sorry to have seen him so little. Wish him health and wisdom and a safe return to his father, for a great inheritance is no light matter. And now, sahibs, go in peace."

Murphy smiled politely but vaguely, while Alister muttered something.

"Stay in peace, Munshi sahib," Peter said.

"True Mohammedans," said the Khan, "do not eat pig and do not drink wine. They also have their foreskins cut."

He surveyed No. 2 Platoon with a fierce grin.

"For myself," he said, "I eat pork and I drink alcohol and I do not give a good God-damn who has a foreskin and who has not. Indeed, I have reason to believe that a foreskin keeps the flesh tender and – how do you say? – sensitive, and so makes for an increase of pleasure."

He grinned again, rather as if he had a stock of foreskins at his disposal which he would be happy to distribute on request to those deprived.

"And so," said the Khan, "I am not a religious man. I am unclean. I am defiled." He put his left hand down to his flank and started to fiddle with the empty sword-frog which hung there. "I acknowledge Allah and I respect his prophet, but there is an end of it. If I went into a Mosque, I should take my shoes off, but I should not go inside to pray, I should go inside looking for Subadar Doraini Mahmet, a religious man if ever there was one, who lost fifty rupees to me at dice ten years ago, when I too was a Subadar, and has not yet paid. So every time I see a Mosque, I say to myself, 'Perhaps that hound Doraini Mahmet is in there praying, I will go in and demand my due.' I have not yet found him, my Cadets, but one day I shall, and it will be a black day for Doraini Mahmet, that I promise him.

"But why do I tell you all this? Simply to show that I, Gilzai Khan, am not a man for prayer or fast or thrusting my God upon my fellow men.

"In brief, my brothers, I know and mind my business, and I expect others, whether Mohammedan or Hindu, to mind theirs. But this is what they will not do. Hindu and Mohammedan, they are for ever calling down curses upon each other and draining each other's blood and slicing off each other's parts because the foreskin has been cut or not cut, as the case may be.

"And so what is a man to do? Ignore this folly you say; but this folly is everywhere in India and may not be ignored. A sea of folly over the earth, my brothers – which will turn to a sea of blood the first minute the King Emperor withdraws his might and his men. Ignore it? We shall be swimming in it – those of us who are still here. As for you, you will be gone. But as for me . . . this is my country, so here I must stay. And when the knives come out, mine too must come out, to protect my own people. I cannot stand by and watch while Hindus slaughter Moslems, however much I may condemn the folly of both. A man must fight for his own kind, and if that kind and another kind take arms against each other in the one country that both believe to be their own, then a man were better unborn than live to see it."

And then one evening a few days later they heard that Muscateer was dead.

"Dead, sir? Dead of *jaundice*?"

"They say he had a dodgy liver," Captain Detterling said. "Funny, that. His old governor's is made of brass."

"Bad news, Molly. Muscateer's done for. I've just had a wire from his Commandant."

"Oh. Oh dear. Oh dear. Oh dear. Oh dear."

The Marquis Canteloupe handed his wife the Commandant's telegram and went to the window. Outside, February
lay long and blank over the Wiltshire fields.

"I thought," said Lady Canteloupe eventually, "that cousin
Detterling's letter said he was all right."

"Some time ago, that was. Poisoned in a wog cook-shop,
Detterling said, but not to worry. Seems he was wrong. Jaundice, that telegram says. Something to do with the liver, ain't
it?"

"My father had it. Twice."

"I s'pose Muscateer gets it from him. Not your fault, old
girl. Pity it's too late for another, though." He turned back
to look through the window. "When there's all this."

"He was such a kind boy," Molly Canteloupe said.

"It'll all be wasted on my bloody brother Stephen. Or
Alfred. Should either of 'em live to collect it."

"Why should this happen to such a kind boy?"

"Ask me another," Lord Canteloupe said.

And with that he left the room and then the house, and
walked sharply across his demesne to a small boat house which,
until now, no one had ever entered during the winter. Someone had locked it until the summer should come, but Canteloupe, knowing what he wanted and being a man unaccus-
tomed to hindrance, kicked the door in with one blow of his
foot, and then dragged a rowing boat down into the creek
which lapped into the open end of the shed. Once seated in the
boat, he fitted the oars in the rowlocks and coaxed his way
down the narrow creek, shoving at the banks with his oar-
blades to gain passage and correct his course.

Very soon he reached the river. Without hesitation he
turned upstream and rowed towards a distant wood; but Canteloupe, facing to stern as he rowed, could not see the wood:
his view was of marshy flats lined with willow that stretched
silently away, growing dim and white in the lurking mist; and
ever between him and this view, sitting in the stern and holding the steering ropes, was a lightly flickering shade, now of a
little boy in baggy shorts, grinning gaily at the start of a new
day—

'Daddy, daddy, Mr Synge at school says there's going to be a war soon. *Is* there? And when will it be my turn to row?'

—now of a furry and pustular ephebe in worn corduroys—

'Father, I'm worried about mother. She gets so lonely while you're away fighting.'

—and now of a fine young man, stretched lazily across the seat with his long legs thrust out in front of him and crossed at the ankle, with eyes that smiled even when his face was grave, with large, brown capable hands—

'So you've come home, Papa, just when I'm going off to join up. Lucky for me the war in the East is over, though I don't care for the sound of this new bomb.'

So Canteloupe came, as they had always come, to the trees which spread their branches over the river; only now the trees were leafless and he could see the low, grey sky above; and when he came out on the other side of them, into a meadow which there was, it was not like coming out of a dark tunnel (as it always used to be) but more like emerging from a narrow street into an empty square. But if this was different, the voices were the same: 'Daddy, Daddy . . . Father . . . Papa. Tell me the story about the knight, the knight who was murdered in this meadow.'

And when he heard these voices, the unhappy man at last bowed his head and wept. Hitherto he had kept his face straight and stern, like a face on a tomb, as became a nobleman of ancient line who was visited with great misfortune; but now that the voices had asked for the story which he had told so many times, he shipped his oars and bowed his head and wept, babbling out the story as the tears ran down his face, interrupting it, now and then, to pray for the souls of the murdered knight and his own lovely son . . . until the kindly river, seeing that he would row no more that day, took his boat in its slow stream and carried him back again through the trees, the way that he had come.

"Your trousers are muddy, dear."

"I've been down to the river."

"I see. I've been thinking. We can have him brought home, you know. Even if they've already . . . We could still have him brought home. Then he could be here, which is only right."

"He'll sleep sound enough where he is," said the Marquis Canteloupe. "Look 'ee here, Molly. We'll speak no more of Muscateer in this house. He was our boy, and now he's dead, and there's an end of that."

And so Geoffrey Humbert Charles fitzAvon Julius d'Azincourt Sarum, called by courtesy of England the Earl of Muscateer, went to his long home in Bangalore, riding on a gun-carriage drawn by his comrades, as a soldier should. Gilzai Khan and Major Baxter marched in front of him and Sergeant-Major Cruxtable waddled behind, while the drums and bugles of a nearby British Battalion played him bravely on his way. In the graveyard of the Garrison Church, amidst the hideous but durable monuments of three generations of sahibs, he was received by a Chaplain with the rank of full colonel, who introduced him to his new quarters with unctuous aplomb; after which a firing party let off several rounds of blank over him without serious misadventure. Captain Detterling, as the nearest relative present, then cast the first dust upon the coffin; the Commandant of the O.T.S. succeeded him; and it was just as the Commandant was returning the trowel to the Chaplain that something quite appalling occurred.

Gilzai Khan began to keen.

At first no one knew what it was or who. There was a sound that might have been the wind on a winter shore, followed closely by another which might have been made by a rutting cat, and then a series of long wails reminiscent of faulty plumbing in a Bloomsbury hotel. Everyone looked about in some alarm, while Major Baxter took the trowel from the Chaplain and did his bit with it, but no one was any nearer to an explanation either of the noise or its meaning until C.S.M. Cruxtable, who knew a thing or two in his quiet way, moved quickly round the grave in order to accost Gilzai Khan, who was standing behind Detterling and the Chaplain and was therefore concealed from the other mourners. What Cruxtable intended to do when he reached the Khan nobody would ever know; for before the confrontation could take place, the Khan moved forward to take his turn with the trowel, and while he was doing this he really let rip.

By this time it was clear to all present what was happening and why, and reactions were various. C.S.M. Cruxtable shrugged his shoulders and rolled back to his former place. The Chaplain stood with his mouth open, rather as if he expected someone to put a jelly baby into it. The Commandant gritted his teeth and flared his lips, like a neighing horse. Major Baxter scratched his arsehole vigorously. Alister Mortleman was working his face in fury. And the other Cadets looked sad and foolish because a man whom they trusted was letting them down. Only Captain Detterling seemed unaffected by what was happening, and he it was that saved the situation. As Gilzai Khan stepped back from the grave, flourishing the trowel over his head and screeching like a banshee, Detterling stepped forward to embrace him, and in a loud, clear voice that all might hear thanked him, in the name of the Marquis Canteloupe, for the tribute which the Khan had paid to his son.

"The noble Lord his father shall hear of this," said Captain Detterling, "and send his greeting over the ocean to Gilzai Khan."

This remark settled everyone, including Gilzai Khan. The senior men present were comfortably confirmed in their view that only white men could deal with natives, while the Cadets, except for the furious Alister, felt that Gil' Khan, after all, had done something rather splendid after his own fashion.

So it was in an atmosphere of relief and good will that they all adjourned to Ley Wong's Chinese Restaurant for the wake.

Why Ley Wong's should have been chosen for this purpose rather than Wellesley Mess, no one was quite sure. Possibly Detterling (who was in charge of this part of the arrangements) had thought that Ley Wong would do the thing better;

possibly the Commandant had persuaded him that to have a funeral feast going full blast in the middle of the O.T.S. at noon would be bad for discipline. However this might be, Ley Wong's was where they went, and a very nice change it made.

Present were all members of Muscateer's Platoon with their Commander, Captain Gilzai Khan, and also the Commandant, Major Baxter as O.C. C Company, Captain Detterling, Sergeant-Major Cruxtable and the Bugle-Major who had led the Drums and Bugles during the morning's ceremony. So although they had been allotted the largest private room, there was rather a crush; and since Ley Wong had laid on a Chinese banquet of thirty-five courses, each one more elaborately spiced than the last, their faces were soon dripping with sweat, which was mopped up by two attendants who made an unceasing circuit of the banqueters carrying towels soaked in buckets of jasmine water. After the fifteenth course, Cruxtable and the Bugle-Major retired, being the only two present who did not either hold or aspire to commissioned rank; after the twentieth course the Commandant withdrew to keep an appointment with the Resident; and after the twenty-fifth Major Baxter excused himself on the ground of work waiting for him in the Company Office. This left only the principal mourners, if you could call them that, who by this time, with the exceptions of Captain Detterling and Peter Morrison, were exceedingly drunk. As Gilzai Khan had told the Cadets, his nominal adherence to Islam did not inhibit him in the article of alcohol, of which he consumed twice as much as anybody else with perhaps two-thirds of the effect; and even Barry Strange, who was normally cautious when the wine-cups glistened, had caught the spirit of the occasion and was busy downing bumpers with Wanker Murphy.

As drunk as anyone else, but by no means as happy, was Alister Mortleman, who gave the impression of biding his time. This he judged to have come when he saw Gilzai Khan leaning across the table to associate himself in a bumper with Murphy and Barry. As the Khan's glass came across to touch those of the other two, and as Barry smiled a welcome first to the Khan's glass and then to the Khan himself, Alister pushed back his chair, lurched round the table, and rapped the Khan sharply on the shoulder three times.

"Yes, Cadet Mortleman?" said the Khan, not looking at Alister but smiling back at Barry instead.

"British Officers," said Alister, "don't do that sort of thing. They don't make a beastly caterwauling at a funeral."

"I am not a British Officer," said the Khan, still smiling at Barry.

"You hold the King's Commission. *The King's Commission*," Alister screamed.

Whereupon everyone else was silent and the Khan, though still looking at Barry, no longer smiled.

"That does not prevent me," said the Khan, "from sorrowing for a dead friend."

"But he *wasn't* a friend," said Alister in a high, wild voice: "you hardly even knew him."

At last Gilzai Khan turned to face Alister.

"He was my man, and I knew his quality."

"You stinking black snob."

Gilzai Khan got to his feet, slapped Alister smartly but not very hard across the cheek, sat down again, raised his glass to Barry, and drained it.

"I could report you for that," Alister squealed; "you'd be sacked."

"But you won't, Cadet Mortleman. Because you are an Englishman, and whatever your faults you do not bear tales. Besides, it was, as you know, a challenge."

"Now look here, you two," began Peter Morrison from across the table. He turned to Detterling for assistance, but Detterling pursed his lips and poured himself more wine.

"Necessity," Detterling said. "Those two were bound to have a row in the end."

"But a challenge, sir? A duel?"

"It's often happened in the best circles."

"They're both drunk."

"So much the better. Neither of them will get hurt."

And Detterling looked across with interest to see how the affair would progress. As for the Cadets of No. 2 Pl., what with the heat and the succulent dishes of food which were still being served, what with the pools of spilled wine and the broken glass and the ubiquitous scent of jasmine, most of them clearly regarded the whole business as totally unreal, as a kind of cabaret got up to round off a memorable entertainment; and even those who were more alive to what was going forward took their cue from Detterling and looked on without apprehension or partiality. Apart from Peter Morrison, only Barry Strange seemed to fear any serious threat; but when he started to get up, presumably to intercede between his two friends, the Khan shook his head and frowned so heavily that Barry at once huddled back into his seat.

"Now," said the Khan to Alister. "I am the challenger, so the choice of weapons is with you. But since I shall destroy you, with any weapon known to either of us, within thirty seconds, you will allow me to make a suggestion. A contest, Cadet Mortleman, which will injure neither of us and will therefore make no scandal; a contest in which, indeed, I shall have the advantage of experience but you will have the advantage of youth; a contest for which we are both somewhat unmanned by drink, but you no more than I."

And with that Gilzai Khan clapped his hands and beckoned to Ley Wong, into whose ear he whispered at some length.

"Now, gentlemen all," he said, as Ley Wong bowed himself from the room, "what you are about to see is to be a secret between us as comrades of the same Platoon. By the memory of the friend whom we have buried, you will all swear yourselves to silence. All raise your right hand and repeat after me. . . .

"By the memory of the Muscateer bahadur do I swear to keep silence when I leave this room."

Three minutes later, a string of six girls was ushered through the door by Ley Wong. Two were Indian, slim and delicate; two Malayan, plump and dimpled; and two were Indo-Burmese half-breeds, childish in face yet full in figure : and all were naked above the waist.

"You choose first, Cadet Mortleman," said the Khan : "one, two or three. The contest is this : which of us shall prove his manhood the more times in twenty minutes. So choose up to three girls and then go about it as you please; they will obey your slightest order. But remember one thing: when I say 'prove your manhood', you must be seen to have done so. You understand?"

Alister nodded.

"And the judge of that," said the Khan, turning to Peter, "shall be you, Morrison huzoor. You, so to speak, shall award the hits."

"Oh, I say," Peter began, but the Khan ignored his incipient protest and turned away to strip. As did Alister. Two couches were now deposited by servants in the narrow but adequate space between that side of the table, which was opposite Peter, and the wall; while those sitting in that area withdrew their chairs to either side in order to give Peter a clear view. It was a measure either of the Khan's authority, or of the amount that had been drunk, or of both, that no one except Peter seemed to think any of this in the least extraordinary. Indeed many Cadets were making fairly obvious preparations to enjoy themselves fully on their own account.

When Alister and Gilzai Khan were both fully stripped, Alister chose two girls, a Malayan and an Indo-Burmese, and motioned them both to sit on his couch. Of the remaining four, the Khan chose three, two of whom, rather surprisingly, were the Indians and the other the second Malayan. While the un-selected girl slipped quietly from the room, the Khan instructed one Indian to go to his couch and his other two girls to stand off on one side. He then looked at Peter.

"Give the signal, huzoor," he said. "Remember: twenty minutes."

Peter gaped. Detterling produced a gold hunter and placed it in front of him.

"Starters' orders," Detterling said: "don't keep 'em hang-ing about."

"Er . . . go," Peter said absurdly, and each contestant leapt to his own pitch.

The Khan did not bother to undress his girl; he merely opened his legs slightly (showing two ugly white scars, one on each hairy thigh and both about three inches below his crutch) and made her apply a simple manual technique. Alister was more elaborate; he fiddled rather foolishly with the skirts of the Malayan before bringing the other girl's head to his lap. Crudity paid off : for the Khan was the first to show, inside a minute, with a magnificent rainbow which arched over the table and splashed down, amid a delighted cheer from the Cadets, within a foot of Detterling's hunter. But Alister was not far behind; twenty seconds later he lifted the head of the Indo-Burmese and showed himself to Peter as he scored a palpable point, though less spectacular than the Khan's. Meanwhile he had succeeded in uncovering the Malayan; he spread her thighs quickly, plunged in while still erect, and set to work with a powerful yet unhurried action of the hips and pelvis.

At the same time the Khan, who had dismissed his first Indian, was toying gently with his Malayan's fesses, while encouraging the second Indian to amuse herself just in front of him. Rightly considering that it would be some minutes before he was called on to judge a second coup for either party, Peter took a look round the audience. Murphy, as might have been expected, was stroking himself glutinously and taking no trouble to hide the fact; Zaccharias was doing the same, but furtively, with prim, genteel little movements. Other Cadets, in twos and threes, were setting up primitive mutual arrangements, while yet others were simply staring at one or other of the two principal tableaux as though at the ark of God. Barry, sitting next to Murphy, was ignoring him entirely and gazing, with an attention that was part puzzled, part wistful and part resentful, straight at the Khan's swelling groin . . . on to which, having first lifted her into the air with both hands and dangled her over him while he took aim, the Khan now clapped the splayed Malayan, making her buttocks squelch like a sponge. He then proceeded to joggle her quickly up and down, looking intently, the while, at the gracefully self-administering Indian, and thirty seconds later, with a yell of triumph, extricated himself from his subordinate position just in time to give Peter clear proof of a second score.

Alister, once again, was not far behind. He had been going

very, very easily in the conventional position, and now flattened one of his Malayan's legs, rolled sideways off her and over it, and presented Peter with an ungenerous but indubitable emission. Eight minutes to go and all square: could either – or both – of them manage another goal?

Once again, Peter glanced round at the audience. Most of the twosomes and threesomes were still going full swing, but the facile Murphy had finished his business and shut up shop, and was lugubriously eyeing Zaccharias, who just then gave a mean little moan of fulfilment and sat quite still. Barry was looking as intently as ever at the Khan, though now with a thoughtful and academic air, his former hurtness and bewilderment having given place to an objective appreciation of efficacy and style.

But the Khan was now failing. His weapon had drooped and died; the first Indian girl, whose expert touch had done so much for him at the outset, was powerless to rouse it; and the auto-erotic exhibition of the second Indian had now lost all interest for him. For a moment his eyes hardened while he took a snap decision . . . as a result of which he turned on to his stomach and called on all three of his hand-maidens to gouge at his bottom with their finger-nails.

Alister, who was also fading, hit on an equally sophisticated means of resuscitation: he commanded the pair at his disposal to make love to one another while he took himself in hand. The girls obeyed with such evident enthusiasm that they set up an almost visible aura of lust all about them, thus giving a powerful stimulus to Alister, who lubricated his renewed rigidity from a small decanter of olive oil thoughtfully provided by Ley Wong and then, sweating fiercely, half forced and half insinuated himself through the back entrance of the Indo-Burmese. The latter raised her head and mewed horribly, a protest which might seriously have disrupted Alister's concentration – had not the Malayan swiftly forced her friend's face down again, back to the feast which she was proffering, and so closed her mouth for good.

Since the Khan was still on his belly, no one could tell how he was faring. His eyes were closed and his face was calm; but every now and then he would beat the couch sharply with his right palm, indicating to his girls that they should operate yet faster and fiercer on his bottom, which was already flecked with blood. At last he gave a kind of stentorian yap, turned on his side to show incipient renascence, pulled his Malayan down beside him, and sited his piece between her large, firm breasts, which she squeezed together until they engulfed it. The Khan now sought to complete the process of repriming it by a series of slow, heaving thrusts. His face was no longer calm; it was split by a savage grin, while his eyes seemed to be staring desperately into the distance, as though at a quarry which he could just see flickering before him through the trees.

"You must give them the time, old chap," said Detterling to Peter.

"Three minutes to go, gentlemen," said Peter, reading from Detterling's watch.

Alister was now working with a steady and elegant circular movement of his crutch, giving huge and slobbering grunts that might have signalled the oncome either of success or of exhaustion. The Khan was grinding like a millstone, jaw locked and teeth clenched, while drops of sweat bubbled on his bald scalp. His two Indians stood close to his face, fingering themselves and each other, and the Khan now brought his eyes back from the far quarry in the forest to dwell on their activities. As he did so, a light of triumph appeared on his face and he started to grind faster and shorter. Alister, meanwhile, kept the same steady rhythm, but with each revolution his action was growing just perceptibly weaker.

"Sixty seconds, gentlemen," Peter said.

And now, all other amusements being either concluded or suspended, the entire Platoon was watching the two champions as they bid for the winning throw. The look of triumph on the Khan's face was growing fiercer every moment, while Alister was visibly sagging in trunk and thigh.

"Eleven to four on Gilzai Khan," said Detterling.

And indeed the match seemed all but finished in the Khan's favour – when suddenly the goddess, laughter-loving Aphrodite, flew down from Olympus to Alister's aid. For just as he was about to sink back defeated, his Malayan girl, who had been twitching and jerking for some time under the clever tongue of the Indo-Burmese, let out a high, thin wail of ecstasy. Since her face was directly below the loins of the Indo-Burmese and Alister's dangling sack, the breath of her long cry warmed his prostate at the same moment as her gross abandonment refurbished his desire. His whole body pricked and quivered; he gave four short but savage stabs at intervals of three seconds; and then withdrew to show a tiny but palpable pearl at the end of his blood-red wand.

There was a gasp of applause from the Cadets and a quick, wry pout from the Khan, who knew that this must mean a third notch for his rival. But there was still a good chance that he would score an equaliser. For at this very moment he was easing out from under his Malayan's breasts and kneeling up to show himself rampant and ready. A last fond stroke with his own palm, and a mighty quivering ensued. A mighty, an heroic, a magnificent quivering : but no moisture. Gilzai Khan had already been drained dry.

Peter looked at Detterling.

"Does that count?" he said, handing back Detterling's watch.

"No, huzoor, it does not," said Gilzai Khan, cradling his throbbing but infertile tuber. "No rain, no harvest." He rose from his couch and limped, gallant and priapic, to where Alister lay panting and sobbing into the Malayan's navel.

"You have beat me fair and square, Mortleman huzoor," said the Khan. "With this weapon" – he tweaked himself – "you are the better man. And now we shall be brothers, shall we not?"

Alister thrust out a trembling hand and the Khan took it in both of his own. Then he removed his right hand only, turned and beckoned to Barry, and hugged him, when he came, with his right arm.

"You must see your friend safe home, little Officer Cadet," he said; "and then you will come to me, that we may talk of the day's events."

Barry nodded gravely, and bent over Alister. The Khan

dragged himself back to his couch, sat down very heavily, and started to dress. Detterling rose from his chair.

"An interesting old luncheon," he said to Peter. "I should like to see Canteloupe's face when he gets the bill . . . particularly with those girls added on. Good afternoon to you, Mr Morrison."

Peter shoved Detterling aside, trampled through upturned chairs and sprawled Cadets to the door, and galloped down the corridor to the public restaurant, which was empty at this hour of the day except for Ley Wong, who was counting his till.

"Ley Wong," Peter said: "find me one piece girlie. NOW."

The next morning the Cadets of No. 2 Pl. were both excited and morose; excited by their memories of the previous afternoon, and morose because the common round appeared, by contrast, to be somewhat drab. For them, they felt, there could now be no new thing under the sun. In order to restore them to a sense of duty, the Khan devoted an entire period, which was scheduled as 'Current Affairs', to a conscientious account of the sources and symptoms of venereal disease.

"Gonorrhoea," said the Khan, "or the clap. This disagreeable sickness declares itself between three days and three weeks after intercourse with an infected person. It is important that the men whom you will command should be clearly instructed as to the signs which herald its arrival, so that they may report sick immediately and before infecting their comrades."

"But how could they do that, Gil' Khan?"

"A diseased male," said the Khan patiently, "can infect the anus of another male, who can in turn infect the penis of a third."

"Oh, *Gil' Khan. . . .*"

I wonder if I've got it, thought Peter Morrison. But surely not; she was such a sweet little thing that she must have been clean. Three days to three weeks, the Khan says. I can't be sure for three weeks. But I *am* sure. 'Something rather special,' Ley Wong said – and he wouldn't want to risk his good name by serving up damaged goods. Something rather special, a Eurasian, a blackie-white, but more white than blackie, 'Oooh,' she said, 'how big and hard he is, put 'im between my breasts, no, first show me how you do it to yourself, naughty boy, and I will show you how I do it to myself . . . so, with the handle of the hair-brush, it passes the time when you are lonely, but we are not lonely now, there, between my breasts, and I will kiss 'im, so, he is so strong, he is throbbing, he is throbbing – a fountain, a fountain, welling up between my breasts. . . . All gone, naughty boy, all gone. But you are a strong naughty boy, and you have time (yes?), and money (yes?), so you will stay longer and I will teach you many things. But first we wash 'im . . . and then we dry 'im . . . and then we powder 'im – so – and then we leave 'im for a little, and kiss, and tickle on the neck and the ears, and talk of other matters. . . .'

"Morrison huzoor, do you hear me?"

"I hear you, Gil' Khan."

"Your customary look of intelligent attention is absent from your face."

"I apologise, Gil' Khan. Just for a moment I was thinking of . . . other matters."

"Well, huzoor, you will not think of other matters if you get the pox, so hear what Gilzai Khan now says of it. Syphilis, my brothers, or the Great Pox. Unlike gonorrhoea, syphilis is a killer for sure. It makes itself evident, any time between ten and a hundred days after intercourse with an infected person, in the form of a lesion or chancre or ulcer at the point of infection. This lesion or chancre or ulcer is a wet sore which takes on all the hues of the rainbow, and gradually spreads itself, unless treated, eating away the fair flesh, whether it be your white flesh, or my brown, or Ley Wong's yellow, or the nigger's black. The most memorable description of such a sore and its growth is to be found in a piece of traditional English verse :

" 'I took it to the doctor,' "

Gilzai Khan incongruously quoted,

" 'Who said, "Where did you knock her?"
I said, "Down where the green grass blows."
He said, "Quicker than a twinkle
That pimple on your winkle
        Will be bigger than a red, red rose." ' "

A red rose, thought Peter. 'My name is Margaret Rose,' the
girl had said, as they lay there lazily scratching each other's
buttocks, 'Margaret Rose Engineer, I am named after our
princess. What is your name?' 'Peter.' 'Peter what? You need
not fear to tell me.' 'Peter Morrison.' 'Where do you live, Peter
Morrison?' 'I live in England, Margaret Rose, on a farm in
Norfolk, not far from the sea. It is winter there now, and the
fields are black and hard. But soon the spring will come and
then the summer, and my fields – for they will be mine when
my father dies – my fields will be rich with the new corn.'

'Tell me more about your home, Peter Morrison.' 'There
are clumps of birch and pine, which whisper in the breezes
which blow from the sea. There is a church too, and near the
church a little field . . . where we play at cricket from the first
day of May until the first day of October.'

'And all this will be yours?' 'Yes. I had an elder brother,
Margaret Rose, but he was killed some time ago, fighting for
the King. Like the brothers of many of my friends. We are the
lucky ones, I suppose. We were too young to fight, and so we
inherit the land for which they fell.'

'Do not be sad, Peter. Kiss me. And now there. And now
there – see how the nipple rises. There too, lest the other nipple
be jealous. And there. And there. And with the point of the
tongue . . . just . . . *there* . . . And now I will kiss you. There,
and there . . . and there. And see, he is big and strong again.
Now, what shall we do to make 'im pleasure? Tickle him, so,
and stroke him, so, and scratch 'im, very lightly, so. . . .' 'God
oh God, how marvellous. Oh God Oh Christ Oh God.' 'And
then . . . we mount 'im, very carefully, so. And then we ride
'im . . . ride 'im . . . ride 'im. . . . Oh sweet God, I am coming,
Peter Morrison, you must come too when I tell you, not just
yet, he is making me come, he is so big and strong, swelling

inside me, making me come, now, Peter, now, Peter, *now*, Peter, NOW . . . spurt, spurt, spurt, *spurt your hot lovely spunk.' 'Sweet Jesus Christ,* MAKE IT NEVER STOP.'

". . . So do not forget, my Cadets. Tell your men to wear sheaths, and wash themselves immediately after, and use the disinfectant cream that is for issue. And tell them that if they do not, the spirochaete will smash their noses and leave twin black holes between their rotting cheeks. . . ."

'. . . So we wash 'im and dry 'im and powder 'im and give 'im one last kiss. There. And now you must go, Peter.' 'Why?' 'Please do not ask.' 'Very well. But I can come again soon?' 'Of course. But give warning. Through Ley Wong is best.' 'I understand. This is for you, Margaret Rose.' 'Good. That is a generous present, most generous. And do not forget the old lady who will show you out. She is shrivelled and ugly now; but once she was so beautiful, just like me. Come again soon, Peter Morrison, and tell me more of your home in England. . . .'

"Morrison huzoor, let me repeat my question. What precautions will you tell your men to take?"

"Wash 'im and dry 'im and powder 'im – I mean, wear a sheath, wash afterwards, and use the disinfectant cream that is for issue."

"Good, huzoor. Perhaps you have been listening after all."

The old woman who had shown him out. When he had given her ten rupees, she had made a salaam. Something in the gesture had been familiar; it had been precisely the same in style and timing as the gesture which Margaret Rose had made when he handed her her 'present'. His immediate thought had been that the older woman must have taught the younger. 'Once she was so beautiful, just like me.' She still was rather like her – though very much darker in the face. The same eyes, the same mouth, the same hands (which had accepted the ten-rupee note). Her mother. Margaret Rose's mother, serving her daughter as a whore's maid. What kind of woman did that make of her? For that matter, what kind of woman did it make of Margaret Rose? 'We mount 'im, very carefully, so . . . and then we ride 'im . . . ride 'im . . . ride 'im.

. . .' That was the kind of woman it made of her, and for that
he would go again, though the maid were twenty times her
mother and his own to boot.

The next 'Current Affairs' period, one week later, was not
about venereal disease and it was not taken by Gilzai Khan.
It was about the situation which the British faced in India and
it was taken by Captain Detterling.

"Riots," Captain Detterling said: "in Bombay, in Madras,
in Calcutta, there have been ugly riots. The Commandant
thought it would be more . . . tactful . . . if I were to discuss
these with you instead of Gilzai Khan, who is rather annoyed
as a result. He says that his assessment would have been quite
as accurate as mine, and come to that, gentlemen, he is right.
The Commandant requires, however, that on this issue British
Cadets should be instructed by a British Officer.

"These riots, gentlemen. They have arisen because the
Indians are still uncertain what we intend. Now that the war
is over they want us to declare ourselves. As indeed, you might
say, we have – because the Prime Minister has made it known
that he wishes to quit India. But this is too vague, the Indians
reply: no date has been given, no concrete arrangements have
been made. The Indians are asking when and how, and as yet
there has been no answer.

"But then how could there be, gentlemen? To hand over
the rule of a vast continent – of an Empire, no less – is a serious
matter. One cannot just get up and go, leaving one's empty
chair to the first bully boy who can sit down in it. Suitable
replacements must be found, money must be discussed, continued restraint and protection must be ensured for those who
should be protected and restrained. Good men must be trained
and their weapons tested; bad men must be disarmed and their
guns spiked. In short, there must be a complex and laborious
programme – such as no one has yet had the time or the pre-
sumption to draw up.

"And how long will it now take to draw up? Gentlemen,
you may well ask. India is an Augean stable which we must

cleanse before leaving it; how does one even begin to schedule such a terrible task? Unlike Hercules, we are not of divine descent...."

"So what did Detterling bahadur say?" asked Gilzai Khan, when he saw No. 2 Pl. later. "About the riots?"

"He said that they have been caused by our failure to declare our detailed plans," Peter Morrison told him.

"That is right."

"And he said that even to formulate such plans is almost impossible."

"Again, that is right. And you will be under such pressure to leave that you will go before the plans are properly formulated. In any case, what plans does one formulate to keep greedy and superstitious men from each other's throats? How will you satisfy both Moslem and Hindu?"

"Some sort of compromise, Gil' Khan?"

"Neither side will be satisfied unless it is given everything. I hear this afternoon that there are new riots – Moslem riots – in Karachi. The Moslems are demanding the complete expulsion of the Hindu community. What does one do with people who make demands such as these? They are my people, but I say they are mad. Listen to me, my children." Gilzai Khan lifted the empty sword-frog from his flank and slapped it back again. "Such people must be ruled with a long, sharp sword, and the King Emperor alone is strong enough to wield it."

"I was looking forward to coming to India," said Barry Strange at dinner in Wellesley Mess, "but now I'm jolly glad we'll be leaving it when we're commissioned. All these riots and things. It makes a man uncomfortable."

"According to what Colonel Glastonbury said at Khalyan," Peter reminded him, "most of us are now intended for British Battalions in the Far East. That could easily mean British Battalions here in India."

"There's a lot of the Far East which isn't India," said Barry.
"And a lot which is."

"You sound as if you want to stay here."

"I never want to stay where I'm not wanted," Peter said.
"But we may be *needed*. To see that the hand-over goes
smoothly."

"Not much chance of it doing that, from what the Khan was
saying."

"And from what Detterling was saying," Alister Mortleman
put in, "it'll be years before we hand over anyhow."

"And meanwhile, more and more nasty temper and more
and more riots," said Barry. "Myself, I don't at all look forward to putting down riots."

"It 'ud be a sight easier," Alister said, "if we were allowed
to shoot 'em dead. But for every dead wog, a hundred politicians howl their heads off."

"That's as it should be," said Peter. "The rights of the
Indian population must be respected."

"Even when they're rioting against us?"

"They don't know what they're doing, most of them.
They're the dupes of trained agitators, who whip 'em into mob
hysteria."

"Rabble," said Alister.

"People," said Barry. "One can't just mow them down."

"You two just wait till you're on the wrong end of a riot,"
Alister told them, "and find out how you feel then."

"I hope I shall never find out," Barry said. "I might be
ashamed of myself when I did."

"Just so, Barrikins. You might be ashamed of yourself, but
you'd still be feeling what I'm saying – that you wanted to
shoot them all dead. But I don't think you need worry."
Alister leaned across the table and addressed his two friends in
a confidential whisper. "I picked up a rumour today. It seems
that after we're commissioned here, they'll probably send us
all home. *Not* to units in the Far East, but home."

"Why on earth should they do that?"

"The Labour Government are keen to bring everyone home
as soon as possible. They want the Army demobilised because

they think it'll make them popular and anyway they don't care for Armies."

"But there's too much still to be done. We have military responsibilities all over the place."

"They're getting shot of those as fast as they can – even if it means just dropping them down the lats. Bring the boys home, that's the cry. And apparently that includes us."

"Where did you hear this?"

"It's pretty clear from the English papers."

"About *us*, I mean."

"C.S.M. Cruxtable. He's trying to find out what's happened to poor Muscateer's Part One Pay Book, and he had me in to ask if I could help. I told him what little I knew about it, and then we got chatting for a bit. He's a chatty sort of bloke."

"I don't know that one need pay much attention to Cruxtable," Peter said. "There's been nothing official – not as far as we're concerned."

"Always listen to a Sergeant-Major," Alister said. "One word from a Sergeant-Major is worth three official announcements."

"My brothers used to say that too," mused Barry, "or something of the kind. The Sergeant-Major's jokes, they used to say, are the Field Marshal's nightmares."

"So that's what they're saying," said Barry to Gilzai Khan later that evening: "that we'll all be sent back to England as soon as we're commissioned."

"I do not know how that will be," said the Khan. "I am not in the Commandant's confidence here. Nor in anyone else's."

"Oh, surely. Everyone likes you. *We* do."

"You are not on the staff, huzoor."

"Captain Detterling does, I know."

"The bahadur Detterling likes me well enough, I think. But I am not in his confidence. I am an Indian, to whom he does not tell secrets."

"This isn't a secret. It's a rumour going around everywhere."

"But the truth, or the falsehood, behind the rumour – that is still secret."

"I suppose so. . . . Does it make you sad, Gil' Khan? When they don't tell you things, I mean."

"It makes me uneasy. One does not know . . . quite what is in store."

"None of us can know that."

"One can be told what is *intended*. It is a very uncomfortable thing, little Cadet, when all one's colleagues know what is intended and oneself does not. People break off what they are saying, and give knowing looks at one, and take each other into corners so that one shall not hear them."

"Is that what they're doing to you?"

"Lately. They always did, of course, but lately I have noticed it more."

"Why?"

"You ask too many questions, huzoor. The whole evening you have been asking questions."

"I'm sorry, Gil' Khan. There. . . . Does that make up for it?"

"It does, and more. But you must go now. It is late and you are tired."

Gilzai Khan started to lift the mosquito net.

"No, I'm not. Please let me stay a little longer. Please . . . my Khan."

"How can I refuse? Oh, my little Englishman, you make my heart to yearn."

"And you make mine, Gil' Khan, and you make mine."

". . . Oh, God, Peter, you will make me die, Peter, now, Peter, *now*, Peter, NOW."

"Now, now, now, now . . . NOW."

Some while later, Margaret Rose said:

"Next time I will teach you to do it like the dogs do it. When shall you come?"

"Not for a little, I'm afraid. We're going to Jungle Camp."

"You are going away?" (Sharply.)

"Not far. Not for long."

"How long?"

"Ten days. Starting the day after tomorrow."

"Then you can come tomorrow evening."

"No, Margaret Rose. Tomorrow evening we must pack and make ready. We leave soon after midnight."

"But you will come as soon as you get back?"

"You know I shall."

"I will be lonely for you. I shall use the hair-brush and think of you. You too must do it to yourself and think of me. Let us agree on a time, and then we shall both know that the other is doing it too."

"There is not much privacy in camp."

"You will find a place. Let us say . . . ten o'clock at night."

"Every night?"

"No. Too often will spoil it. Two nights from now, and every third night after that."

"All right."

"Yes. For now – for ten days – it is all right. But what shall I do when you go for ever?"

To this question there could be no answer.

"Some time you will go," said Margaret Rose, "and then all the British will go. Then they will murder us, me and my – old lady."

"Murder you?"

"Yes. They hate us because we are neither one thing nor the other. Blackie-whites. Half-castes."

"No one could murder anyone as lovely as you."

"You do not know them. 'Half-caste whore,' they call me. 'Kill her,' they will say, 'kill her because she is unclean' – not because I am a whore, you understand, but because I am a half-caste. 'Kill her,' they will scream, '—and take her money.' "

"Oh, Margaret . . . Margaret Rose. But the British are still here now. We shall be here for some time yet. And so shall I."

"You. You do not care about me. You pay me and you mess me and that is all."

"Don't be bitter. I'm . . . very fond of you."

"And you forget me the minute you go out of the door. Until your flesh gets hard again."

"It's hard again already. Margaret Rose: teach me to do it like the dogs do it."

"You will be generous?"

"You know I will."

"With your heart as well as your rupees?"

"I will think of you when I go out of the door, if that's what you mean. And I've promised to remember you when I'm away at camp."

"Then I will give you something good to remember. Before we do it like the dogs, we must court each other like the dogs. Get on to your hands and knees, Peter. So. Now. I am wagging my tail, see, and I give a sniff-sniff there, and a lick-lick there, and then I squat like this. . . , . And now you, Peter, wag your tail – good, good – and a sniff and a lick and a nip, and a sniff and a lick and a nip. . . . Nice doggie, nice doggie, lift your back leg so, and oh my goodness me. . . ."

Jungle Camp was rough. On the first day the Cadets did a forced march through the jungle (which was really only heavy bush, but quite disagreeable enough) with no rations for twelve hours and only as much water as they could carry in their water-bottles. After this, Peter was too tired to think of Margaret Rose, though their first engagement had been fixed for ten that night. On the second day, No. 2 Pl. was 'cut off' and had to man a defensive position for twenty-four hours; this time they were allowed rations but no fires to cook them. On the third day, Gilzai Khan taught them about jungle ambushes, with particular emphasis on garotting scouts : 'Over his head with the noose, my Cadets, and then squeeze till his eyes burst like plums.' On the fourth day, they practised wading along jungle streams (about twenty miles of them), after which Peter was again too tired to keep his second mental tryst with Margaret Rose. And on the fifth day Captain Detterling arrived at the camp with a face as long as a tunnel.

At first no one could understand why he looked so despondent, for the news which he brought was good. Substantially, it consisted of official confirmation of the rumour that all the Cadets, when commissioned, were to be posted back to the U.K., or at any rate to Europe, and not to units in the Far East. What was more, Detterling told them, the date on which they would pass out from the O.T.S. had been provisionally brought forward by one month, which meant that they now had barely eight weeks' training left. There were, however, some awkward complications about the regiments to which they would be assigned, particularly in the case of the so-called 'Indian Army Cadets'. The British Infantry, it appeared, was shortly to be much reduced in strength, and vacancies in all infantry regiments, especially the smarter ones, would be correspondingly fewer; yet on the other hand there were more Cadets than ever to be accommodated, as no Cadet (it now went without saying) would be going to an Indian Regiment. This meant that none of them could depend on being accepted by the regiment of his previous choice, and that many of them (perhaps 100 of the 300 which made up their intake) would be seconded to other arms altogether, such as the Artillery or the Signals, despite their manifest lack of qualification. But with all this, every effort would be made to suit individual preferences; and if they would all be so good as to write careful answers to the questions on the forms which Captain Detterling would now distribute, they might rest assured that action in their interests would be initiated as soon as he and the forms were back in Bangalore.

The prospect of getting their pips a month early and the certainty of returning to Europe more than consoled the Cadets for the possibility of having to serve in banausic regiments. While the more keen-sighted of them might suspect some instability in arrangements which had been so radically and so suddenly revised, they were all too busy filling in Detterling's forms to bother much about that.

" 'First Choice of Regiment'," Alister said: "The Rifle Brigade. I see we have to list four more. I suppose one may as well put down Barry's shower second."

"The Wessex Fusiliers are not a shower," Barry said.

"Will they still take you?" Peter asked Barry.

"I hope so. Captain Detterling said that family connections would still count for a good deal."

"Well, I've got none there, but I shall try for them too," Peter said, "since the Indian Army's out. What chance do you think I've got?"

"You're a J.U.O. You should get your choice if anyone does."

"We'll see about that. 'Choice of Station in Europe other than U.K.' I think Italy might be rather nice."

"The Macaronis all steal things," said Alister. "What about Germany? I hear you can have all the women you want for a packet of Gold Flake."

"Or Austria," said Barry: "I've always wanted to go to Vienna."

"Excuse my interrupting your plans for the Grand Tour," said Detterling from behind them, "but I want a private word with Morrison."

This took just two minutes, and incidentally explained why Detterling was looking so unhappy. For it appeared that when he left for Bangalore the next morning, he was to take with him not only the completed forms but also 14477929 Officer Cadet (J.U.O.) Morrison, P., who was required for interview with the Commandant in order to defend himself against a complaint laid against him by Miss Margaret Rose Engineer.

They travelled back to Bangalore in a fifteen-hundredweight truck. Detterling was in the cab with the driver; Peter was in the open and very dusty rear, along with Detterling's expensive camping equipment, which took up most of the room, and Sergeant-Major Cruxtable, who took up all the rest.

"And what, Sergeant-Major," said Peter with false cheeriness from his place inside Detterling's camp bath, "is taking *you* back to Bangalore?"

"Lord Muscateer's Part One Pay Book," Cruxtable said. "It's still not been found, so I've got to make an extra special search of everywhere. Office, bashas, messes, hospital – the lot."

"Why the fuss?"

"He's not officially dead until his Part One Pay Book has been handed over to Records for cancellation. So he's still on the roll for rations and pay. It's downright embarrassing. Next thing you know, they'll want to dig him up again, because the poor bleeder's not entitled to his coffin. Being as how he's not dead, you understand."

"He first missed it up at Khalyan. It's probably still there."

"Only we can't tell 'em that, Mr Morrison, because when you all got here the Company Commander signed for you as having arrived complete with Scale Nine Equipment and all requisite documents. We didn't check, you see. So we can't go back on that now, or the Company Commander will be down shit alley."

"What'll happen if you never find it?"

"Lord Muscateer's pay will be docked by so much a week until he's paid for one grave, Officer Cadet for the use of, which he's occupying under false pretences."

"You can't mean it."

"Stranger things have happened, laddie. Still, I dare say he can afford it. He'll have quite a nice credit balance building up with the Paymaster by now. . . . And what's this spot of bother you've gone and got into?"

At first Peter would not answer this; but when Cruxtable displayed total indifference as to whether he was told or not, Peter changed his mind and told him.

". . . Only I don't know what she's complaining about. I never made her do anything she didn't want to and I paid up on the nail."

"It's some trick to get more, Mr Morrison. Does she think you're rich?"

"I don't know why she should. Yes, I do. I told her once that my family has land in Norfolk."

"That'll be it, then. She's smelt money."

"Then why didn't she ask for it? She didn't need to go to the Commandant; the threat would have been quite enough.

Anyhow, I can't think what she can possibly have told him."

"Doesn't matter," said Cruxtable with sombre relish; "as things are nowadays, these bloody wogs only have to open their mouths and dribble, and everyone in the world's on their side against us. No one wants to know the truth of it. They're just for the wogs and against us – and so are half our own people, come to that."

"But she's a half-caste. Which means that proper Indians won't support her."

"They'll support her all right," said Sergeant-Major Cruxtable, "if they think it'll do down *you*."

"The sum of the thing is this," the Commandant said. "That girl swears that you promised to marry her, and that on the strength of that promise she let you have your wicked way with her. And now, she says, she's pregnant."

"So she may well be, sir. By anyone in Bangalore."

"My dear fellow, we all know that." The Commandant arranged his stubby hands as though he were holding reins and then spurred the chair-leg beneath him. "But the point is, she's threatenin' trouble and she'll get support. You know how vulnerable we are just now. Any excuse will do to get at us, and this one's good for riots all over Southern India."

Oh, Margaret Rose, how could you? I lusted, yes, but so did you (or so you made me believe), and I was always tender.

"What does she want, sir?"

"She wants you to marry her. Which really means that she wants a passage to England. I don't think she cares for the smell of things out here, and I can't say I blame her."

A passage to England. For her and (no doubt) her old mother.

"I never promised anything of the kind."

"Of course not."

"And of course I can't marry her."

"My dear Morrison, you don't have to tell me that. Now, if you were an N.C.O., it might be different. N.C.O.s often

marry whores, and I believe that they can make very good
wives. But a gentleman can't marry a chee-chee."

"And so where, sir, do we go from there?"

"That's just it." The Commandant shook up the reins and
petulantly spurred the chair-leg. "If only you chaps would do
as we ask. We do *ask* you to keep away from girls like that,
because this is just the sort of thing that always comes of it.
As you now see for yourself."

"If it's money she wants, sir, I think my father—"

"—No. I gathered from Detterling that you could run to
plenty of conkers, so I put it to her straight. No good. She wants
marriage. As I say, she wants to get out of India – because the
way the wicket's goin' to start shapin' here, Morrison, she
reckons it needs much more than money to keep her bails on.
So if she doesn't get her way, she's goin' to make trouble; and
to stop that trouble I shall have to punish you, and the only
punishment severe enough to have the desired effect will be
your dismissal from this O.T.S. And even then we shan't have
heard the last of it."

"Punish me for what, sir?"

"In *their* eyes, for abusin' this girl's confidence; and in our
eyes, for stickin' yer finger in the wrong honey-pot. *You were
told when you got here not to go ruttin' with native sluts.* Not
that we'd bother about that, if the wind was right, but as it is
we just can't help it. It's not really a punishment, it's . . . it's an
act of policy."

"But whichever it is, it's been settled on?"

"Yes. I'm sorry, Morrison."

"And if I *should* agree to marry her?"

"You'd go even quicker." A vicious back-kick at the chair-
leg. "Officers don't marry Eurasian trash. We had to put up
with it from a few ranker officers during the war, but all that's
over now."

"So there's no hope at all, sir?"

"None . . . unless you yourself can persuade her to haul
down her colours. I've done my best, God knows, and I've got
nowhere at all. But I can give you five days, Morrison – until
your intake returns from Jungle Camp. If you fix her before

then, and show me that you've fixed her, then everything will be toodle-pip. If not, then it's juldi jao, my dear Morrison, for you."

Peter's first movement was to go to see Ley Wong.

"This girlie, Ley Wong : she do me one piece harm."

Ley Wong was very sorry, but there was no accounting for human vagary.

"Colonel Glastonbury, he be angry when he learn."

Ley Wong regretted to hear it; but the Colonel was a man of the world and would doubtless perceive, on due consideration, that such misfortunes were bound to occur from time to time and owed nothing to the malice of Ley Wong. Had not the English a saying, that those who touched pitch must risk defilement?

"You can do nothing then?"

But of course Ley Wong could do something. He could arrange another girl for the Sahib during the remainder of his stay in Bangalore. In all the circumstances, he would allow the Sahib a very generous discount indeed.

"Listen, Ley Wong. I no want new girlie. I want that *this* girlie closee one piece mouth."

The Sahib should recollect that the spoken word was beyond recall. As Ley Wong understood the matter, the damage was already done.

"Not if you get her to unsay what she has said."

Ley Wong deposed that since Margaret Rose had already refused money the only thing which would now change her mind was fear. Although he would normally have been able to operate very effectively on this basis, in the present instance the girl had solicited the protection of the authorities and was therefore not to be tampered with by prudent men.

Then Peter called Ley Wong a fucking yellow bastard and was politely bowed out of the Restaurant.

It was only after this futile exhibition of ill temper that Peter began to realise the true nature of the disaster which now faced him. Hitherto he had assumed, despite Detterling's doleful face and the Commandant's very lucid exposition of the guiding factors, that there must be some fairly easy way of settling the affair. In all his career to date, whether at school or in the Army, Peter had behaved with intelligent propriety; which is to say that he had informed himself which rules were seriously enforced by the authorities (as opposed to those rules which were kept on the books merely for the look of the thing) and had obeyed them to the letter. On arriving in India, therefore, he had paid keen attention to Colonel Glastonbury and Captain Detterling, and from their tone and attitudes he had concluded (among much else) that the rules which enjoined sexual abstinence need not be closely observed, provided only that one paid one's way like a gentleman. The official exhortation to the contrary he had taken to be simply a form of satisfying residual public hypocrisies; and indeed the Commandant, in one of his softer utterances during the recent interview, had in effect upheld this view. 'Not that we'd worry about that,' the Commandant had said, 'if the wind was right. . . .'

But now that he came to look at it all more carefully, Peter saw just how significant this last clause was. 'If the wind was right. . . .' The trouble about the wind was that it was something elemental, something which could not be controlled or 'fixed'. The wind blew where it listed; and while it was not, as a rule, strong enough to disrupt upper-class amusements, every now and again it gave a maleficent blast from the wrong quarter and ruined the picnic. This was what had happened now. He had taken his trousers off to frolic on the grass, and the wind had caught them up and carried them off to the tree-tops. Nor was this wind a mere sportive breeze, sent by one of the minor and more corrupt rural deities who might have been bought off by a congenial offering; the wind, in this case, was an ice-cold gale, and it blew from political Necessity. Whether the British authorities liked it or not, they were now compelled to punish him.

As the victim of Necessity, then, he would receive a great deal of sympathy, had indeed already received some from the

Commandant; but the fact remained that he was trouserless and would cut a very sorry figure when he went home to his friends and parents. He was threatened both with disgrace and with ridicule. The voices of sympathy would soon be replaced by the reproaches of his father and the snickers of light-minded contemporaries. ('Have you heard about po-faced Peter Morrison? Chucked out of Bangalore for humping a black tart.') But there was even worse to it than that; for while he could endure reproach and could certainly face down malice, he could not bear to go home unworthy of his land. He had come forth, as all men who held land should do, to show his love and loyalty to his sovereign, whose vassals, in a sense, his father and himself still conceived themselves to be. If he returned having been refused the King's Commission he would have dishonoured the land for which, as he saw it, he was now doing his knight-service.

And if he had dishonoured his land, he could not return to it. He could not thrive on acres to which he had been false and his title to which would now be a mockery. As he set out to visit Margaret Rose, his mood was not one of anger or indignation or even of anxiety, it was simply one of sorrow. It was his intention to go down on his knees and plead with her to spare his fields from the shame which threatened them and to spare himself from being exiled for ever.

But when he reached the handsome suburban house in which Margaret Rose had her apartments, he found Gilzai Khan on the doorstep. The Khan smiled savagely and played a tattoo on his left buttock with his empty sword-frog.

"Do not go in, huzoor."

"Gil' Khan. . . . When did you get back from Jungle Camp?"

The Khan shrugged and smiled again, dismissing the question as trivial. For a few moments Peter played with the theory that he too was one of Margaret Rose's clients, and that his desire for her had become so fierce that he had arranged the day off from camp in order to come to her. But if so, he would hardly be spending his time on the doorstep, and in any case it was clear from his demeanour that he regarded himself in some sort as a sentry.

"Excuse me, Gil' Khan, but I want to go in and see someone."

"The person you want, huzoor, will soon be coming out."

And sure enough, the door now opened and four large men emerged through it. Two of them were holding Margaret Rose, and two of them her old maid (or mother). A van sidled up the drive from nowhere, and inside ten seconds the four men and the two women had disappeared into the back of it. Margaret Rose neither spoke to Peter, as she was taken past, nor looked at him; he was not sure she had even known he was there.

Gilzai Khan, who had stepped down to the rear of the van behind the rest of them, thrust his bald head into it.

"It was as I told you?" he called.

"It was as you told us," said a voice from inside.

Then the back doors slammed and the van drove unobtrusively off.

Gilzai Khan remounted the steps, took the stupefied Peter by the arm, and walked him away down the drive.

"And now, my dear Peter," said the Khan, using the Christian name for the first time, "we will go to see the Commandant. Later you will eat with me, and then we shall return to the camp together tomorrow morning."

"I think I'm supposed to stay in Bangalore."

"No need, not now."

"I don't understand, Gil' Khan."

"By and by," said the Khan, "it will all be made very plain."

"You're lucky, Mr Morrison," the Commandant said some hours later. "The cloak and dagger boys have got a quarrel with that slut of yours, so *she* won't be shouting the odds any longer."

"Do you mean, sir . . . they're going to charge her with something?"

"Not charge her," said Gilzai Khan; "do a deal with her. Her offence is not really serious as such offences go. It will be enough if she will undertake to leave Mysore State and not to reside within twenty-five miles of any military cantonment or establishment."

The Commandant took up the reins and spurred his chair-leg.

"She's been warned off the course," he said. "Provided she stays off, no one will trouble her. But just let her stick the tip of her nose back into the ring . . . leave alone start pestering me with complaints about my Cadets . . . and she'll go down till Domesday."

"But what is her offence, sir? Trying to blackmail me?"

"No. So far as that went she had a pretty good board, as I told you. She was sure of native support, for one thing. But now she's done something else which will make the Indians drop her flat."

"What, sir?"

"I don't understand the ins and outs, but according to the chappies who flushed her out today she's been running a cloak and dagger racket of her own."

"Surely the Indians will approve of that?"

"No. She doesn't seem to be connected with any of the Indian movements – so that means she's been doing it just for the cash. Her game was papers and passports – that sort of thing – which might have been very useful to them. But she was just pulling in the mangoes on her tod. In short, she's been unpatriotic, as they'll see it, and her a half-caste anyhow, so they'll leave her to rot."

"But if she's been selling passports and so on, sir, she'll surely go to prison as well?"

"It seems the evidence isn't very ample. Our people in that line would sooner do a deal than throw the lawbooks at her. Captain Khan knows more than I do, so ask him."

Gilzai Khan, standing just behind Peter, chuckled lightly.

"And meanwhile," the Commandant said by way of peroration, "all this gets you off the hook. So thank your stars, young Morrison, and don't go gobbling the first juicy fly that floats along the water, because next time you may get reeled in and gaffed in the guts for good."

"You are no doubt thinking," said Gilzai Khan to Peter (in a curry kitchen, out of bounds to all ranks, to which he had taken Peter for dinner), "that the unmasking of Miss Engineer has been most opportune. I have reason for wishing you to know rather more about it."

"I'm not sure I want to."

"It will be good for you, huzoor. For some people – like our beloved Commandant – it is good that they should know only what suits them. They do not appreciate life's ironies and would only be perturbed by them. However, in you I think we have a genuine student of human folly, and as one such student to another I shall be happy to tell you certain things which I know and the Commandant does not. Try this chutney: it contains an interesting spice based on the seed of the poppy."

"Would that be sensible?"

"For you, yes, because you are a stable man and firm of purpose. In the same way, this knowledge I shall now impart is safe with you but would not be with all men. Now, huzoor, as I say: there are some things the Commandant does know and some he does not. What he does know is that a certain document was found in Miss Engineer's apartment, and that this has created a strong suspicion that she was trafficking in military and other identification papers. Since the evidence is scanty, however, the authorities are prepared to waive prosecution on condition she goes away and, as you would say, keeps her nose clean. 'You stick to being a whore,' they will tell her, 'and we will all love you. But no more documents, if you please, and keep your pretty fingers off the soldiers. And now, Miss Engineer, you may show us how grateful you are to us before you depart.' That is how it will be with her. Have some more of the pilau, Peter, and another stuffed paratha with this sauce."

"Thank you, Gil' Khan."

"All this, the Commandant knows. He also knows, though

he did not see fit to tell you, that the document that was found was Lord Muscateer's Part One Pay Book—"

"—Good lord. I never thought that Muscateer—"

"—Which," continued the Khan, "since Part One Pay Books carry no photographs, could serve someone for a short time as a very useful means of identification. A small thing really, and not worth much, but if Miss Engineer could steal pay books, she could also steal Officers' Identity Cards and whichever; and hence it has been deduced that she was running a market in such things. Deduced but not really proven; and herself not arraigned but simply removed."

"Sergeant-Major Cruxtable has been going mad looking for that Pay Book. He says Muscateer won't be officially dead till it's found."

"Well, now it is found, and the Muscateer bahadur can sleep in official peace."

"But look here, Gil' Khan. Muscateer went into hospital only a day or two after we got here. He *couldn't* have been with Margaret Rose."

"He *could* have been, huzoor. In that first day or two."

"She was one of Ley Wong's girls. Muscateer didn't meet Ley Wong until two hours before he was taken ill."

"That," said the Khan, "is one of the things the Commandant does not know. Another thing he does not know – and neither do those perspicacious gentlemen from the Special Branch – is that I myself, as you would say, planted Lord Muscateer's Pay Book."

Gilzai Khan paused for this to sink in.

"When the bahadur was ill," he went on, "I was with him one morning, and he said to me, 'Gilzai Khan, I am much troubled, I have lost my Part One Pay Book, and they keep asking for it.' 'Very well,' I said, 'I will look for it in your basha.' I looked for it and I found it – in the middle of the bahadur's Holy Bible, a present from the Begum his mother. But before I could give it to him he was dead, and in my sorrow I thought of other things than his Pay Book.

"But then, my dear Peter . . . when I heard from Captain Detterling at the Camp about your trouble . . . I remembered.

So I came back to Bangalore on the ration truck early this morning, and I took the Pay Book, and I presented myself as a client to Miss Engineer, with whom I had much jolly pleasure. But when she leaves the room to put the money which I give her in a safe place, I open a drawer and pop in the Pay Book – and later I go to the authorities to tell them that I have suspicions of Miss Engineer. They come to search – and in ten minutes it is all finished, as you saw. Tell me, my friend : was this not well done?"

Gilzai Khan looked like a boastful ten year old.

"You did it for me?" said Peter slowly.

"For you, and for your friend Mortleman, who is now my friend, and for your friend, the little Strange, who . . . who is also my friend. They would be sad if you were to leave them now. And I, Morrison huzoor, if you were to leave me."

"I was going . . . to beg her to stop what she was doing to me. She might have listened, perhaps."

"No. She is hard, that one. She is frigid, did you know?"

"But I always found . . . strong signs of response."

"So did. I. Faked, huzoor. A little olive oil, clever use of the muscles and the voice while pretending to orgasm. 'Oh, he is spurting inside me,' " Gilzai Khan mimicked in a high voice, " 'he spurts so beautiful that I shall die of it.' Well done and worth the money, huzoor : nevertheless, faked."

"You're sure?"

"Of course. If she came like that – really came – with all of her clients, she'd be dead before the sun went down."

"I thought . . . that it was only for me."

"You were meant to think that. Did she teach you to make love like the dogs do it?"

"Ye-e-es."

"Well," said Gilzai Khan, "you should have lifted your leg and pissed down her lying throat."

Peter had missed the better part of two days at Jungle Camp by the time he arrived back there with Gilzai Khan, and as far as that went he was not at all sorry. While he was away, he now heard, there had been more forced marches and almost continual deprivation. Both Barry and Alister had strange, lean looks on their faces, as if they had just joined a religious sect and were obsessed with their own new-found righteousness. It was plain that they regarded Peter, however irrationally, as a deserter; and the account which he gave of his absence (a prosaic story about personal documents which had gone astray in Delhi and needed immediate renewal and signature) did nothing to diminish their contempt. Gilzai Khan's defection had also been marked, and he too was coldly received.

But by the end of the eighth day, during which No. 2 Pl. stormed a derelict temple and Wanker Murphy had his thigh broken by falling masonry, good humour had been restored all round. Murphy's misfortune made everyone feel even more manly than before; and the inconvenience of having to carry him back to camp on a stretcher was largely borne by Peter and the Khan, whose popularity revived in consequence. On the ninth day they swam across a reservoir in battle order, cut their way through ten miles of trackless bush, and climbed from inside a ravine to attack a position from the rear; and on the tenth and last day they erected an *ad hoc* jungle fortress big enough to hold a Company and then burnt it down by way of celebration. In their own minds (thought Peter sadly) they were now lords of the jungle.

But when they arrived back in Bangalore late on the day after, loud and swaggering as Mohocks, the pride of No. 2 Pl. was instantly brought to the dust. Their leader, they learned, was to be taken : Gilzai Khan was dismissed the O.T.S.

"But *why*, sir?"

"He's broken the rules," Captain Detterling said : "an Indian can't get away with that."

"What rules?" Peter asked.

"Regulation Safety Precautions for Use of Live Ammunition from Automatic Weapons during Training on Assault Courses.

He neglected to fire on a fixed line, and sprayed bullets under your noses."

"That was *weeks* ago."

"Another thing," Captain Detterling said: "his political attitudes – i.e. pro-British – are not considered suitable."

"What?"

"I mean it. The Labour Government wants to hand this country over to the Indians, and the Indians can't wait to get hold of it. So the correct attitude for a King's Indian Officer just now is friendly obedience to the British, qualified by determination to be independent as soon as it's feasible; *not* feudal loyalty, openly proclaimed, to the Crown. It's been decided that his appointment here was a mistake."

"Decided by whom?"

"In one word, Delhi."

"Even so, sir, we might have been told more tactfully. Why was it all so sudden? We get back from Jungle Camp, and hardly has Gil' Khan got out of his truck when he's hustled away to the Commandant. And five minutes later the news is all round the bashas. That's no way to treat a good man – even if his politics are out of the fashion."

"My dear fellow, I entirely agree. But there is something else."

They've found out what he did for me, Peter thought, and trembled at the backs of his knees.

"This man Murphy, who was broken up at camp. He was brought into the hospital here delirious. The Matron reported that he was . . . babbling about an orgy at Ley Wong's."

"Oh?"

"Yes. But of course nobody believed *that* story."

"Of course not."

"The trouble was, Murphy was also carrying on about Gilzai Khan and one of the Cadets. He wasn't very clear, but it seems he wanted to own up to spotting 'em through a window one afternoon and tossing himself off while he watched. He thought he was dying, you see."

"And that story they do believe?"

"Yes. The Commandant's very old-fashioned about what he

calls 'the vices of Sodom'. Hence his lack of ceremony with the Khan."

"Did Murphy name the Cadet?"

"No. And now that he's come to his senses he denies the whole thing."

Peter gave a snort of relief.

"Which means," said Detterling, "that the Cadet's in the clear, whoever *he* may be. But Murphy was plain enough about the Khan, whatever else, so there's an end of him."

"He'll have to leave the Army?"

"No – or not for the time being. It's clear that Murphy's not going to tell the tale a second time, and anyhow they don't want a scandal of that kind. So the official reason they'll give for relieving the Khan of his job here will be that business on the Assault Course – which will look much better in the book. But if it were only that . . . that and his politics . . . they'd have let him stay till you all passed out, which would have looked better still."

"When does he go?"

"Day after tomorrow."

"We must give him a dinner – say good-bye."

"The Commandant won't like it."

"It will . . . 'look much better'."

"Yes," said Detterling. "Yes, I think we can get the Commandant to see it like that. I'll promise him that I'll be there to make sure there are no vices of Sodom."

So once again they all assembled at Ley Wong's. Although the feast provided was not quite as elaborate as that with which they had celebrated the obsequies of Muscateer, it was quite splendid enough. Ley Wong had proposed that he should serve the classical Chinese fare which friends offered to one who was going into long exile, and the suggestion had been judged apt. Exile, it appeared, warranted only twenty-three courses, as compared to the thirty-five which they had consumed in honour of the dead; but as Captain Detterling observed, on that occasion the bill had gone to Lord Canteloupe (who had paid without demur and by return of post), whereas this time they must foot it themselves.

And quite apart from the food and drink, there was another substantial item of expense. After dinner had been eaten but while the wine was still plentiful, Barry Strange left the room and returned with Gilzai Khan's black Sam Browne belt. This he buckled on to the Khan, after which he invited him to stand. Peter Morrison now came forward, bearing a sheathed Light Infantry sword, which he fastened into Gilzai Khan's empty sword-frog, kneeling in the manner of a 'squire.

"To show gratitude," he said, "and to pay honour. Go well, Gilzai Khan."

"Go well," chorused the Cadets, raising their glasses to drink: "go well, Gilzai Khan."

Gilzai Khan grinned like a fiend. He stepped up on to his chair and thence on to the table. Then he drew his new sword, kissed the hilt and brought it to the carry, raised the hilt to his lips to kiss it once again, and dipped the point in salute.

"Stay well," he said, his voice cracking very slightly: "stay well, my children . . . my brothers . . . my Cadets."

PART THREE

THE YOUNG KNIGHTS

DOWN THE STEPS from the rostrum on the saluting base came the Right Honourable Edwin Turbot, M.P., late Minister for Public Order in the wartime coalition Government, now the Conservative third of a three-man all-party Parliamentary fact-finding mission to British India. Having quit the steps for *terra firma*, the ex-Minister thrust his rump out behind him, as if inviting the Commandant in his immediate rear to commit a carnal act, clasped his hands over the shaft of his buttocks to make sure that nothing of the kind in fact occurred, and set off at a brisk shuffle to review the ranks of Officer Cadets.

Passing Out Parades at Bangalore were normally presided over by General Officers or distinguished members of the Indian Administration. On this occasion, however, since the local prestige of the Raj was insecure to say the least of it and since riots were threatening for one reason or another in every corner of Mysore State, it had been felt that discretion was more requisite than ceremony, and that such discretion might be combined with propriety by inviting one of the three M.P.s from the fact-finding mission (which was associated in the Indian mind with arrangements for Independence) to inspect the parade and take the salute. The Labour M.P., who had been approached first both as a member of the ruling party and as the dowdiest and therefore most suitable of the trio, had declined to take part in any military function; the Liberal M.P. had shown altogether too much interest in the whole affair; and so the job had fallen at last to Edwin Turbot, who was an old hand at this sort of game but who, it was feared, might lend rather too grand (or even imperial) an air to the proceedings.

Although the ex-Minister had been dissuaded from dressing in a frock coat and had eventually been coaxed into an appro-

priate suit of dark grey flannel, now that he was out in front
of the parade he was beyond any man's control and intended
to give himself full value. Later on he would be making a
speech; just now he was face to face with the Cadets at close
quarters and he was determined they should know it. None of
this sneaking down the line with a neutral simper aimed over
everybody's head – not for the Right Honourable Edwin
Turbot.

"You there," he barked at the third Cadet he came to;
"who won the Battle of Plassey?"

"Clive, sir," said the Cadet, who luckily belonged to one of
the Grammar School platoons and so had a working acquaint-
ance with history.

I hope, thought Peter Morrison, who as J.U.O. was standing out in front of No. 2 Pl. C Coy, that he's not going to ask
my lot that kind of question. Nor did he; Edwin Turbot recognised proper gentlemen when he saw them and was too much
of one himself to take advantage of their predictable lack of
common knowledge. In any case, he had more important
questions for *this* particular class of young officer.

"These rows with the natives," he said to Peter: "have they
taught you how to cope with them?"

"We have been trained in Duties in Aid of the Civil Power,"
Peter said, and followed Turbot along the front rank of No. 2
Pl.

"Ump," said the ex-Minister, and stopped in front of Barry.

"You're Barry Strange," he said.

"Sir."

"How's your father?"

"Well, thank you, sir, when last I heard."

"And your brothers?"

"Dead, sir."

"Ump," said Turbot lightly. "Lucky thing your mother's
still got you. . . . Duties in Aid of the Civil Power," he resumed
to Peter as they passed on, "and what do you" – to Zaccharias
– "understand by *those*?"

"Keeping order, sir."

"Yes. I know a thing or two about that. Easy in England –

so far, that is – because the lower classes have always been a pretty decent lot. But the point is" – this over his shoulder to the Commandant – "what do you teach these boys here?"

"To keep their heads," said the Commandant, giving a sharp tug on the reins, "when things get rough."

"And have *you*," said Turbot to Zaccharias, "been taught to keep your head?"

"Yes, sir, of course, sir," said Zaccharias with a giggle.

"Ump," said Edwin Turbot, and shuffled on to the next platoon.

But of course, reflected Peter, as he saluted and went back to his station, keeping one's head was something which one could only learn by experience, and none of them had had so much as five seconds of that. What the Commandant presumably meant was that they had all been instructed in the set procedure which, if they followed it exactly, would guarantee that no one could blame them for anything later on. The great thing (as Gilzai Khan's dull but decent successor had repeated to them every five minutes in all three of their 'Action in Aid' periods) was that an Officer must never order his men to fire on a mob unless requested to do so by a Magistrate or equivalent representative of the Civil Power; and that even after such a request had been received, an Officer should still not give a fire order until the request had been put into writing and the Magistrate induced to sign it. For it appeared that panicky officials (of whatever colour) were apt to urge the use of bullets and then deny, at all subsequent Enquiries, that they had done so, thus leaving the military commander to sink in the quagmires of shit into which the least drop of spilt blood was always transformed by the politicians.

'And as we all know,' Gil' Khan's successor had said, 'Labour politicians are particularly adept at doing this and particularly keen on it. If you want to lose your commission, the fastest way I know is to scratch an Indian. He may be an escaped murderer, and leading a mob which has already sacked every town from Karachi to Cape Cormorin, but you just touch him – without a Magistrate's signature – and every socialist in Westminster will be squealing for your head.'

All right, thought Peter now, as he watched Edwin Turbot mount the rostrum and take out the notes for his address; so far it's simple; get a signature before you shoot, and even the politicians can't touch you; but what about the Furies, the avengers of crime against brotherhood – do *they* respect the contract?

"For all of you," said Edwin Turbot in a mellow, effortless voice which carried easily over the parade ground, "this is a very great day : certainly the greatest in your young lives so far, and possibly the greatest which you will ever know. For you are receiving the King's Commission. You are being entrusted with the care and command of His Majesty's soldiers – and more than this : there is a sense in which you are being dubbed as knights. These days, of course, titular knighthoods go only to old men, most of whom have served their sovereign at the desk rather than on the battle field – many of whom, indeed, have done nothing more than present large sums of money to approved causes. But there was a time when knighthoods went to the young – to the young, the pure and the brave, who took a vow to fear God, honour their liege lords and where possible to exercise their skill and chivalry in aid of the weak, the poor and the oppressed.

"As it happens," Turbot went on, his tone shifting from the exhortative to the confidential, "there are plenty of such people around you here." He smiled in embarrassment and apology, like the headmaster of a preparatory school about to explain the facts of life of those leaving that term. "Despite many years of British rule, this is still a corrupt and superstitious country, in which peasants are strangled by moneylenders, priests obstruct necessary social reform in the name of unspeakable gods, and smooth-tongued native politicians urge the innocent to revolt in order that they may the more savagely exploit them after we, their British protectors, have gone."

The Commandant stirred uneasily, hoping that no Indian reporters were present. Edwin Turbot smiled even more apologetically than before (the headmaster now explaining to his leavers that certain older boys would try to touch their 'parts' and that this must on no account be permitted) and started to mix a well-practised huskiness into his otherwise bland speech-making voice.

"The result is that there is and will be riot and bloodshed, for which you will be blamed and which, at the same time, you will be relied upon to prevent. In such circumstances, there is one overwhelming temptation to which you must never succumb. I refer, of course, to that weakness which is some-times called 'pity' or 'compassion': being sorry for the poor misguided rioters, among whom there will be many young men of your own age and even little children, you may feel an impulse of mercy, you may, in a fatal moment of softness, wish to give in, to hold your hand, to put by the rod of justice which is yours to wield. If you do, you are lost. You will be failing those poor wretches of rioters, the very people to whom you owe your knightly aid – which should be given in the form of a short, sharp, memorable lesson that will teach them, in their own interest, to desist."

Dear God, thought Peter, rocking back and forth on his toes to prevent himself from feeling dizzy: how much longer will he keep us? Has no one told him that 99 per cent of those who stand here are starting tomorrow morning for Bombay and the boat back home? That only three of us out of 300 will ever come near a riot? And if someone has told him, thought Peter, light-headed in the blazing sun, has he nevertheless decided to give this lecture just for those three? Just for those three – aye, there's the rub. . . .

'You'll be glad to know,' Captain Detterling had said to Peter a few days earlier, 'that the three of you will be staying together.'

'In the Wessex Fusiliers, sir?'

'That's right. Strange always had them down as first choice. As for you and Mortleman, the Rifle Brigade won't touch Mortleman, because his father's a bad lot, and the Indian Army won't touch you because you're white. So since both of you named the Wessex Fusiliers on those forms you had, there it is.'

'But the Wessex Fusiliers must know we both really wanted something else. Didn't they resent that? I mean, some regiments have to take what they can get, but the Wessex Fusiliers are rather grand.'

'In their middle-class way, yes,' said Detterling. 'Quite grand enough to pick and choose rather than be picked and chosen. In fact, I think they'd have turned you and Mortleman down if it hadn't been for one thing.'

'Oh?'

'Barry Strange wrote to the Colonel of the Regiment and said you were his friends.'

'Rather bold for a Cadet?'

'They know him there, you see . . .

> You come here where your brothers came,
> To the old school years ago . . .

. . . That kind of thing. One quite sees why they're a good regiment – *in* their middle-class way.'

'Well, sir, thank you for telling me.'

'That's not quite all. You're staying out here – all three of you.'

'But . . . the whole lot of us are going home.'

'Except the three of you. There's a Battalion of the Wessex Fusiliers at Berhampore. The First.'

'There are British Battalions all over India,' said Peter, refusing to believe, 'but they said that none of us was going to them. They *said* we were all going home.'

'And now I'm *saying* that Strange and Mortleman and you are staying out here. Just before the First Wessex moved to Berhampore, something went wrong with the water in the Officers' Mess and seven of 'em died of cholera. So they're very short and they've asked Delhi to let them have you.'

'That's all very well, sir. But I was *told* I was going home, I was looking forward to going h—'

'—Oh, for God's sake stop whining,' Detterling had said. 'What would they think of you – and of Strange's letter to the Colonel – if they could hear you now?'

'I'm sorry, sir.'

'I'm afraid you're going to be even sorrier. The Wessex Fusiliers,' Detterling went on thoughtfully, '*are* a good regiment, they're dead loyal to their own people, and they'd sooner burn in Hades than show their backs. But . . .'

'But what?'

'You know what Wellington said of them? "The steadiest Officers in England – and the dullest in Europe." Something like that.'

But at least, Peter thought now, they couldn't be as dull as the Right Honourable Edwin Turbot, who was at last (thank God) winding up.

"You may think," said Turbot, "that it has been rather odd of me to say so much about your duties in Aid of the Civil Power, when most of you, as I understand it, are going home to England very shortly. But let me put it to you like this. Even back in England the times are . . . peculiar. Certain classes of people have expected a great deal of a new popular Government, and have been, inevitably, disappointed. They are going to go on being disappointed until they learn that even popular Governments cannot perform miracles. Meanwhile, suppose, just suppose, that discontent were to give rise to widespread strikes – a National Strike perhaps – with the serious civil disorder that might well be concomitant? I think you take my point, gentlemen. Not the least duty of a knight at arms is to defend his own hearth against the lawless . . . whether they come from without or within. What I have said today, about dealing with riots in this country, can be applied, *mutatis mutandis*, to events which might occur considerably nearer home."

You cunning old bugger, Peter thought, keeping the sting in the tail. Well, if I've got to shoot civilians, I'd sooner shoot brown ones than white, and that's all about that. So perhaps it's as well that I'm staying in India after all. Not that it could ever come to shooting in England . . . *or could it?*

But this train of speculation was now interrupted by commands in preparation for the March Past. The Cadets would march past, in Column of Platoons . . . by the *right*, wham, tampity bam, and slam into Old Towler. Away they marched at a sharp light infantry pace to the end of the parade ground, where they wheeled and wheeled again to march back past

Edwin Turbot, who raised his hat in response to the 'Eyes Right' and let fall a tiny tear (which nobody saw) as he thought how soon these clean bright limbs would be shrunk to skin and gristle, and that of these 300 lovely paladins not one would be alive in ninety years. But the young knights themselves were discommoded by no such reflections; for in a few minutes they would put on for the first time the emblems of authority, and a man who dons a new uniform has ever thought himself immortal. The time had come at last to gird themselves in new splendour, to sit in glory and drink deep.

Most of them, of course, drank much too deep, and on the morning after it was rather a sorry crowd of new Officers that boarded the train at Bangalore Station, bound for the boat at Bombay. Peter, Alister and Barry, who were not leaving for Berhampore until the next day, were there to see them off.

"It's too bad," Second Lieutenant Zaccharias complained to them on the platform: "they're making us travel just like when we came here. Like cattle in so many trucks."

"When you're moving 300 people all together," Peter explained rather heavily, "you can't afford to pamper them."

"You should have proper respect for their rank."

"Where everyone has the same rank, nobody has any rank," said Alister contentiously: "moving 300 subalterns is the same as moving 300 sepoys. If you all had Wagon Lits, the train would stretch from here to Poona."

"No one said anything about Wagon Lits," grizzled Zaccharias: "all I want is the respect which is due to me as an Officer."

"You're not an Officer yet," said Barry, "not a real one. You won't be that until you're doing an Officer's job in a proper unit."

"That's right," said Alister; "for the time being you're just cargo."

"Well, at least," said Zaccharias spitefully, "the cargo's going home." He shoved a beggar out of the way with the flat of his foot and moved off to join the queue of disgruntled

Second Lieutenants who were slowly filing into the nearest coach. "Go and see poor old Murphy in hospital before you go," he called back to Peter, "and tell him not to beat his meat to pieces before they let him out."

Peter, Barry and Alister stood and watched as the row of new-dubbed knights, sweaty and twitching with crapula, crept past them and into the train.

"Good-bye, Julian . . . good-bye, George . . ."

The metal crests above the vizors glittered in the sun, the Sphinx, the Bugle Horn, the Cross of Malta; Britannia and the Castle and the Lamb. "Good-bye, Jimmy . . . good luck, Monty . . . happy days, Jeremy . . . see you, Paul . . ."

"What are you three doing, hanging about? Get in the queue, will you."

This from an unknown R.S.M. accompanying an unknown Captain who was commanding the train to Bombay.

"We're seeing our friends off, Sergeant-Major."

"I am an R.S.M. You don't call *me* plain Sergeant-Major."

"I am an Officer. You call *me* 'sir'."

"Then stop cluttering up this platform, *sir*."

"We shall stay here as long as we please, *Regimental Sergeant-Major*."

"I am speaking, sir, for the Officer i/c Train."

"For Christ's *sake*," said the Officer i/c Train and shambled on up the platform.

The R.S.M. pranced about at his heels.

"Must keep a tidy platform, sir."

"For Christ's *sake*, R.S.M. Clapham. Too early in the morning."

The Harp of Ulster, the Rose of Lancaster, the Horse of Kent. "Good-bye, Nicholas . . . good-bye, Sandy . . . keep it clean, Oscar . . ." The Crown of Cornwall and the Plume of Wales.

"Good-bye. Good-bye. Good-bye."

And then the train was gone and the platform was empty, except for several hundred Indians, who were sleeping in neat rows, and for Sergeant-Major Cruxtable, who was still waving down the line.

"Lonely, now they're all gone," said Cruxtable, as he turned towards the three who were left.

"Yes, ' said Peter. All four looked at each other with drooping mouths.

"Zaccharias was right," said Barry, breaking the long silence : "we must go and see Murphy before we leave."

"I'm going that way too, gentlemen," said Cruxtable; "I've got some documents for him to sign."

They picked their way out of the station.

"What will happen to Murphy?" asked Alister. "Has he been commissioned like the rest of us?"

"He has been, sir," said Cruxtable, "and then he hasn't."

"Well, which?"

"He's been in hospital ever since Jungle Camp," the Sergeant-Major explained patiently, "so he's missed too much training to be commissioned with the rest of you gentlemen. By rights, he ought to be back-squadded to another company when he comes out and finish his training with them."

"But there's only Indians left here."

"Precisely, sir. He can't go in with them but equally he can't pass out with you, and then again he can't stay in hospital as a Cadet because official as from yesterday there are no white Cadets on strength in this station. It'd be unfair to bust him down to Private, and he wouldn't do as a Sergeant, so he's been posted across – on paper – to the Education Corps, on the ground he's passed his School Certificate in French and Scripture, and it just so happens the Education Corps has a vacancy for one Officer in their establishment at Delhi. Now, Captain Murphy's done enough basic officer training for *that* mob, so—"

"—*Captain* Murphy?"

"Yes, sir," said Cruxtable with grim amusement. "The vacancy carries an acting Captaincy. Odd how things turn out."

But Acting Captain Murphy, whose thigh was still in plaster, was not a happy man. "I sometimes think I'm going to be lying here for ever," he whined, while Cruxtable fussed about arranging the documents.

"Zaccharias says you're not to beat your meat," said Alister.

"That's no way to talk to your superior."

"As Regimental Officers," said Barry, "we are not account-able to Captains in the Education Corps. If you and I were washed up on a desert island, *I* should be in command of us both."

"But *I* should be drawing a Captain's screw."

"Not yet you're not, sir, anyway," said Cruxtable, giving Murphy a pen and a pile of papers. "You can call yourself 'Captain' but you don't start drawing the money till you get to Delhi."

"What's the use?" moaned Murphy. "I'll be here at least another month. You three are going away tomorrow. There's no one left at the O.T.S. but blacks. There'll be no one to come and see me except C.S.M. Cruxtable—"

"—And not even him in a week or so," said Cruxtable gently, "but I'll make sure the local padre remembers you're here."

"Oh, fuck the padre. Everyone's leaving. And for the last month the staff in here has been changing every day. Very soon now no one will even know who I am. Don't you see?" Murphy concentrated his features as if making some abnormal mental effort. "A man only has an identity," he said slowly, "if he's among people who recognise him . . . who can vouch for who and what he is. When everyone who knows me has left Bangalore, I might be anyone at all."

"You sign them papers," said Cruxtable soothingly, "and you'll get written order from Delhi in good time. They'll say exactly who and what you are."

"*If* they ever get to me. I can't receive written orders unless someone knows that I'm the person they're meant for . . . or unless I can prove it. Now," said Murphy in shrill accusation, "have you got an Officer's Identity Card for me?"

" 'Fraid not, sir. You're a special case. Your Officer's Iden-tity Card will come from Delhi with your orders."

"There you are, you see. Until I get it I'm nobody, and as long as I'm nobody I can't possibly get it."

From the looks on their faces, Alister and Barry were thinking that Murphy was making a silly fuss. Peter was not so sure, and neither, he fancied, was Cruxtable, for all his reassuring words.

Although Murphy was not the brightest of men, he had clearly examined his situation with some care, while lying in his distressful bed, and somehow he had hit upon an important truth : that it was no good a man's knowing who he was unless other people knew it too. Leave aside the metaphysical questions which it raised, this truth had always been particularly applicable to official or military matters; better soldiers than Murphy had slipped through a crack in the floor, so to speak, and been left forgotten to rot beneath the boards. Cruxtable, Peter now thought, had probably sensed this uneasy factor in Murphy's predicament and sensed, moreover, that in the present fluid state of the Raj in India such a factor was more than usually liable to operate. But what could Cruxtable do about it? He was a Sergeant-Major whose job it was to fill in forms and collect signatures. No one would thank him to interfere further. So it was up to him, Peter, as a commissioned Officer, to make sure that Murphy's fears were allayed and his affairs put on a sound footing.

"I'll see Detterling about it," he said to Murphy.

"Captain Detterling's off, sir. In three days' time, to Delhi."

"Then he can put in a word there. He can make sure that everyone concerned knows exactly how Mr – er, Captain Murphy is placed down here."

Murphy brightened a little. Cruxtable shook his head gloomily, thereby admitting that his smooth bedside manner of minutes before had been fraudulent, and collected up the signed documents. They all said Good-bye to Murphy and trooped down the empty ward. Looking back to wave from the door, Peter observed that Captain Murphy was already beating his meat under the bed-clothes.

Outside the hospital they met Captain Detterling, who, he told them, had been there to sign a certificate which exonerated the hospital staff from any blame for losing Lord Muscateer's Part One Pay Book.

"Why worry, now it's been found?" said Peter.

"They always like to find out just who it was that lost things in the first place," Cruxtable told him.

"Murphy's afraid they're going to lose *him*," said Peter to Detterling. "I've promised him you'd see things straight in Delhi."

"Oh, yes," said Detterling easily. "But of course it's a long way . . . these days . . . between here and Delhi."

Cruxtable sniffed audibly, as if to observe that fate would take its course despite all human intervention.

"Well, at least *you* lot have got your orders signed and sealed," he said. "Look in at the office this afternoon to say good-bye, and I'll give you your railway warrants for to-morrow."

He saluted Detterling and waddled off.

"Where will he go from here?" asked Alister.

"Regimental stores somewhere," said Detterling, "or a desk in an Orderly Room. I see him next to a huge stove, full of red hot coke, drinking endless mugs of thick, sweet tea."

"Not in India surely?"

"Metaphorically," said Detterling, "men like Cruxtable take their stoves and their mugs of tea with them wherever they go, much as wandering players carry their props. The stove is the symbol and the centre of Cruxtable's entire way of life – or any other old soldier's. And talking of old soldiers, I have news of a friend of ours. Gilzai Khan."

Barry shuffled his feet about. Alister looked up with interest and affection. Peter smiled rather daintily. A squad of Sikh Cadets marched past them and gave them an 'Eyes Right'. Although the movement was punctiliously executed, it was somehow an accusation rather than a courtesy, reminding them all that their time was running out and that in a few days, even a few hours, they would no longer have the right to loiter on this ground. So they began walking slowly towards the Commandant's Headquarters, where, after all, they might still be acknowledged to have some business; but as they walked unfamiliar orders given in unfamiliar accents came to them from the parade ground, declaring that this was now an alien place. Crowded but empty, Peter thought; empty of all

that for us has made it both school and home for the last sixteen weeks. As far as we four are concerned the O.T.S. is now
as deserted as if grass were already growing through the floors
of our bashas and jungle weeds were creeping along the
verandahs.

"So what news, sir," he said at last, "what news of Gilzai
Khan?"

"He's resigned his commission."

"Because . . . because of what happened here?"

"On the face of it, one must suppose so. But there's something very odd about it all."

"I'm sure," said Barry, "that whatever Gilzai Khan has done
is as plain and honest as the day."

"Hear, hear," Alister said.

"Well, you're both wrong," said Detterling, his voice crack-
ling with irritation. "When he left here he went to his Regimental Depot up in the North and was given a job training
recruits. Not exactly what one would have expected after
everything that went on here" – he glanced with a mixture of
malice and apology at the blushing Barry – "but then the
Indian Army, just like the British, is notorious for repeating its
mistakes. Anyhow, after a month or so all was going quite well
– when suddenly he formed up, out of the blue, and said he
wanted to resign immediately. And it turned out that because
of his age and the terms of his engagement and one thing and
another they'd have to let him do just that. They couldn't even
make him stay till he'd finished training his current intake of
recruits."

"How do you know all this, sir?" Peter asked.

"Giles Glastonbury has been taking an interest . . . for this
reason and that."

"What reason?" said Barry.

Detterling shrugged this to one side, implying with a quick
twist of his mouth that men of the world must answer some
questions for themselves.

"According to the letter I had from Giles this morning," he
went on, "they begged Gilzai Khan to stay on till they could
find a replacement, but he just wouldn't listen. He wanted to

go, and he was entitled to go, and he was going – there and then. Now what strikes any of you as being peculiar about all this?"

"Gil' Khan was a loyal man," said Peter, "who loved the Army and his Regiment. You'd think he'd agree to waive his rights and help them out for a few weeks more."

"Exactly. And come to that, why resign at all? He has no other life, and if the Indian Army was prepared to keep him on after the row here—"

"—Was it prepared to keep him on?"

"Giles says yes. Strictly speaking, a decision still had to be taken at the time the Khan resigned, but it was pretty certain that he was going to be forgiven – or at any rate pardoned – and so he had already been told. Officers like Gilzai Khan don't grow on bushes."

"So he couldn't have been resigning in order to get out before he was kicked out?"

"It seems not."

"Perhaps," said Barry, "he didn't like the idea of being 'pardoned'?"

"Then why wait as long as he did? He'd known the form for weeks and was apparently quite happy. Then he's into the Colonel's office like a jack-in-the-box one morning, and waving them all good-bye three days later. Only he didn't even wave them good-bye. As soon as his papers were stamped he vanished without a word. And this from his Regimental H.Q., remember. There were men there he'd known for over twenty years, and he didn't even bother to say good-bye."

"But this is dreadful," said Barry. "He always set such store by proper good-byes. Even if it was just for a few hours—" He broke off in some confusion. "I mean, something must have been terribly wrong," he said. "But whatever could it have been?"

" 'What song the Sirens sang,' " Detterling said, " 'or what name Achilles assumed when he hid himself among women, though puzzling questions, are not beyond all conjecture.' I'll be seeing Giles in a few days, and I'll let you know if there's anything new. Good-bye for now, chums," he said, abruptly but pleasantly. "I'll hope to see you some time in Berhampore. It's not that far from Delhi."

"Good-bye, sir . . ."

"You shouldn't call me 'sir' any more."

He shook hands with the three of them and then walked away down the avenue which led to the Commandant's office. Indian Cadets saluted him as he went, and he returned their salutes; but they did not look at his face, nor he at theirs.

"Now," said the Senior Subaltern, "repeat after me: 'I, Peter Morrison, do most faithfully swear, on this drum and by my blood . . .' "

"I, Peter Morrison, do most faithfully swear, on this drum and by my blood . . ."

" '. . . That this regiment shall be my house . . .' "

". . . That this regiment shall be my house . . ."

" '. . . That its sons shall be my brothers . . .' "

". . . That its sons shall be my brothers . . ."

" '. . . And that its honour shall be my honour to cherish and avenge. . . .' "

Peter was kneeling on his right knee and resting his right hand, palm upward, on the parchment of a corded drum. The Senior Subaltern, who was reading the oath from what looked like a small leather diary, knelt opposite him, also on one knee and on either side of the Senior Subaltern knelt the two Subalterns next in standing, both of them pointing bare swords at Peter's throat. To one side stood the Adjutant, in mounted dress, his sword sheathed; behind Peter were Barry and Alister, waiting their turn; and behind them again were all the Subaltern Officers of the First Battalion, the Wessex Fusiliers, who were there to bear witness.

" '. . . And this, I swear it by my blood . . .' "

The Subaltern on Peter's left shifted his point from Peter's throat and dipped it down and across to nick his palm. Peter turned his hand over and pressed his palm hard down on to the parchment.

". . . And this, I swear it by my blood, on this drum do I

swear it, and by the souls of all those who have answered its call."

"I stand here for them," said the Adjutant, "and I am to tell you this. Now that your blood is on the drum, you must answer its call, as they did, to the death. From now until your dying day, if you receive word, written or spoken, that 'The drum is beaten', you are thereby summoned to return to it, wherever you may be and wherever it may be. And so now, for the first time : The drum is beaten, friend; the drum is in Berhampore."

"I have come to Berhampore," Peter said, "to answer the drum."

"He has come to Berhampore," said all the Subalterns together (except Barry and Alister), "to answer the drum. Come, friend, and stand among us."

Then Peter went to stand among his new comrades while Barry and Alister took the oath in their turn. After this the Adjutant led the Subalterns, with the newcomers at their head, through double doors and into a spacious dining room, which was almost filled by a table some forty yards long and ready laid for dinner. There was no cloth; the table was polished jet black; at the centre was a grotesque representation, nearly four feet high, of an Edwardian castle keep; and at the far end was a huge and triangular pile of drums, which made a kind of wigwam or canopy over the President's chair. Seated on this was the Lieutenant-Colonel Commanding and grouped about his wigwam were his Field Officers and Captains. Peter, Barry and Alister stood in a row at the bottom of the table and, "We have come to Berhampore," they shouted down its length, "to answer the drum."

"Then sit, friends, and eat," replied the Colonel, indicating that they and the Adjutant should occupy the four places nearest to him. At last, Peter felt, someone was showing a little common sense; but in fact they were not allowed to sit down until the invitation had been repeated to each one of them by each one of the Captains and Majors present, all of whom had to be personally assured that they had come to Berhampore to answer the drum.

Nor was the food up to much when they finally sat down to eat it. Although there was plenty of it, smoothly served by immaculate bearers, it was coarse in substance and unloved in the cooking; and as for the wine, it was beyond human charity.

"We usually drink beer," said the Adjutant to Peter, "but of course we make a special thing of it when we dine new fellows in. Sorry there's so little of the silver here – we had to pack it away for the duration."

"But you've got the centre-piece, I see," said Peter: "it's very . . . remarkable."

"That, with the drums and this table, we take everywhere we go. It's a model of part of the Depot. Reminds us of home."

"What about the Colours? Haven't you brought them?"

"No. The drums serve much the same purpose and in wartime one must save space on troopships. By the way, Morrison," said the Adjutant shyly, "I think I should tell you that in this regiment the Adjutant, like the Field Officers, is addressed as 'sir' by subalterns, even off duty."

"As you say, sir."

"I know it's not the fashionable thing to do, but we have our own ways, you see."

The Adjutant, who was called Captain Thomas Oake, was an exceedingly nice man, Peter thought, and probably not a fool, but he did rather put one in mind of Wellington's remark, as quoted by Detterling, about the dullness of the Wessex Fusiliers. A quick look down the table now confirmed the Duke's apophthegm: the square, honest, weathered faces, all guzzling away as if this were the first and last meal of the month, gave little promise of wit or gaiety (though some promise of jollity, perhaps, which was another matter). Captain Oake's face differed from the rest in being slightly rhombic; no doubt it had once been square enough, but some accident of life or war had given its entire structure a right-handed slant, which endowed its owner with the look of a benevolent ghoul. As for the Colonel, who was called Brockworthy, his make and scale were massive; his capital block sat on his body block like a cornice on a very squat column. To such men as these, Peter reflected, his two friends and even himself must seem dainty to the point of decadence; and indeed the Colonel, between vast mouthfuls of meat and potato, was already directing some very suspicious looks at Alister.

"Interesting ceremony we've just been through," said Alister, pushing away a plate still two-thirds full; "but the thing is, Colonel, what do you do if someone doesn't turn up? When he's summoned by the drum, I mean."

"We obliterate his name, Mr Mortleman; he ceases to exist."

Alister took a draught of wine and winced energetically.

"But isn't that rather . . . unreal? Like those Jewish families who hold a funeral if one of their children marries a gentile."

"I am not well up in Jewish customs."

"Take it from me, Colonel, that's what they do. They behave as if the offending son or daughter were dead."

"Then there is no comparison between their behaviour and ours. We do not behave as if the offender was dead: we behave as if he had never existed."

The Colonel turned sharply from Alister to Barry Strange, whom he had known since Barry was in the nursery.

"Do you think," he said in a small, petulant voice which came oddly from such an exterior, "that we shall . . . understand Mortleman here? He seems rather big in the mouth."

"Nerves, sir," Barry said. "He always tries to impress new people. It's because of that he can't eat his dinner."

"Nerves, boy? This is not, you know, a nervous regiment."

"Not quite nerves, sir. Over-excitement."

"This is not an excitable regiment."

"Take my word for it," said Barry boldly: "Alister Mortleman is all right."

"We have taken your word for it, Strange; that's why he's here. Let's hope you weren't wrong about him, that's all. But I like the look of your other friend, Morrison; he seems so calm. A J.U.O. at Bangalore, I hear?"

"That's right, sir."

"And talking of Bangalore, Strange, there's some tale going round about an Indian you were friendly with."

"Our Platoon Commander. We all liked him."

"But he left very suddenly?"

"A mistake, sir. There was a bad mistake."

"So long as it wasn't yours, boy. I've known your family a very long time, and I should hate you to make a bad mistake."

"No one could be mistaken about Gilzai Khan."

"Ah, but you've just told me that someone was."

"Gilzai Khan himself, sir. He made the mistake of being too good for the place. He broke silly little rules and upset silly little men. And he made no secret of being pro-British. With politics as they are now, a pro-British Indian teaching British Cadets was bound to be inconvenient."

"Inconvenient to whom?"

"To Delhi, sir. It would annoy all the politicians both at home and in India, and they'd take it out on Delhi. So the Khan had to go, from Bangalore at any rate. He made the mistake of being the only honest man among a crew of jackals."

"I must say, Strange, you too seem to be getting a bit big in the mouth. In my day we never even mentioned such matters. Is that what Bangalore has done for you all?"

"Not Bangalore, sir. Just two officers – Gil' Khan and another one called Detterling. They enjoyed frank conversations."

"Detterling . . . Detterling . . . There's some story there, if only I could remember. A cavalryman, was he?"

"Yes, sir. Earl Hamilton's Light Dragoons."

"By God, yes. I've got it now."

"Got what, sir?"

"It's not a story for your ears, boy, though you'll hear it some day, I suppose." And then leaning forward, "Did you hear that, Oake?" called the Colonel to the Adjutant. "Detterling was instructing at Bangalore."

Captain Oake shook his rhombus in gentle deprecation.

"Understand this," the Colonel yapped next: "I'll thank you all to forget anything that Captain Detterling may have taught you." He turned on Alister like an inquisitor. "What have *you* got to say about Bangalore?" he asked.

While Alister was saying it, and the Colonel was not much liking it, and Barry was trying to hold the ring, Peter turned to Captain Oake.

"What's wrong with Detterling?" he inquired.

"Nothing was ever proved," said Oake, "so I'm not even going to hint at it. It might not be true, after all. The C.O. hates the cavalry and always believes the worst of them."

"Hates the cavalry . . . sir?"

"He thinks they're flashy and rich. This is a poor regiment, Morrison, as you've probably gathered already." Captain Oake searched his teeth with his tongue, as though seeking for some consolation in this state of affairs. "Which is a good thing," he said, suddenly finding it. "You see, all we have is the regiment, so we think the more of it. Hence all that business you went through just now. Mind you, you won't find any of that in the wartime battalions. But the First Battalion's still got quite a lot of regulars who know the proper form." He searched his teeth again and again found what he sought. "Most regulars go looking for cushy appointments in wartime," he said without malice, "like Detterling. But with us the regulars stay put with the regiment."

" 'The drum is beaten'?"

"Not only that. We just . . . feel more at home. This is *our place*. That's why we always bring this table along. By the way, did they teach you about riots in Bangalore? Duties in Aid of the Civil Power?"

"A few periods, sir. Are you expecting trouble?"

"We've been told to, and we're making preparations. The C.O. doesn't like it because he says it interferes with proper training. . . ."

". . . Good solid training," the Colonel was saying to Barry and Alister; "you don't seem to have had nearly enough of it at Bangalore. Well, that's what we believe in here. Good solid training six days of the week and Church Parade on the seventh."

"What for?" said Alister.

"Obvious, isn't it? Got to give 'em something to do, even on Sunday."

"Not the Church Parades, Colonel. The good solid training. What for? What *role* are you contemplating?"

Barry shuddered.

"Doing what has to be done," the Colonel said.

"Precisely. And what will that be?"

"Not your business to know. Or mine, come to that."

"Then how can we train for it?"

"We keep fit, sir, and we learn to do as we're told without asking damn silly questions. That's how we train for it," the Colonel said.

After a number of toasts, to the King, the Colonel in Chief, the Colonel Commandant, the Five Counties of Wessex, and absent friends, there followed a series of party games such as the Fusiliers always played after dinner on great occasions. Alister had been hoping for a little roulette, but nothing of that kind ever occurred among the Wessex Fusiliers; *their* games consisted in making someone lie down on the floor and seeing how many people could stand on him all together before he fainted, that kind of a thing. There was a particular favourite called Blind Man's Buffet, in which the 'Buffer', having been blindfolded, was turned loose to rove round the room swinging heavy punches wherever he would. He might punch the furniture, in which case he could hurt himself very nastily; or he might punch his fellow Fusiliers, in which case he could hurt them very nastily. Since he was in any case bound to keep punching at a steady rate no matter what he might hit, while the rest of the players were on their honour to remain absolutely still throughout (even when a knockout punch was coming straight at them), this game was held with good reason to be a test of character.

Alister, who was one of the first to have his eyes covered, earned general contempt by punching too softly and only at stomach level.

"Aim them hard at the jaw, man," the Colonel said.

Whereupon Alister, judging the direction and elevation by the voice, aimed one hard (as he thought) at the Colonel's jaw, and cracked his knuckles viciously on a stone wall-bracket. This misfortune raised hearty Fusilier laughter; for it seemed that the Colonel had some minor ventriloquial skill and was accustomed to undo tiros in this manner.

Peter, who didn't care much for this sort of game, took up his ground in what he thought would be a safe place, in the rear of the Mess Piano. But this was just the area in which experienced players, who knew the local course, went looking for skulkers; and he received a terrific clout across the chops from the 'Buffer' who succeeded Alister, an elderly lieutenant whe resembled a peasant *en fête* by Brueghel and had been commissioned in the field at Imphal.

In accordance with the rules of this entertainment, and after the ten seconds allowed for his recovery, Peter as having been 'buffed' now became the 'Buffer'. While he was being blind-folded, most of the other players shifted, as was permitted, to new ground; only Barry and one or two more elected to stay put, this being an old stratagem based on the assumption that no 'Buffer' would try to find a target in a place which would probably have been vacated. Meanwhile the Adjutant finished knotting the handkerchief behind Peter's head and gave the traditional command 'Buffo', whereupon all present assumed the correct upright position (with jaw slightly jutting to give the 'Buffer' a sporting chance) in which they were bound to remain frozen all through the coming 'Buffaloo' or 'Buff-up'.

"Buffo-Buffo," Captain Oake then said – the signal for Peter to start buffing.

Peter, not much wishing to hit anyone and particularly not wishing to hit Barry, buffed his way to where he knew Barry had previously been and therefore ought not to be now. He swung mightily into what he thought was empty air, buffed Barry bang between the eyes and laid him as flat as a flounder – except, that is, for Barry's head, which cracked against the leg of the Second in Command's armchair and there remained, fixed in a vertical position, as though split and secured by the sharp edge at the angle of the chair-leg.

"Wango," the Adjutant said, indicating by this formula a disaster of sufficient magnitude to unfreeze all other players.

These gathered round Barry, silently (since Wessex Fusiliers do not greet catastrophe with chatter) and leaving a decent space, so that Barry might breathe, should he still be able to, and the M.O. might do his stuff. But the wretched fellow couldn't even begin; for Peter, not understanding the com-mand 'Wango', and forgetting in his dismay at having hit someone that a 'Buff' automatically terminated the current 'Buffaloo', went on thrashing and caught the M.O. a horrible blow in the throat, causing him to crumple like a Guy in a bonfire. "Wango-wango," insisted the Adjutant to Peter – and himself went down for the count.

"Wango-wango-*wango*," the Colonel piped.

And now the Colonel himself would have been felled by Peter's leg-of-mutton fist, had not Alister deflected it in its path, and then whipped the handkerchief up over Peter's eyes.

"Lay off, Peterkin," Alister said.

Several Fusilier faces twitched with disapproval of the endearment, but in the main concern lay with the fallen. Captain Oake was speedily revived when someone squirted soda into his face; the doctor was eventually brought to his feet by some sharp kicks in the anus from the Colonel ("Get up, damn your eyes, and do your job"); but Barry, beneath whose neck was a pool of blood, was not to be dealt with, as even the Colonel saw, by such peremptory means. In the end, Peter and Alister got him laid out on a sofa; and the rather shaky Adjutant examined the back of his skull, while the medico retired, after his first look, to be violently sick in a corner.

"Plucky performance," said the Colonel. "All the same, those Strange .boys. Stood there as steady as a rock and took what was coming."

"For Christ's sake," said Captain Oake in a casual tone (to avoid creating alarm), "fetch that doctor back here."

But the M.O. was still being sick.

"Pity we can't train our own," said the Colonel; "these outside fellows never come up to the scratch."

"It's this bleeding," said Alister : "it won't stop."

"Oh God, oh Christ, oh God," said Peter. "It's all my fault."

"Don't *you* start," said the Colonel. He went over to the sideboard and seized the whisky bottle. "First disinfect in case," he said, sluicing whisky into the red crevice which gaped beneath Barry's fair hair, "and then sew the bloody hole up. Have to shave the hair first, though. You" – to Alister – "fetch a razor. Cut-throat – you're the sort of chap that has one. *You*" – to the Senior Subaltern – "go to the M.I. Room for the kit. And *you*" – to Peter – "get ready to hold his hand if he comes to. There's nothing to it," he announced to his officers at large : "done it dozens of times."

"Perhaps, sir," the Adjutant began, "if we were to wait until the M.O.—"

"—Bloody man's pissed as a dhobi's arsehole. You leave it to me. Took a dooli-bearer's leg off once – beautiful job – and dug a bullet out of Bunjy Brewster's guts in '41. Common sense, that's all you need," said the Colonel, taking a razor from the breathless Alister, "and a bit of an eye for the thing."

He opened the razor and balanced it with care; then, with surprising gentleness, he began to coax the hair away from Barry's scalp.

"More whisky," he said, and swabbed the blood away with it. "Give me that needle and thread. . . . And now, just watch, all of you, and then you subalterns can have a go for yourselves. One stitch each should just about do the job – like . . . *that*. Bloody useful bit of training," he said, straightening up again, "so you're lucky to have the chance. And don't botch the poor little bugger up."

And then all the subalterns queued up, without a word and in strict order of seniority, to take their turn at stitching Barry's head.

Peter stuck a neat little flag into the area marked 'Ranges' on his wall-map of Berhampore. That was where Alister's Platoon was spending the day : Alister's Platoon, as he now reflected, but not commanded by Alister, who had been detailed off, as 'second-in-command and under instruction', to a Rifle Platoon which was commanded by one of the senior Lieutenants. Alister's conversation on the dining-in night had displeased the Colonel, and this rather humiliating appointment had been the result.

Barry, on the other hand, had won everybody's approval by his stout behaviour during the 'Buff-up', and so he had been given a Rifle Platoon all of his own. In fact, however, this was the first day on which he had been fit enough to command it;

for on the morning after the 'Buff-up', the M.O., pale and smelling of vomit, had examined his stitches, given a low moan of horror, and sent Barry off, heavily drugged, to remain under observation in the Military Hospital at Delhi. There Barry stayed for some days, then returned, minus the stitches and apparently none the worse, except for an ugly bump at the base of his skull (which in the Colonel's opinion only made him look more 'manly'); but the instructions he carried said he was to go to bed immediately and stay there for another week. Why? the Colonel wanted to know : it was all mere pampering. Possible delayed concussion, the M.O. told him, and threatened to report him to the Director of Medical Services unless Barry was allowed to follow the instructions to the letter. So to bed Barry had gone, and was much visited by all his new colleagues, who sat round him in groups of five or six for hour after hour, apparently concerned to prevent his being bored but neither saying nor doing anything at all to obviate boredom. 'The Colonel's sent them to make sure he doesn't play with himself,' Alister explained to Peter : 'it's the kind of thing they worry about here.' But however that might be, Barry had now at last been declared fit for duty, and this very morning he was taking the field with his new Platoon to practise the Frontal Assault on the Old Polo Ground. . . .

. . . In the centre of which Peter now pinned another flag to record Barry's location. He now had just three more flags to dispose of : one for the C.O., who was out inspecting the Training; one for the Adjutant, who was sitting in the office next door; and one for himself, as Intelligence Officer. The Adjutant and himself ('ADJ' and 'I.O.') he stuck side by side in a shaded area marked 'Admin. Block'; that much was easily done. But what to do about the Colonel? Since Peter had the whole of the rest of the morning to give to the problem, he took his time about it. Should he work out the C.O.'s probable route and move the flag every few minutes accordingly? Or should he pin the flag at a point equidistant from every place at which training was in progress? The latter method would be inexact; the former too conjectural.

The Adjutant now came in, as he quite often did. He liked

Peter, so Peter had very soon realised, and this was why Peter had been given his present job.

'It sounds very grand – Intelligence Officer,' Thomas Oake had said; 'but in fact, you know, you're just a glorified messenger boy. And when you're not being fagged for messages all you do is keep the map, which is simple routine. But you'll be at the centre of things . . . if you take my point.'

Peter took the point and had been very glad of the appointment. The work, if leisurely, had more subtleties to it than the Adjutant had suggested. What was more, the Adjutant's propinquity was pleasant, provided one observed the proper forms, and his conversation rich in unexpected insights.

"Getting on all right?" the Adjutant said now.

This was his unvaried excuse for dropping in for a chat.

"Slight problem over the C.O., sir. He's moving about this morning. I'm not sure how to place him."

"Ah," said Oake, frowning slightly. "He should have given you a breakdown of his route and the exact times at which he intends to reach every stage of it."

"Perhaps I should have asked him?"

"No. It's not for you or me to ask our Commanding Officer where he's going. It's for him to tell us. If he doesn't, we assume he has reasons for secrecy."

"He can't want to be secret this morning, sir."

"No. He just forgot."

Not a very serious omission, Peter thought; but it was clear that the Adjutant took a different view. His face was puzzled, hurt and apprehensive.

"The Colonel," he said at last, "is a marvellous fighting soldier, but he doesn't bother much about standard procedure. Suppose the General paid us a visit and asked to be taken to him? We'd have quite a job finding him, and that wouldn't look good."

Oake smiled wistfully at Peter and then went on:

"You think I'm making a silly fuss, don't you? And probably, as far as this morning goes, no harm will have been done. But this kind of casual behaviour . . . this disregard of the *rules* . . . presents serious dangers."

"I should have thought . . . sir . . . that the Colonel was very keen on keeping the rules."

"Keen that others should, certainly. For himself . . . he has his own set. I'm going to say something rather disloyal, Peter, because I think that you and I have to prepare ourselves for . . . possible difficulties."

The Adjutant closed his eyes and was silent for so long that he might have fallen asleep on his feet. But eventually he opened his right eye, then his left, and lumbered over to Peter's map.

"A Company," he said, rapping it lightly with his fore-finger, "is going over the Assault Course. B is on the Range, C engaged in elementary tactical movements by platoons. The Band is practising for the Retreat Parade next month, and everyone else is busy with administration or interior economy. What does all this suggest to you?"

"An infantry battalion engaged in routine training."

"Which is to say training for a field role. The only trouble is that we have been warned – we have been commanded – to train with a view to something else as well – to keeping the King's peace. Duties in time of civil disorder, action in case of riot – that is what Delhi has told us to prepare for, and that is why we are really here. And so we are repeatedly reminded by missives from Brigade, and higher, two or three times a week. But how much training, since you have been here, Peter, has this Battalion done to prepare it to cope with civil riot?"

"Surely," said Peter slowly, "we have to submit copies of our Training Programmes. So Brigade . . . and higher . . . must be satisfied from these that we're doing as they wish. Otherwise they'd be down here like a ton of bricks."

"They would be if they knew what was really happening. They *ought* to be, Peter. But as it is, well, Berhampore is rather out of the way, and the war's just over, and they're all having a good time while the set-up still lasts – so they're taking our Programmes on trust. And of course on paper it's all sound enough. On paper, according to the Programmes, each Com-pany is spending three days a week training for Duties in Aid of the Civil Power. Just as it should be. But the truth is that those days never dawn. At the last minute the Colonel always thinks of something else. 'A Coy's looking sluggish,' he tells me: 'route march for them tomorrow.' 'But sir,' I say, 'tomorrow's one of their days for Riot Drill.' 'Never mind that,' he says; 'they won't be fit for anything at all until they've had some exercise.' " The Adjutant lifted both arms from his sides. "And it's the same all the time." He let his arms fall again. "Not one Company has done a day's training in Riot Drill for the last six weeks."

"Why has the C.O. . . . . discountenanced it?" said Peter carefully.

"He thinks other things are more important. He thinks we're still training for the war."

"Sir?"

"Oh, he knows it's over, of course. But part of him, a big part, refuses to admit it. You see, all his life he's wanted one thing – to lead this regiment in battle. He's seen enough action, God knows, but to him that was just a preparation for his real destiny – to command the First Battalion, *his* Battalion, of the Wessex Fusiliers in the face of the enemy. And now he's got command all right – but it's just too late. And much of the time he can't believe it. He *can't believe* that God would have given him the command he's always prayed for without also giving him the battle."

"Won't riot duties do instead, sir?"

"Fighting civilians, Peter? You might just as well offer St. George a stray dog instead of a dragon."

"Yet stray dogs must be dealt with, I suppose?"

"Indeed they must. But they have to be captured, not killed. The techniques are different."

"The net and not the lance?"

"You might say so. But meanwhile the Colonel is sharpening his lance . . ."

". . . And disdains to learn to cast the net . . ."

". . . Which takes a light hand and lots of practice."

A long silence.

"What are you going to do, sir?" Peter said at length.

"I'm going to give lectures to the Platoon Commanders.

Every evening, starting next Monday. I shall tell the C.O. they're on Regimental History, but in fact they'll be about Riot Duties and the rest. I shall suggest ways in which chaps might practise their Platoons, at such odd times as may be available. They'll take the hint, I think."

"No good having a quiet word with the Company Commanders as well?"

"No. Most of them think like the Colonel. Action involving civilians is beneath their dignity as soldiers. And they'd think I was going beyond myself to interfere."

"I see, sir. But suppose the C.O. turns up at these lectures?"

"Then for as long as he stays they'll be about Regimental History. No harm done, as far as that goes. Though the whole thing's going to seem a bit odd, I'm afraid. . . ."

"As you say, sir, the chaps will take the hint. They'll see what's going on all right. But there's something else." Peter pondered for a few seconds. "Have you thought . . . how the Colonel will react . . . when and if there *are* riots? Will he be able to face facts? And take charge of the situation?"

"He'll hang his head in shame, that he and his regiment should have to do with any action so grubby and contemptible. Meanwhile, the Platoon Commanders will do what is necessary . . . I hope . . . and in the intervals of overseeing them, I shall offer the Colonel what comfort I may by pretending that he is coping with it all without dishonour. I'm fond of him, you see, and I don't want his feelings to be hurt."

Thomas Oake wandered to the door, gently shaking his head.

"And for this morning, sir?" Peter called after him. "What shall I do with his flag?"

Peter held this up and waved it in front of the map. Captain Oake looked back and considered.

"Stick it in by the Assault Course," he advised. "That's where he'll be happiest, bless his heart."

"What I want to know," said Alister a few evenings later, "is what the hell we're doing here anyhow."

"Routine training prior to undertaking an active role in the field – for one thing," Peter said.

"What field?"

"In time of peace," said Barry rather earnestly, "the Army prepares itself for the next war."

"The next war will be a different affair. The Atom Bomb will see to that. Frontal attacks and field firing – that's all I've done for a fortnight. Now one Atom Bomb," said Alister sourly, "could do the work of a million frontal attacks and ten million men in five seconds."

"The Atom Bomb's not fair," said Barry. "Anyhow, no one will dare use it."

"The enemy will if we don't. Anyway, we *have* used it."

"And learnt how horrible it is. In future," said Barry, "there will have to be an agreement by both sides not to use it any more. Otherwise the whole earth will be blown up."

"Big red balls to that," Alister said. "That's just what people like you were saying when gun-powder first came in – but they all went on using it like anything . . . except for a few poor suckers who still insisted on training archers. Which is more or less what they're doing to us here. All this rubbish they're teaching us – it's as though they were training us to use the longbow after the invention of the musket."

Alister was not enjoying being second-in-command of a Platoon. The snub rankled, and the crustiness and pedantry of his Platoon Commander had completed his disillusionment with those processes of warfare which were favoured by the Wessex Fusiliers. But although Alister's bitterness was largely due to personal slight, he had, as Peter reflected, a sound point for debate. "One has to accept," Peter now said, "that there will always be a *local* need of the military methods which we are at present practising. You can't plaster every square inch with Atom Bombs."

"I don't see why not."

"They're expensive," Barry said.

"All right," Alister conceded, "let's say we're training for a local and tactical role in the next war. Why are we doing it in Berhampore, of all places?"

"We're here because we're here," said Barry, quoting his Platoon Sergeant.

"Not entirely," said Peter, who now felt it was up to him to do a little proselytising on the Adjutant's behalf. "We're here to maintain internal security in India. During a time of political transition."

"We are, are we? A fat lot of training we've done for that."

"Ah," said Peter tactfully. "The Adjutant tells me that from now on we shall be hearing more about it. He's giving lectures on Riot Duty and so on – starting Monday."

"Riot Duty," said Barry with disdain. "I don't care for the sound of that."

"No more does the Colonel. But something has to be done in preparation, so the Adjutant says."

Barry looked stubborn.

"That's for the Colonel to decide."

"No doubt," said Peter disingenuously; "but I'm sure Tom Oake would never start on anything without the Colonel's approval. Or at least his tacit approval."

But Barry shook his head sternly, repudiating the Civil Role. Barry had loved the Colonel since childhood and instinctively shared his attitudes; quelling riots was no business for a soldier, he thought; he had not won his spurs for that.

"What it is to be near the seats of the mighty," Alister was saying to Peter. "So we're really here to keep the natives in order?"

"We were warned it might come to that a long time ago. You remember what Gil' Khan used to say? We've discussed the possibility often enough between us."

"As a hypothesis," Alister said.

"As a nightmare," capped Barry.

"I never believed it could happen," Alister went on. "Or not after we were told we were going home. And then, when we came here after all, I'd somehow managed to forget about it. Picketing streets, firing on mobs – it just doesn't fit with all this." He waved a hand in the direction of the Mess, the home of the Drum. "It's not what a Regiment like this is for."

"I entirely agree," Barry said.

"All this field firing and what have you, it may be a bloody waste of time, but one *can* just about put up with it – even with the temperature at 190 in the shade. Exhausting and futile, yes, but at least it doesn't make one positively sick to think about."

"And do Civil Duties make you positively sick to think about?"

"Like Barry, I loathe the idea of them."

"You used to take a tougher view," said Peter. "Back at Bangalore."

"I told you, that was all hypothetical. The reality smells rather different."

"It hasn't come to reality yet. But if it does," said Peter, "need one be so faddy about it? After all, we shall only be doing what is needed. We shall be protecting the people of India against agitators and bullies. We shall be preventing looting and chaos. We shall be upholding the rights of religious minorities."

"We shall be doing the dirty work," said Barry; "*we* shall become the untouchables."

"That's right," said Alister: "I didn't come all this way to be a street-cleaner. That's what it'll add up to – cleaning up the mess. *Their* fucking mess."

"We helped to make it."

"Nonsense. If we hadn't been here, things would have been far worse. This country is such a bleeding shambles that no one could have done any better. All this filth and disease, all these damn silly sects and flea-bitten cows. Millions of syphilitics breeding like flies in dung. The truth is, we ought to be glad they want to rule themselves. Let 'em get on with it, I say. Let's for God's sake go away and leave them to rot in their own muck. And then at least no one will be able to blame us any more."

"We shall be blamed all right," said Peter. "Haven't you understood? There's a new way of thinking these days. We are always wrong, however hard we try, and *they* – the subject races, the natives, the masses wherever they may be – *they* are always the wronged, no matter how stupid or dirty or criminal they may be. That's what democracy means, Alister. So when we leave this country, if anything at all goes right, *they'll* be congratulated and what they've achieved without us will be paraded endlessly under our noses. But if the least little thing goes wrong—"

"—And just about everything will—"

"—It'll be *our* fault because we once presumed to govern them, and the failure will be flung in our faces. I tell you, we'll have them hanging round our necks until the end of time."

"Well, if we're going to be blamed whatever happens," said Alister, "about the best thing we can do is let 'em massacre each other – as that's what they seem to want. The more riots the better. So many less mouths to feed."

"It won't just be Hindu against Moslem. It'll be both of them against us. But whatever it is, we can't just ignore it. We owe them better than that."

"We owe them nothing."

"Then we owe ourselves better than that. We want to be able . . . to stand right with ourselves when it's over."

"I'll settle for keeping my hands clean," said Alister; "quite literally, just that."

"Right," Barry said.

"In fact," said Peter, "we shall all three of us do just what we are told to do. That much at least is clear. So if I were you, I'd wait and see what the Adjutant has to say in his lectures. . . ."

"The whole thing begins and ends with this," the Adjutant said: "everything will be all right so long as you stay on your side of the line and they stay on theirs."

The Adjutant was addressing the Senior Subaltern and all Subaltern Officers. Since the lecture was being delivered in their spare time, some of those present looked sulky or impatient; most, however, were listening with an appearance of polite attention. They had been told to be there, so there they were; and if Captain Oake was talking about riots and not about Regimental History (the subject proclaimed in Orders), that was all the same to them. No doubt he had his reasons; or possibly the programme had been changed at the last minute without their hearing of it. In any case, it did not do to show surprise or curiosity, leave alone resentment; in the Wessex Fusiliers one took things as they came, giving thanks that they were no worse. An hour's lecture on any topic under the moon was much preferable to (say) an all-night exercise. If you only sat still and pretended to listen, it would soon be over.

"So the first thing you do," Captain Oake pursued, "is to paint a long, straight, thick white line right across the street. When you've done that, you set up notices in every language spoken locally and any others you happen to know, stating that anyone who crosses the line is in danger of being shot. You then retire some way behind it and set up a barrier. Any questions so far?"

As it happened, the Adjutant had decided not to deceive the Colonel, who would have been very offended if he had ever found out. Having received his commander's willing permission, some days before, to lecture the Subalterns on their Regimental History, Tom Oake had then approached him, on the afternoon before this first session, and diffidently enquired whether it might not be prudent to give a little instruction about Riot Duties instead – 'just to keep those Johnnies in Delhi happy'. Although the Colonel had not much cared for this proposal, he had conceded that it could do no harm, and he had apparently felt (so Oake told Peter later on) that the Adjutant's purpose of lecturing Subalterns and Subalterns only put the distasteful subject of Aid to the Civil Power in its correct and inferior place. Since Captains and Majors were not to be bothered, the whole affair became an unimportant chore, much like fire drill, which was offhandedly thrown at junior men to be gone through once a month 'just in case'. On this basis, the C.O. had given Oake his blessing, merely requiring of him that he would in fact deliver the more seemly lectures on Regimental History as soon as the course on Civil Aid was concluded.

"You set up a barrier," the Adjutant repeated. "Any questions?"

"Yes, sir," said Peter (by pre-arrangement, in order 'to wake 'em all up'): "suppose you haven't time to do all this? Suppose you're called out in a hurry and things are already in full swing?"

"Good question," said the Adjutant. "I wonder no one else thought of it. Let's have more attention, gentlemen, please."

The polite faces of the Subalterns now became serious. If the Adjutant wanted a show of more attention before he got it over with, then by all means let him have it. It was as easy to look serious as to look merely polite, and doubtless the Senior Subaltern would frame a question or two later on to complete the pretence. Come to that, it was a pity he hadn't been the first to break; bad show, letting this Peter-come-lately-Morrison get in ahead like that, making them all look fools. Officious fellow, Morrison; the Adjutant's new favourite, it seemed.

"But although the problem which Mr Morrison has raised is very pertinent," Thomas Oake went on, "we'll leave it until later. First, let's get the basic procedure straight. As things are, then, we've got a thick white line and notices saying, 'So far but no farther'; and some twenty yards behind it we have ourselves, in platoon strength, let us say, and stationed behind a barricade, if materials for one are available. There is one more important item of equipment: a loud-speaker, through which, for the benefit of the illiterate, the prohibitions on the notice-boards may be conveyed from mouth to ear. . . ."

"Platoon will move to the left in threes," shouted Alister: "le-e-e-ft . . . *hunnn*."

"Don't bray, man," his Platoon Commander said from behind him. "You can't expect to be given a platoon of your own if you're going to bray at them like a donkey."

"I should leave all that to the Platoon Sergeant," Alister said. "It's his job."

"Don't answer back. Now march the Platoon up to the Rifle Butts and wait there till I join you. And I don't expect to find you all sitting about smoking. Think of something useful for them to do—"

"—Like what?—"

"—And see that they do it. And any more insolence out of you, Mr Mortleman, and I'll wheel you in front of the Commanding Officer."

"I am instructed," said Barry to his Platoon, which was seated round him in a half circle on the ground, "to issue a routine reminder about the use of Early Treatment Packets."

The men guffawed.

"Quiet," the Sergeant said: "listen to Mr Strange."

"Thank you, Sergeant. If you intend to go with a woman, any of you, you should call at the Early Treatment Centre and collect a small packet – this – which contains a tube of disinfectant cream and one rubber sheath. During intercourse you will wear the sheath—"

"But sir," said the Platoon wag, "wearing them things spoils it."

"And not wearing them may spoil you. If you want to rot away with sores," said Barry vigorously, "like that beggar outside the barrack gate who's got no lips left, then by all means do it without a sheath. Meanwhile, my friend, you will listen without interrupting. . . ."

"Very good, Mr Strange, sir," said the Platoon Sergeant later on; "that bit about the beggar, very good. They can see him for themselves, you see. You really had them listening after that."

"Our position on the map, Mr Morrison?"

"Map reference 076492, sir. Small casuarina copse at southwest corner of tank."

The Battalion was having a night exercise.

"I can't see the tank."

"Just over that rise, sir. . . ."

". . . And there we are, bang on. Very good, Mr Morrison," the Colonel said. "Now kindly make a round of the Company Commanders and tell them all to prepare to advance at dawn."

"Excuse me, sir," said the Adjutant, "but can't we use the wireless for that?"

"They'll all have ballsed their sets up by now. Word of mouth is more reliable. They won't be able to balls Morrison up. Got that, Morrison? Tell 'em, ready to advance at dawn."

"Exact time, sir?" said the Adjutant apologetically.

"How the hell should I know? What time is dawn, Mr Morrison?"

"0452 hours, sir."

"You seem to have all the answers. 0452 hours it is then. Now on your way. But before you go . . . have a nice swig from my flask."

"Thank you, sir."

"Thank *you*, Mr Morrison, thank *you*."

". . . Right," said Tom Oake to the assembled Subalterns; "so you've got the Magistrate's written permission to fire. Now you must give a proper fire order. Don't just tell 'em to loose off into the crowd; pick out the leader, and order them to aim at him. . . ."

And so the days went on, bringing Alister to proficiency in his word of command but not to a command of his own; bringing Barry to undisputed mastery of his Platoon; bringing Peter to the kind of Intelligence required of an Intelligence Officer; bringing Thomas Oake to the end of his lectures on Duties in Aid of the Civil Power, and to the beginning of those on Regimental History; and bringing, of all things, Wanker Murphy to Berhampore.

"There's a Major Murphy to see you, sir," said the Orderly Room Quartermaster Sergeant one morning.

"*Who?*" Peter said.

"Major Murphy, sir, of the Education Corps."

And Murphy rolled into the room, all got up in riding boots and breeches and carrying an ivory-handled hunting crop.

"Peter, my dear chap. No formalities, please."

Murphy preened and postured, then sat down on Peter's desk and started pleasuring himself with the crop-handle.

"Murphy. What the devil are you doing in that rig?"

"A Field Officer, as you may have heard, is entitled to wear mounted dress."

"If he rides a horse. I didn't know they had them in the Education Corps."

"I'm only in the Education Corps nominally. Actually I'm now a courier. That's why I'm here. To liaise with you."

"And you came here on a horse?"

"The uniform is symbolic of the office," said Murphy, very seriously. "In fact I have my own staff car and a driver to drive it."

"I see. And how did all this come about?"

"Well, my commission as Captain came through all right – it seems Detterling saw after that, like you asked him to – but when I got to Delhi they said that the appointment had been dispensed with after all because the Education Corps in India was packing up. But there *was* an appointment for a Major, to go round doing secret liaison. Carrying messages which were 'for hand of Officer only'. Top level stuff. I'm known," said Murphy with pardonable pomp, "as the Viceroy's Galloper."

"And why did *you* get the job?"

"No one else wanted it, and I was spare. Funny, that. You'd have thought they'd all have jumped at it."

"Yes. . . . Shouldn't the Viceroy's Galloper be transferred to a smarter Regiment?"

"I was told about that. It seems they're all very busy and it'll take some time for the transfer to come through. Eventually I'm going to belong to Lord Curzon's Horse. But for the time being, they said, would I mind continuing in the Education Corps?"

"Nominally."

"That's it."

"Did Detterling have anything to do with it all?'

"As a matter of fact, yes. He knew what had happened about the other thing, of course, so he suggested me for this.

He took me to see that fellow Glastonbury, the one who came to Khalyan that time. 'You're just the chap we're looking for,' Glastonbury said. Then he explained about Lord Curzon's Horse and all that, and I was promoted on the spot."

"Well, congratulations. What happened to the last chap who had the job?"

"I didn't think to ask."

"Hmm. And what brings you here, Murphy? You want the Colonel, I suppose?"

"No. I want you."

"The Adjutant, you mean? He's just next door."

"No. You."

"I'm only the Intelligence Officer."

"You," Murphy said.

"For Christ's sake, Murphy. What does the Viceroy's Galloper want with me?"

"It's what Colonel Glastonbury wants with you. It's so secret I wasn't even allowed to write it down."

"Then I'm not sure I want to hear it. There's a nasty smell here, Murphy."

"Anyway, I've got to tell you and you've got to listen. It's all about Gilzai Khan."

"Ah," said Peter, abandoning caution at the sound of the well-loved name.

"He's somewhere in this area, getting up trouble among the Mohammedans. He's telling them that they'll be massacred by the Hindus if the British leave India. He's urging them to oppose self-government and to petition for us to stay on here."

"Sounds true to form."

"I dare say. But Delhi doesn't like it."

"Why not? He's pro-British, isn't he?"

"That's just what's embarrassing them. Official British Policy, Labour Party Policy, is *anti*-British, if you follow me. The idea is to hand the whole bloody boiling over to the Indians as soon as possible, and then run for it before the balloon goes up."

"Surely . . . we're going to stay until we've made proper arrangements."

"That might have been the idea once, but the wheeze now is just to get out fast. So we don't want people asking us to stay. And the better the reasons they give, the less we want it."

"In other words, the Khan is telling the plain but inconvenient truth—"

"—Which is getting on Delhi's tits—"

"—So they want him to shut his mouth."

"They want *you* to shut his mouth," Murphy said.

"Don't be absurd."

"I'm not being. I am to remind you of that awkward affair about Margaret Rose Engineer, which could still be dug up again and used against you, and I am to tell you that Delhi expects your absolute co-operation."

"What can I possibly do about it? The Khan wouldn't listen to me about a thing like this . . . even if I knew how to find him."

"There's someone else who could find him easily enough, isn't there?" Murphy said.

Peter opened his mouth and shut it again. Murphy stroked himself voluptuously with his riding crop.

"If Barry Strange put the word round the bazaar that he wanted to see Gilzai Khan," said Murphy, "the Khan would come running with his mouth watering and his tail wagging. I wonder he hasn't come already."

"Murphy. We simply cannot be having this conversation."

"I don't see why not. We are wondering why Gil' Khan, given he's in the neighbourhood, hasn't yet been to see his little friend, and we conclude, I think, that he's having a busy time of it and just hasn't heard that Barry is here. As I was saying, however, a word in the bazaar will soon put that right. And once you've tethered the juicy little kid, along comes the tiger."

"Perhaps. But the Khan is not going to be persuaded – not even by Barry – to hold his tongue over this Moslem business. You know how he feels about it."

"My dear Peter, when the tiger comes for the bait, you don't argue with him or try to reform him. You take more radical measures."

"WHAT ARE YOU SAYING, MURPHY?"

"That it would be easier and neater if Gilzai Khan's mouth was closed for good. At least, that is the opinion in Delhi."

"Glastonbury's opinion?"

"He certainly passed it on. But I think it must have originated a bit higher."

"Does Detterling know anything about it?"

"If he does, he hasn't favoured me with his comments."

"Let's get this straight, Murphy," said Peter carefully. "Gilzai Khan is a retired officer of comparatively low rank who is trying to influence local Moslem opinion in a way which annoys Delhi—"

"—And London . . ."

"—And are you seriously telling me that just because of that they want him . . . done away with?"

"Not just because of that. They're afraid of what he may become. He's a remarkable chap, as both you and I are well aware. If he once gets started, there's no knowing where he'll end. Berhampore today, all India tomorrow."

"And so they have sent you . . . to tell me . . . to . . . to do *what* exactly?"

"They didn't go into detail. The general drift is clear enough, I think."

"But Murphy, Gil' Khan is my friend. And even if he wasn't, I'm not a trained assassin. I just would not know how to do this."

"Then you'd better start thinking, Peter. Because if you disoblige Delhi, Delhi is going to disoblige you by raking up dear little Margaret Rose Engineer and using her to get you cashiered. Drummed out, my dear."

"I did nothing wrong."

"You consorted with a Eurasian girl of under sixteen – statutory rape, even if she was a whore – made her pregnant, and deserted her. That's what they're going to throw at you, Morrison – unless they hear good news from Berhampore within four weeks from now. Four weeks, I was told to say. Quite generous, really."

Then Major Murphy of the Education Corps, Galloper to the

Viceroy of India, removed his bum from Peter's desk, raised his riding whip to the peak of his cap in salute, and waddled out of Peter's office.

"Who was that chap with you this morning?" the Adjutant asked.

"An old chum from Bangalore, sir. Friendly visit."

"He took up enough of your time, I must say."

"I had to be polite, sir. Through some preposterous series of chances he's become Viceroy's Galloper – or that's what he calls himself."

"Oh. It used to be a splendid thing, but the character of the appointment has changed, I'm told. There's no more galloping to be done, just crawling about with secret orders. The kind of orders no decent man would dare send through the post."

"I see. He was never really a friend, just a Cadet in my Platoon. But I thought it as well to be polite. Anyone from Delhi . . ."

"You were quite right about that, Peter. I only hope he had no secret orders for you, ha ha."

"Ha ha."

"The last chap who had the job died of D.T.s," said Tom Oake, reminiscing, "and I think the one before was killed in a street brawl somewhere. Let's hope your friend is more lucky."

"He isn't a friend."

"Your fellow Cadet then. You should really have brought him through, you know, and introduced him. Anyone from Delhi, as you say . . ."

"He was in a hurry."

"Not to judge from the time he spent with you."

"You wouldn't have liked him, sir."

"I could have judged for myself about that."

"Please believe me, sir," said Peter desperately; "I was doing you a service by keeping Murphy out of your office. He leaves a trail of slime like a slug."

"If you put it like that," said the Adjutant gently, "I'll say

no more about it. But on the next occasion someone from outside calls on you in your office, Peter, just let me know what's
going on, will you? We're not running a coffee house, you
know, we're running a Battalion Headquarters."

The next occasion came just three days later, and the caller
was Gilzai Khan. He was dressed in European clothes, baggy
grey trousers, a crumpled alpaca jacket and an open-necked
shirt, all of which made him look like a mildly left-wing don of
the late nineteen-thirties. Since both the Colonel and the
Adjutant were out on the drill square, supervising a rehearsal
of the forthcoming Retreat Parade, Peter had no need to
introduce his guest.

"Morrison huzoor."

"Gilzai Khan."

They shook hands politely.

"I'd been told you were round here," said Peter, picking his
words, "and I was going to try to get hold of you."

"Were you indeed, huzoor? And who told you I was in the
vicinity?"

"I had word from Delhi. They say . . . that you have gone
into politics."

"They told you what kind of politics?"

"Yes."

"Then why did you want to see me?"

"For old times' sake."

Gilzai Khan accepted this and smiled his pleasure.

"Ah. That is why I have come."

Peter nodded and smiled back. Both men waited for the
other to speak.

"How did you get in?" said Peter at last.

"They think I am a Munshi who has come to be interviewed.
An Intelligence Officer might wish to keep up his Urdu."

"He might. In fact, I think my Adjutant would rather
approve."

"But in fact, huzoor, you will not be employing this particular Munshi. I have come for the first and last time. I found out

by accident that you and your two friends were here, and I have come . . . to see you only, Peter . . . and to tell you a message."

"You don't want to see Barry Strange?"

The Khan shrugged.

"Have you told him I am in Berhampore?"

"Not yet. I only heard a few days ago, and I've been thinking it over."

"Like a good Intelligence Officer. No, huzoor. I do not wish to see Barry Strange. He liked the soldier but might not care for the politician. It is the same with Master Mortleman. Salute them from me, if you will, and there let it rest. And now, my message."

"What message, Gilzai Khan?"

"I learnt you were here," said the Khan, "because we have procured a roll of your Battalion. We wished to know your exact strength, you understand?"

"I understand."

"And we have made our plans accordingly." The Khan nodded as though commending his own ingenuity. "To begin with, a petition will go to Delhi, asking for a guarantee that the British will stay at least long enough and in at least sufficient numbers to protect Moslem communities – and Hindu communities too, come to that – wherever it may be necessary. The petition will be ignored. At best there will be an evasive reply. We shall then organise strikes and riots, very much the usual kind of thing; and we also propose, at a later stage, to block the railway line. We shall lie across it, huzoor, and there will be too many of us for your Battalion to remove. We have worked it all out very carefully, you see. But what I most wish to tell you is this. If it is possible, stay away from the railway line – you, and the little Strange, and the lanky Mortleman – right away from the railway. It is a warning, Peter, from one friend to another, and, as you say, for old times' sake."

There was a long silence. Then Peter said: "How did you get into this, Gil' Khan? Why did you ever leave the Army?"

"I care for my poor country, huzoor. The only hope of avoiding unbelievable massacres is for the British to stay. Or if they must leave, to leave very gradually. *Someone* must urge this."

"When we go, surely the Indian Army will keep order?"

"An Indian Army with Indian Officers?" The Khan spat on the floor. "The kind they are now training at Bangalore? Most of them could not command a pi-dog. Besides, the Army itself will be split – into Mohammedan regiments and Hindu regiments – and their way of keeping order will be to add to the slaughter. Hindu regiments will be sent to Hindu towns where they will simply kill the Moslems. It will be easier and far less dangerous than trying to restrain their Hindu brethren. But that is still in the future and none of it need concern you. I am here to tell you to keep away from the railway here in Berhampore."

"When will the trouble here start?"

"Soon. Our local petition goes to Delhi tomorrow. If we hear nothing after two weeks, the trouble will start. Slowly, then more quickly later on. It is later on you must avoid the railway."

And now Peter had decided what to do. For three days and nights after the apparition of Murphy he had pondered and found no answer: now he began to see his way plain.

"You have helped me twice, Gilzai Khan," Peter said. "You saved me from disgrace at Bangalore, and you have warned me here. What use your warning can be to me—"

"—Obey it, huzoor, obey it—"

"—What use it can be to me, or to my friends, I am not sure. Soldiers, as you know better than anyone, must go where they are told. But the warning is kindly meant and kindly taken. Now I must repay the debt."

"There is no debt. There has simply been truth between friends."

"And now there must be more of it." Peter paused. "They mean to kill you, Gilzai Khan," he said, "and they don't at all care how they do it."

The Khan bared his teeth and rubbed his nose.

"I am not surprised," he said. "How do you know of it?"

"By the same means I knew you were here. You remember a Cadet called Murphy?"

"I remember," said the Khan. "Mean and rather fat. His thigh was broken."

"And has now mended, leaving him meaner and fatter."

And then Peter told Gilzai Khan of Major Murphy's visit and all that had been said.

"Truth," he concluded, "between friends."

"So they want you to do it, do they?" The Khan grinned like a vampire. "On pain of disgrace?"

"That could be a bluff, of course. They'd have to find the girl for a start. God alone knows where she is by now."

"There are ways of discovering."

"They'd have to explain why they'd dropped it for so long."

"They could do that too. New evidence, they could say."

"I dare say they could. . . . Meanwhile, I thought I should warn you of their intentions."

"And your own, huzoor?"

"I intend to obey the rules," Peter said, "as I was always taught."

"The rules of honour? Or the rules for survival?"

"I have been taught to regard them as the same. Tell no lies and do as you would be done by. That way one cannot go far wrong."

"Let us indeed hope not." Gilzai Khan rose and walked to the door. "Stay well, huzoor," he said. "Stay well, and stay away from the railway, and see your friends do the same."

"I shall do my best. Go well . . . Gilzai Khan."

"Who was that Indian coming away from your office?" the Adjutant said.

"I thought of employing a Munshi. But that one won't do."

"Why not? He looked a better type than most of 'em. Held himself well. Walked smartly."

"And an excellent teacher for all I know. But he is . . . too familiar."

"That's no good then," the Adjutant said.

"Sir . . . ?"

"Yes, Peter?"

"I was wondering if I might have a day or two's leave. I rather want to go to Delhi."

"Why?"

"To see friends. To check up on something."

"Afraid not, old chap. I'd like to oblige, but this morning we had a special order over the wire. No leave to be granted to any personnel for any reason whatever until further notice. It looks as if they think trouble's really on the way."

"I need only be gone for thirty-six hours."

"Sorry, Peter," said Tom Oake rather sharply; "no can do."

So that's that, Peter thought: he was on his own, and had no way of confirming that Murphy's message was genuine. But then why should he doubt it? Murphy had neither the imagination nor the motive to fake it, and Murphy's credentials – the staff car and the Corporal Driver, if not the riding boots – were impressive. True, he had offered only oral authority for the instructions which he had passed on; but then, as he had remarked at the time, prudent men did not put their signatures under instructions of this nature. They just employed the Murphies of this world. So be it.

"Sorry to have bothered you, sir," he said to the Adjutant; "it isn't really as pressing as all that."

As Peter saw it, he had four duties: one to his Battalion in Berhampore, one to his superiors in Delhi, one to Gilzai Khan, and one, not the least, to himself. The problem was to reconcile them all: to perform each one without dereliction of any other.

His duty to his Battalion was simple enough: all he had to do was to obey whatever orders he was given. Much the same, he supposed, was true of his duty to Delhi. If, as he must now assume, Murphy's message was genuine, he must understand that Delhi wanted the Khan to be silenced and had chosen himself to silence him. Nor did Delhi's decision, objectively regarded, seem altogether unreasonable (though hardly very 'British'). These were difficult days, and if the Khan was setting out to make them yet more difficult, he deserved just about everything he got. If a man deliberately sowed violence, no matter how selfless his intentions, he must expect to reap it.

In Peter's view, Gilzai Khan was probably right: the withdrawal of the British would certainly lead to hideous bloodshed and was therefore to be deprecated. However, it was not Peter's duty to hold views, it was his duty to act in accordance with those of his seniors. Plainly, Delhi meant business; very well then; if one Indian must die in order that he should cease to vex an already sorely vexed Administration, on a political level at least Peter saw no particular objection. His experience as a Head of House at school had inclined him to believe in a broadly democratic method, which, however, must necessarily be liable to certain, as it were, backstairs adjustments. In order to keep people quiet, one either had to suppress them or let them have their way; it was easier and more civilised to let them have their way; but in order to let them have it, one had quietly to remove certain nuisances, from time to time, and undertake certain very dirty jobs. The removal of Gilzai Khan was just such a job: a democratically elected government in England, and a huge majority of Indian citizens, wanted the British out of India; and if the Khan was trying, by violent means, to sabotage those who were working to this end, then the Khan was better . . . out of the way. Politically the thing was as clear as a bell; Gilzai Khan's passing bell.

But there were other levels, personal and moral, on which it was not so clear. To begin with, it was Peter himself who had been given charge to . . . put the Khan out of the way; and secondly, the Khan was a friend of whom Peter was very fond and to whom he owed nothing but gratitude. What then, in all the circumstances, was his duty to Gilzai Khan? To respect the friend, Peter thought, and therefore to warn the man. This he had done. But on the other hand he owed no duty to the Khan as rebel. He might shoot down a rebel Indian with no scruple whatever. And yet . . . could he really separate the two in his mind? For there was always love to be reckoned with. When the rebel's body crumpled, would he not see the lineaments of Gilzai Khan? If he destroyed the criminal, would he not still mourn the man? Worst of all, would not killing the

Khan be a sin against brotherhood? A sin – *the* sin – which the Furies punished above all others and from which there could be no absolution at all, no matter how invidious the Khan's own offence might be.

Peter did not wish to be pursued by the Furies, a reflection which brought him, at last, to his duty to himself. This duty, on consideration, he defined as continuing in his career with his honour, both public and private, still intact. To do this, it was apparently necessary, first, to kill the Khan (else Delhi would destroy Peter himself); secondly, to do so in such a way that he need feel no personal blame (or remorse and the Furies would consume him); and thirdly, to avoid scandal or remark in the course of performance (for Delhi, that dealt in oral messages through Major Murphy, would certainly never acknowledge its responsibility for his orders).

There was only one way of achieving all this in combination – the way he had suddenly seen just before he gave the Khan his warning. He must obey the old rules of conduct : he must (to put it very generally) tell no lies and do as he would be done by. Translated into a scheme of action, these rules could not only save his public face and his private conscience, they could also solve for him the very tough physical and psychological problems of how to effect the actual killing. As he had told Murphy, he was not a trained assassin; in this particular, as in every other, he would need a rule book to guide him. Well, he had his rule book – the old code of the old school. This he had so far rigorously applied in his dealings with the Khan (to whom he had indeed told no lies and done as he would be done by), and this he would rigorously apply from now on, in his dealings with the Khan and with everybody else. It might be necessary to interpret the text with some subtlety, to read the small print with care and to search out special cases in the Appendices; but he was sure that his plan lay there (if he only read aright), a plan which the good old rules, in their wisdom, both suggested as practicable and recommended as honourable. Of the details, as yet, he was not quite sure; from now on he must read diligently, line by line, until he had sought them out.

PART FOUR

TATTOO

THE BAND of the First Battalion, the Wessex Fusiliers, marched and counter-marched for the last time, halted in the centre of the parade ground, and executed a left turn, in order to face the spectators. The Drum-Major strutted from behind to take post in the van, turned about to face the Band, and raised his silver staff. Holding it vertically to the ground, he carried it slowly away to his right, conjuring a roll of kettle drums, which mounted in prelude to the evening hymn. At last the drums hovered towards climax, and then sank away again as the wind instruments went into the first luscious notes of 'The Day Thou Gavest, Lord, has Ended'.

The Retreat Parade, for which the Band had been rehearsing in the appalling heat every day for over two months, was nearing its end. Two verses of the hymn (unsung) would be followed by the Call itself. Then the Officers and the Guests (who included the Resident and his wife, and a local Nawab) would retire to the Mess for 'sundowners', while the rest of the Battalion tidied up under the R.S.M.

Not that there would be much tidying up to be done. The parade ground must be swept and raked, and the chairs put away. Since only Officers and Guests had these, and since Guests in any number had been reluctant to come to Berhampore for the occasion, there could not be more than 150 chairs set out, and two-thirds of them were empty . . . which made a very lonely and conspicuous figure of a worried little soldier with a huge cane (the Battalion 'Stick-man', or orderly of the day) who could now be seen picking his way through the barren seats towards the two occupied rows at the front of the block.

In the middle of the front row sat the C.O., with the Resident on the right of him and the Resident's Mem-sahib on the left. On the Resident's right was the Nawab, and on the left of the Resident's Mem was Thomas Oake, Adjutant. Peter Morrison, who had been observing the worried little orderly from a standing position (as Steward) on one flank, could now perceive that he was aiming at the Adjutant's rear; and indeed, as the Band went into its second stanza of the Evening Hymn, the orderly managed to squirm between two thin and pith-helmeted ladies in the second row, touched Tom Oake on the shoulder, and saluted fiercely (dislodging one pith helmet with his backward-jutting cane) as Tom turned his head. Peter, still observing from the wing, was now treated to the following silent sequence: as soon as Tom had acknowledged the orderly, the orderly bent forward to talk most urgently into Tom's ear, while the lady whose pith helmet had been knocked off reached indignantly down for it, apparently pressing her nose into the orderly's bottom as she did so; whereupon the orderly, still talking to Tom, gave a wag of his behind, as if to dislodge a fly or some other minor nuisance, and struck the lady hard on the chin with his coccyx. The lady flopped off her chair to the ground; the Stick-man saluted and swivelled, inadvertently trampled on the lady, was walloped by her companion in the pit of his stomach, and barged rapidly away, scattering the empty chairs as he went. Meanwhile, Thomas Oake had leaned across the Resident's Mem (whose face tightened ominously), tapped Colonel Brockworthy on the knee and started to mouth at him through the music. After three seconds of this the Colonel went bright orange, swelled up like a frog, and brought the silent sequence to a close by bawling, over the penultimate bar of the hymn:

"Be damned to all that, Oake. Sit still, will you, and let the thing go on."

But now, in fact, as the Call itself was about to begin, was the proper time to rise. The audience, however, mistaking the import of the C.O.'s outburst and vaguely imagining that some contrariness of Fusilier custom required them to remain seated after all ('Sit still, will you'), sat steadily on . . . except, of course, for the Fusilier Officers, who were certain of the proper drill and now rose as one man – but then, not wishing to embarrass the Guests by pointing up their solecism, immediately sat down again. But by this time the Guests had realised their error and were rising themselves . . . then started to sit again when they saw the Officers do so . . . only to find that the Officers were now rising once more – a split second too late – to join the Guests. At this stage it occurred to both factions that neither could catch the other up unless one of them waited. So each decided to wait for the other to conform, the Officers on their feet and the Guests on their bottoms, until, ten seconds having elapsed with no movement whatever, there was a failure of nerve all round, and both parties moved simultaneously, thus merely reversing their roles yet again and remaining as far as ever from desiderated harmony.

Whether this farce would resolve itself before the end of the Call, and if so, which faction would finally impose its will on the other, were interesting sources of speculation to those not among the privileged. Peter, standing out on his wing, had an absurd desire to shout the odds to the soldiers nearest him, but at once remembered his responsibilities, and also remembered that those responsibilities, to judge from the urgent manner of the now vanished orderly, would very shortly require his presence at Battalion Headquarters. Whatever nonsense was in train among the spectators, there was nothing he could do about it, so he might just as well be first on the scene of action and find out what was going on. If this was what he thought and hoped it was, then his big chance had now come and he could not afford to lose a moment.

He slipped quietly away round the back of the seats and caught up with the little Stick-man not far from the Orderly Room. The Stick-man was being sick, the excitement and the blow in his belly having been too much for him, and at first he was less than helpful.

"Fuckin' whoarre, sir, thumpin' me in ma bloddy ballocks" – vomit, vomit – "how the hell was I to help it?"

"Bad luck," said Peter soothingly. "But what's happened?"

Vomit.

"Now can you tell me what's happened?"

"Fuckin' whoarre banged ma bloddy balls, that's what happened."

"What were you telling Captain Oake?"

"Bloddy wogs seized the station, sir. Pulling up the lines and breaking the lavatory windows. The station maisster rung up – sounded like a bloddy wog hisself – and then the police rung up and all – and told me I'd got to get the Adjutant and the Colonel at once."

"Are the police still on the telephone?"

"Ah s'pose so. They was when Ah went for the Adjutant. Ah feel as if ma bloddy sweetbreads had fell out on the floor and that cowing old whoarre were stomping on them."

Vomit.

Peter went inside. The receiver of the telephone on the Adjutant's desk (which the Stick-man had been left to answer in case of emergency) was off the hook. He picked it up.

"Hullo?"

"Captain Oake? You've taken your time, I must say."

"Second Lieutenant Morrison here; Intelligence Officer."

"I don't want a pip-squeaking wart. I want your Adjutant or your C.O."

"The Adjutant will be here soon. Is there any way I can help meanwhile?"

"I told you, I don't want to talk to a bloody little wart."

"You can keep a civil tongue in your head all the same."

"Don't be insolent. Do you know who I am?"

"I know you're a policeman of some kind."

"I'm Superintendent Willis."

"You can still use a civil tongue, I suppose? Now; what is it you want, Superintendent? The Adjutant may be delayed a few minutes, but I can help to get things going."

Although there was heavy breathing at the other end, Superintendent Willis had apparently seen reason. He answered now with something like respect.

"Very well, Mr Morrison. If you will kindly relay the following information to your Adjutant, and thus set me free to attend to my own duties at last, I shall be most grateful.

"One. Rioters in strength of approximately one thousand

are smashing the station to pieces. An attempt is also being
made to tear up the line. Special squads of rioters are wrecking
the signal boxes at either end of the station.

"Two. The line at both ends of the station is being blocked
by rioters who are lying across it. There are about three hundred of them at either end. No trains can get in or out."

"Are there any trains waiting to get out?"

"Not immediately. But there is a small goods train, with
engine, on the station siding, which is due to leave tonight at
2300 hours.

"Three. There is every sign that this operation has been
carefully pre-planned and that the rioters are being organised
and led by experts."

That fits, Peter thought.

"Four," continued Superintendent Willis. "The police are
hopelessly outnumbered and are having little success in checking the activities of the rioters. We are concentrating on the
protection of the line itself and other vital equipment. But
although both signal boxes have been cut off and surrounded
by detachments of policemen, these detachments have been
unable to recapture the boxes from the rioters or to prevent
them continuing to do serious damage inside.

"Five. The Magistrates have given their reluctant permission for the employment of two Companies of armed riflemen
to assist the police in dealing with the emergency. However, no
ammunition, repeat, no ammunition, will be issued either to
police or Army personnel without the Magistrates' authorisa-
tion.

"Six. The First Battalion, the Wessex Fusiliers, is requested
to provide forthwith the two Companies of riflemen aforesaid,
and to convey them to the north end of the bazaar which lies
half a mile to the east of the station.

"Have you got all that, Mr Morrison?"

"I've got it, Superintendent Willis."

"Then kindly get things moving at the juldi."

The Superintendent rang off sharply. Peter replaced his own
receiver with the care and respect that were due to the King
Emperor's property, then went outside to look for the Stick-

man, who was sitting on the ground groaning and coddling his groin.

"Go and find the Adjutant and the Colonel," said Peter, "and ask them to be so kind as to come here without delay."

"Ma fuckin' knackers, sir."

"Never mind your knackers. They'll be all right if you only stop thinking about them. Now get moving, Fusilier. *At the double.*"

The wretched fellow clambered to his feet and trotted away like an agitated duck, his legs widely splayed, his head well forward, his clasped hands still cradling his parts. Peter returned to the Adjutant's office and began to write down the gist of the Superintendent's message in the appropriate sequence.

Muddle, he thought as he wrote : there is going to be the most God-awful muddle. For the truth was that the Adjutant's lectures on riot procedure had covered only conventional and theoretical situations in which plenty of time was allowed for the preparation and deployment of troops who were already on the ground when the trouble started. Although Peter himself had been put up to enquire what was to be done in more urgent circumstances, when troops might have to be despatched *in medias res*, and although a reply had been promised for later, Thomas Oake had never got round to giving it. He had used the question as a rod for beating an apathetic audience, but had forborne to scourge himself with it . . . for the very simple reason, Peter now surmised, that neither Tom Oake nor anyone else really knew the answer. To contain riotous civilians from carefully established positions was one thing; to go into an attack against them at a few minutes' notice was quite another. The text book had a lot to say about keeping rioters out of stations but precious little helpful advice as to their ejection when once they were in. It was hopefully assumed that anything so embarrassing would never occur.

And indeed it very seldom did occur, because as a rule strong guards were mounted, at the first sign of trouble, over all important areas. In this case, however, that had not been

done, or had only been half-heartedly done, because despite official forebodings (and contrary to what the Khan himself had foretold to Peter) there had been no activity whatever to give early warning. There had been no preliminary strikes, no minor or prefatory riots, no visible disturbance at all. Doubtless, Peter thought, the Khan had changed his plans – and very wisely. He had ordered total peace and quiet – and then WHAM, into a station guarded only by two dozy policemen before anyone could so much as draw breath, the whole plan being conceived and executed with a professional military competence which was not often found among mob agitators, however expert in their trade, and was not, therefore, anticipated in the calculations of the authorities.

All of which, as Peter told himself once more, meant that there was now about to be one enormous muddle; a muddle to which the dilatory behaviour of Tom Oake and the Colonel (where on earth could they be?) would contribute most handsomely. And muddle, of course, was what he, Peter, most wanted. It would give him the framework, or rather the lack of framework, which he needed to come at his object. For in time of muddle a man who had a plan, like his own, which was carefully conceived and founded on definite rules, was in a very strong position; such a man would be the only person who really knew what he was doing, and furthermore the fact that there was muddle would give him ample excuse for bending the rules, his own or other people's, should this be necessary. In the murky conditions which were now about to obtain Peter would have every chance of discharging each one of his four somewhat disparate duties – to Battalion, to Delhi, to the Khan as friend, and to himself – without prejudicing any of the other three.

There was also a fifth and subsidiary duty, to which, having finished his summary of the Superintendent's information, he now gave brief attention. Gilzai Khan had warned him to keep himself, Barry and Alister away from the railway. Whatever changes of plan the Khan had made since his visit, it was reasonable to suppose that the warning still stood, and it was incumbent on him to apply it if this were possible. Where he went himself was his own affair, but he was bound to give Barry and Alister the benefit of the Khan's advice. He had told neither of them that the Khan was in Berhampore (it would only have puzzled Alister and upset Barry), he had therefore said nothing of the visit or the warning, and he did not propose to do so now. (His rule, 'tell no lies', did not bind him to obtrude superfluous truth.) What he did propose was to use his relatively privileged position to keep his friends out of harm's way . . . if he could. In this fashion he would both be conforming with the second of his guiding rules ('do as you would be done by') and also assisting his purpose; for that purpose would not be furthered if either Alister or Barry were to reach the barricades and get a chance view of the Khan on the other side. Quite how they would react, he was uncertain; but he did feel very strongly that their mere presence would inhibit him in his cause.

Having reached this conclusion, Peter was about to go to his own office to examine his map, when the Colonel entered stumpily, made a breathy transit of Oake's office, and disappeared through a connecting door into his own. Tom Oake, who was bringing up in the rear and looking like a cur caught thieving the Sunday joint, beckoned limply to Peter to follow on with him after the Colonel.

"Well?" snapped the Colonel as they came through the door.

Peter lifted his summary.

"Telephone message from Superintendent Willis," he began, "taken by me at 1745 hours on—"

"—I never saw anything like it," the Colonel said: "bloody spectators farting about like a lot of potty sheep."

"Yes, sir," said Tom Oake.

". . . At 1745 hours," Peter continued, "on Wednesday, June the—"

"—And on top of that," said the Colonel, "I'm chivvied out of my own Mess by my own Adjutant, positively bundled out, in front of the Regiment's guests, like a drunk Lance-Corporal in the canteen, just to listen to all this rubbish about riots. Policemen's business. Why can't they cope?"

"It seems there are rather a lot of rioters," Peter said.

"Do please listen to Morrison, sir," implored Tom Oake.

"All right. But this is not soldiering as I understand it. Bloody ignorant spectators who don't know when to stand up at a Retreat parade, and everyone shitting themselves because of a few dozen Indians yelling in the bazaar."

"In the Railway Station, sir," Peter said, and was then allowed to continue without interruption.

"Two Companies?" said Tom Oake when Peter had finished. "Six Platoons. The six Platoons commanded by the six most experienced Subalterns, I think, sir, and never mind what Companies they come from."

"No," said the Colonel. "Can't mix everything up like that. Two proper Companies, as such."

"With respect, sir," said Peter. "All Companies have at least thirty per cent of men down with this new epidemic of diarrhoea. No Company, as such, can muster at proper strength. We'll have to pick right through the Battalion."

"Who asked you?" snapped the Colonel.

But Tom Oake gave Peter a grateful look, and the C.O., on reflection, acknowledged the force of the argument. Peter, who very much favoured Tom Oake's scheme of employing the six senior Subalterns (and thus cutting out Barry's Platoon at least), had slightly fudged his figures to make his point; but figures were not the Colonel's strong suit and Tom Oake was certainly not going to correct them.

"Six separate Platoons then," the Colonel said, "made up to full strength where necessary by other men from their respective Companies. Lieutenants Saunders, Burrows, Clerkhurst, Gieves, Robinson and Flitchley."

Flitchley was the Subaltern who had Alister as second-in-command.

"Flitchley may have something the matter himself, sir," said Peter. "He was complaining in the rears this morning after breakfast."

In fact Flitchley had complained of constipation, but Peter had spoken the truth as far as he went: Flitchley had indeed complained, in the rears, about his bowels, that morning.

"Very well: Massingburd Mundy."

"Good decision, sir," said Tom. "And might I suggest that you take personal command? Since all the Company Commanders will have men out, they'll all have a case for being there if we let them. Which will make a nonsense. One senior commander, and one only : you."

"*You*," said the Colonel, as Tom had hoped. "This isn't my kind of thing. Indians monkeying about in Railway Stations, it's not what I was brought up to. You run it, Oake, and we'll think again if you get buggered up."

"Right, sir. I'll go and get it all moving. Peter, you stay in Headquarters here and keep the map. Put a bed in my office so that you can answer the telephone twenty-four hours a day. I may ring through at any time."

"But, sir, can't I come with you? The Orderly Officer can stand by the phone and my Sergeant is quite competent to keep the map."

The Adjutant pondered.

"Besides, sir, you'll need someone to keep the official log. Minute by minute. You know how important that is – in case there are complaints against us later."

But Thomas Oake, although he would have liked Peter with him, wanted even more to have someone whom he could trust to deal with messages and requests back at base.

"No, old chap. I'll keep my own log. You attend to the telephone and your map, so that you can explain it all to the C.O. whenever he wants."

"I shan't want," said the C.O. miserably. "Mobs in Railway Stations. I haven't given my whole life to the Army to finish up with that."

"There you are, sir. The Colonel doesn't—"

"—You shut up," said the Colonel, "and do what you're told. And if *you're* going to do your stuff, Oake, you'd better get started. It's already dark."

"Sir," said Oake.

Having saluted carefully, he withdrew from the C.O.'s presence at a calm and becoming pace. Peter retired to his own office and prepared special riot flags to stick in his map. The Colonel went back to the Mess, whence all his guests had

departed, and sulked most horribly over a long series of barra
pegs. In such fashion did the Wessex Fusiliers prepare to quell
the insurrection at Berhampore.

"Hullo seven for one," said the R.T. Set in the Adjutant's
office: "how do you hear me? Over."

"One for seven," said Peter: "loud and clear. Over."

"Seven for one. Captain Oake speaking." (The Wessex
Fusiliers were not very strong on radio procedure and security,
both of which the Colonel disdained utterly, 'provided the
bloody things work'.) "Situation report. I confirm that we
have now cleared the station of rioters, also the track itself
within station limits. But about thirty yards – sorry, figures
three-o yards – of the track have been pulled up. Roger so
far?"

"One for seven. Roger so far."

"Seven for one. Continuation of situation report. We have
been unable to clear either of the two – sorry, figures two –
signal boxes, but we have both of them surrounded. It is feared
that all equipment inside them has been effectively dis-
mantled." Tom Oake was fond of occasional litotes. "Nor have
we been able to clear the line outside the station of the rioters
who are lying on it. Both sections on which they are lying
are half a mile in length, and we cannot exert the control
necessary over so large an area. As soon as we take a man
off, he goes along the line and lies down again. Roger so far?
Over."

"One for seven," said Peter. "Suggest as precedent Jebblepoor, 1943."

"You mean figures one-nine-four-three. What happened at
Jebblepoor?"

"The troops were ordered to pee on the rioters, who all went
home for ritual purification. The line was cleared in ten
minutes."

"I think that's rather disgusting, Peter. In any case, the
problem is academic, as there is no point in clearing the line
till the track is repaired in the station."

"What about that goods train? You might get that out off the siding."

"Forgot to tell you. The wagons on the goods train were burnt out last night."

"What was in them?"

"Food for the famine areas round Kisengarh."

"Food for their starving Moslem brothers. Did they know that?"

"Captives report they believed the wagons to be full of whisky en route for G.H.Q. Delhi. They didn't think of checking the crates first."

So even Gilzai Khan's control was not total. Nor was his intelligence service very accurate. Not for the first time, it occurred to Peter that a man accustomed to command trained soldiers must find it a debilitating task to lead rabble. He was just thinking of some pertinent enquiries along these lines, when:

"Seven for one," resumed Tom Oake's voice rather severely. "We are allowing our R.T. procedure to deteriorate, and I can't spend the whole day chatting. Injury state: three men slightly hurt with knife wounds; at least fifty badly affected by heat exhaustion this morning, and another thirty immobilised by diarrhoea.. Please send one Sergeant, four Corporals and seventy-five Fusiliers to replace these. The approaches to the station from the bazaar are clear and well guarded."

"One for seven. Roger. Figures eight-o personnel in all. What are your intentions? Over."

"Seven for one. Superintendent Willis has asked me to hold the station and approaches in case of further attack, which he believes to be imminent."

Ah.

"You agree with him about that?"

"More or less. Those chaps lying on the rails might decide to start up."

"Not if you all pee on them first."

Tom, though he had already disapproved of the suggestion, would enjoy the joke, Peter thought. Tom had a weakness for lavatory jokes, and might wish Peter were there in person to make more of them. Peter himself disliked that kind of humour, but was prepared to serve it up to his master, and now had his reward in the suppressed chuckle which he could hear in Tom's voice.

"That's enough, Peter. Send me those eighty replacements, and rations, et cetera, for a further twenty-four hours. And tell the Colonel that everything's in hand."

"No further instructions, sir? I still can't join you myself?"

Hesitation. Then :

"No. Sorry, Peter. Over and out."

It was now not quite twenty-two hours since the ill-starred Stick-man had first raised the alarm. Through all that time Peter had been confined to his own office or the Adjutant's, in which latter, shortly after the show began, an R.T. Set had been installed to supplement the telephone and ensure for Tom Oake direct contact with his Battalion H.Q. During the course of the night and the morning which followed it reports had come in regularly, and what they amounted to was this : the rioters, unarmed save for knives and clubs, had gradually been driven out of the station at bayonet point. Not a single shot had been fired nor even a single round issued (for the Magistrates had remained resolute about that) and injuries on both sides had been few and minor. But without the use of firearms it had been impossible (as Captain Oake had just said in his latest report) either to recapture the signal boxes (natural forts) or to remove the Moslems who were reclining on the railway line – a job which would in any case require yard by yard control of a large area. Furthermore, one had to remember that although few men had been wounded, over eighty had been put on the sick list.

And so now, at 1500 hours or 3 p.m. on the day which followed the rising, although a reckonable victory had been won, the situation was extremely untidy. Captain Oake's force, inadequate from the beginning, was now badly run down; while the remainder of the Battalion, itself depleted by diarrhoea and responsible for the protection of the barracks, would be able to do no more than provide the bare replacements which had been requested for the station. There, it seemed, further attack might be expected at any moment, attack mounted either by those rioters who had withdrawn or possibly by their hitherto passive brethren just up and down the railway line; and since the Moslem leadership was evidently of high calibre, as these affairs went, and had large numbers at its disposal, the prospect for the Fusiliers in the line was uneasy, to say the least of it. Indeed Tom Oake, Peter thought now, was going to have his work cut out to hold them together; one sharp counter-attack from the rioters, or just one more degree of this heat, might turn the morale, even of the healthy, as fluid as their comrades' bowels.

But he had no time to worry about that now. It was his business, first, to find eighty replacements, second to despatch supplies for another twenty-four hours, and third to reassure Lieutenant-Colonel Brockworthy, who was still sulking, that all was in order ... more or less.

The replacements he instructed the R.S.M. to raise through the Company Sergeant-Majors: one Sergeant, four Corporals and seventy-five Fusiliers. No Officer replacements? the R.S.M. enquired. No; Captain Oake had asked for none.

To raise the supplies, he sent a note by hand of his Intelligence Sergeant: rations and water for 204 men were to be despatched to the station; also cigarettes, soft drinks, etc., which the men could buy if they would. It seemed to him that he had left something out, something that no one had mentioned but was nevertheless essential, yet try as he might he could not think what. Food, drink, purchasable comforts – these had all been arranged for. Medical supplies? The Medical Orderlies were responsible for them. Bedding? Each man took his own as part of the drill. Ammunition? It was already there in Tom's charge, should ever the Magistrates authorise him to issue it. Early Treatment Packets? Don't be silly, they won't have time for *that*. No, whatever it was, he was damned if he could place it, and since no one else had thought of it either, no blame could attach to him. Best drop it then. This was no time to fabricate supererogatory problems.

As for the third of his immediate tasks, which was to reassure the Colonel, this was disagreeable but brief.

"Sir, I've come to tell you—"

"—You're a mess, Morrison. That uniform looks as if you slept in it."

"As a matter of fact, sir, I did. You see—"

"—Yes, I know. You had to stand by the telephone or whatever it was. Understand this, Morrison : in this Regiment we accept no excuse – none at all, sir – for sloppy turn-out. Now what have you come to tell me?"

"Captain Oake says everything's under control."

"So I should hope. Six Platoons of Fusiliers against a few prancing natives. When will he be back?"

"The police want his assistance for a while longer."

"Useless lot, the police. All of them failed for Sandhurst, you know, and went for the second best – tenth best, I should say. All right, Morrison. Now for God's sake go and clean yourself up."

So Peter, leaving the O.R.Q.M.S. to keep watch on the R.T. Set, went to his quarters for a shower and a change. For a few minutes he relaxed, standing in the shower and stroking himself, thinking of Margaret Rose Engineer. ('It's spurting up inside me, more, more, more . . .') But when the fantasy had come to fulfilment ('All gone, all gone') he started to think seriously of serious things. For he now had to decide, within a few hours at most, how to get himself down to the Railway Station. Preferably with Tom Oake's permission, but if this were refused, then without it, he *must* get there before the next morning. If he did not reach the scene of action while action there still was, there would be an end of his plan for God knew how long and almost certainly for much too long. ('Four weeks, I was told to say. Quite generous, really.') Even when he got there, and for all his careful calculations, he would need a lot of luck, and even if he had it he could still very easily fail. But there was no point in dwelling on that; the thing to remember was this – that unless he reached the station while some sort of emergency was still in train, he would have no chance worth the name now or ever.

So how to get there? That evening, at latest that night? It was now four o'clock, so he must act very soon indeed. The

best thing, of course, would be to bamboozle Tom into order-
ing him to come – much better than turning up unbidden and
probably being turned back. But how to bamboozle Tom, who
had already denied him twice? 'You know, Morrison huzoor,'
Gilzai Khan had once said, 'in the Army there is one way,
fallible but always worth trying, of obtaining the orders you
wish to obtain, and that is to pretend that you no longer want
them.' Yes; given Tom Oake's military philosophy, which held
that it was both good and right for junior men to do what they
least wanted, the Khan's formula might well provide the
answer.

As soon as he had put on a clean uniform and had a cup of
tea in the Mess, Peter returned to the Adjutant's office to
relieve the O.R.Q.M.S.

"Any news, Q?"

"Nothing from Captain Oake, sir. The Quartermaster
reports that he has already sent off the supplies, but the R.S.M.
came in to say that there'd be a slight delay over the replacements of personnel."

"Oh, why?"

"The C.O. sent what's left of the Battalion on a route march
this morning. They've only just got back."

"*Route march?* Then who's been guarding the barracks?"

"Normal piquet, sir."

Choking back any further comments on the Colonel's
intransigence, Peter nodded briskly and stepped up to the R.T.
Set.

"Very well, Q. I'll warn Captain Oake. You go and have
your tea."

"Glad to stay with you, sir. It's all quite exciting, isn't it?"

So it might be; but for the next ten minutes or so Peter particularly wanted to be left alone with the wireless.

"I'd be most grateful, Q, if you could find the R.S.M. and
ask him to expedite those replacements."

"He's got all that in hand, sir. As soon as they've had a
meal—"

"—Please do as I ask, Q. I want you to go, yourself in person, and tell the R.S.M. that there is no time at all to be lost."

"Very well, sir."

Hurt by Peter's rejection of his company, irritated by the superfluity of the errand, humiliated at being ordered about by a mere one-pipper, the O.R.Q.M.S. saluted with extreme officiousness and stamped out of the room.

"One for seven," Peter said into the mouthpiece: "fetch Captain Oake. Over."

After a long and sweaty delay (would the O.R.Q.M.S. come bounding back as soon as he'd seen the R.S.M.?) Tom Oake's voice came up over the set.

"Seven for one. Where are my replacements?"

"One for seven. All spare personnel up here have been on a route march. They've just returned, and we're sending your replacements down as soon as possible."

"Route march? Christ, they'll be worn out."

"One for seven. Important information has been received from Delhi. Intelligence sources report that the leader of these riots is almost certainly Captain Gilzai Khan, repeat Gilzai Khan, late of the 43rd Khaipur Light Infantry and recently an instructor at the O.T.S., Bangalore."

And what was wrong with that? He had indeed had the information from Delhi, from the Viceroy's Galloper himself. Tell no lies, and do as you would be done by.

"The suggestion is," Peter continued (his own suggestion, as it happened, but it wasn't his fault if the phrase had an official and authoritative ring), "that in case of further attack you make every effort to seize Gilzai Khan's person, thus depriving the rioters of an experienced and determined leader."

"That's all very well, but he won't be parading about in the front row, now will he?"

"From what is known of his character, that's just what he may be doing."

"Anyhow, I shan't know which he is."

Careful now.

"Second Lieutenants Strange and Mortleman are both

capable of identifying him. Shall I send one of them down to you?"

An easy and natural proposal of the kind which always aroused instant opposition in military minds, just because it *was* easy and natural.

"You know him too, Peter. Better than they do, because you were his J.U.O. It might be best for you to come down here."

Good. He wants me with him. So far he's left me here because he knows I'm reliable on the set and he thinks it would be self-indulgent to take me away from it for the sake of my company. But here's his excuse, made to measure and totally respectable, to do what he really wants. Steady, boy: don't show willing.

"One for seven. Sorry, sir. I've got a lot on here."

"Seven for one. This is an Intelligence Officer's job if ever there was one. Tell Flitchley to take over on the R.T. Set, and come down with the replacements."

So that was it, for the record. 'At 1625 hours, 2/Lt. Morrison was ordered down to the station by Captain Oake.' He had been sent for; though he had pleaded the importance of other duties, had actually displayed reluctance, he had been commanded to go.

"Roger," Peter said: "over and out."

The O.R.Q.M.S. came in and saluted with a bang.

"R.S.M. reports the replacements will be ready to leave in five minutes, sir."

"Tell him to hold it for half an hour, Q. I've got to go with them myself."

"Half an hour, sir?"

"I've got to leave everything in order first."

"The men could have finished their tea properly if we'd known."

"We didn't know. Please send for Mr Flitchley to come and take over the set, while I tidy up the map for him next door."

"Sir."

"And please send instructions to have my kit loaded on to the column. Camp-bed and wash-stand included."

"SIR."

While the furious O.R.Q.M.S., like Lars Porsena, bade messengers go forth in all directions, Peter went into his own office. There was nothing to do on the map; he and his Sergeant had kept that up to the minute. But there was something else that must be done – and thank God the Sergeant was still at tea. Peter unlocked a drawer in his desk, unlocked a sturdy cash box that was inside the drawer, took out six rounds of .38 ammunition, and fitted them carefully into the drum of the revolver which he was carrying on his belt. He should not have possessed these rounds and he should certainly not be taking them with him (let alone loading them) now, as he had no permission to do so. But it was essential that he should have them by him; for the probability was that no ammunition would be officially issued unless matters came to crisis, whereas his plans required that he himself should be able to fire at need. Only as a last resort, to which he prayed that he would never come ('do as you would be done by'); but fire-power he must have in case. Not that he could do much with a .38 revolver, a ladies' weapon, as they always said. However, it would have to serve. It would look very odd if he toted a rifle about, or even a sten gun. Intelligence Officers carried revolvers, and that was that.

He snapped the drum back into the stock, fastened the safety-catch, replaced the pistol in his holster, and returned to the Adjutant's office to wait for Flitchley. In fact he could be ready to leave in ten minutes if Flitchley was prompt and his servants didn't dally with his kit; but he had stipulated half an hour to impress on everybody how little he had expected to be summoned and how difficult it was for him to leave his present charge. To all eyes, he must appear as one who had been surprised and upset by his orders, very far from the man who had anticipated and indeed contrived them.

To further the illusion of his unreadiness, Peter joined the column only seconds before it left for the bazaar, running up in a state of visible agitation and bundling himself into the cab of the leading lorry. It was only when they reached the bazaar, therefore, and the men climbed down to make a tactical approach to the station, that he discovered that both Barry and Alister were there with him – had in fact been travelling in the lorry immediately behind him.

"What the hell are you two doing? No Officers were called for except me."

"Over half my Platoon's among these replacements," said Barry. "Of course I had to come."

"They'll be distributed among the other Platoons. You won't be able to command them."

"I know that. I've come here to be with them."

"Same here," Alister said. "Flitchley can't come with our lot, so I did."

There was a ripple of pleasure among the soldiers near enough to hear this conversation.

"No one told you to come. You'd both better stay here and go back with the lorries."

"I think," said Barry, "that we'll let Captain Oake decide that."

"And now," said Alister, "let's get this lot to the station. Why couldn't we take the lorries right into the station yard?"

"Tom Oake's worried about booby traps."

"Then how does he want us to move?"

"Single file; alternate sections on opposite sides of the street."

"Right," said Alister, and started cheerfully bawling a string of appropriate orders which he had learned, painfully and therefore indelibly, as Flitchley's second-in-command. In thirty seconds flat the men were ready to move off.

"The men are ready to march, sir," said Alister in the correct Fusilier style to Peter, who was technically the senior Officer present. "May I have your permission to give the order?"

"Pray proceed, sir," said Peter, conforming to the idiom.

Alister took post at the head of the leading section and ordered the advance. Barry wanted to join the two sections of his own men, but was asked by Peter to walk with him in the rear.

"Why come looking for trouble?" Peter grumbled: "you said you loathed the very idea of this kind of thing."

"So I do. But if my men must be here, then I must. You've just been in an office these last weeks, Peter. So you haven't had a chance to discover what the whole thing's about. It's only about one thing, really : being there when you're wanted."

"No one wanted you here."

"My men might. They'll feel very awkward and lonely, being scattered round different platoons. But if I'm there to go round and say a word or two, they may not mind so much."

"Flatter yourself, don't you? A little touch of Barry in the night."

Barry flushed and then blinked.

"Do you think I learnt nothing," Peter went on, "being J.U.O. all that time?"

"That was different. Bangalore was a training establishment and we were all Cadets."

"Yes, Officer Cadets. Who are meant to learn that the first thing – the only thing in the end – is to obey orders. You've come here against orders, Barry. So don't blame me if you get more than you bargained for."

"What on earth do you mean by that?"

Remembering the events of that evening months and even years later, Peter often wondered how he would have replied to this question, in what terms, vague or precise, in what tone, wheedling or minatory. In fact, however, he never had to give an answer; because even as the possible combinations of words began to pass through his mind, there was a deafening hiss which seemed to fill all heaven, and they were suddenly walking in cataracts of rain.

The Monsoon.

Which, as every schoolboy knew, had been due in this area any time these last three days. Every schoolboy perhaps, Peter thought, but not, apparently, the Commanding Officer of the First Battalion, the Wessex Fusiliers, to judge from the date he had chosen for his Retreat Parade (no wonder so few guests came), nor indeed the Adjutant and the Quartermaster, who had neglected, between them, to issue the troops with waterproof capes. It was of these he had been thinking, or rather failing to think, when earlier in the afternoon he had told himself that something had been forgotten. Now he knew what. The men only had ground-sheets, which would be pitifully inadequate; by the time the Q.M. had sent down proper capes, they would all be soaked through and through, and since the short-term effect of the heavy rain would be a sharp drop in temperature, there would be some atrocious fevers and an increase in the already endemic diarrhoea.

Splendid, Peter thought. The more disease, the more muddle; the more muddle, the greater his chances of success. True, the arrival of Alister and Barry was a nasty shock, as these two, if once they recognised Gilzai Khan or even knew he was among the rioters, might well prove serious obstacles to Peter's plan; but Tom Oake would probably send them back to barracks, and even if he didn't, the Monsoon, the steaming, streaming, eye-dulling, mind-splitting Monsoon, would be an ally that offered far more assistance than Barry or Alister could possibly effect in hindrance. Thinking of all this, Peter grinned roundly at Barry through the rain and spread his hands, palms upwards, miming the need for charity in their new predicament; and was answered, after just perceptible hesitation, by Barry's puzzled but forgiving smile.

A few minutes later, Alister and the leading section turned into the station yard.

This was an area of sandy earth, some seventy yards square, the top or north side of the square being the façade of the station and the bottom or south side being a continuation of the street along which Alister had led the replacements in a westerly direction from the bazaar. On its east and west sides, the station yard was closed off by high stone walls; while all along the south side it was open to the street, from which it was separated only by a thin strip of concrete that was flush with both yard and street and passed as a kind of pavement. Lining the south of the street was a high and rickety structure of wood, which continued unbroken from a crossing some fifty yards east of the yard to another crossing fifty yards west of it. Into this somewhat rococo building there were doors at every thirty yards or so, these being about ten feet above ground level and approachable from the street by means of exterior staircases, which were most of them little better than step-ladders.

Normally the station yard was crowded with rickshaws, gharries and motor-taxis, all of which would mill round in front of the façade in chaotic competition for custom, except in wet weather, when they would assemble, the yard being un-negotiable, along the street. It was for this alone, in fact, that Berhampore was mildly famous: if you arrived there during the rainy season, you had to convey yourself and your baggage across seventy yards of deep orange mud (the 'Berhampore Quag') to the line of vehicles beyond the concrete strip.

This evening, however, both yard and street were deserted; naturally enough, of course; but the total emptiness of the square was nonetheless disquieting and reminded Peter, as he came into view of the yard, of something more disquieting still. Thomas Oake had said that the approaches to the station from the bazaar were secure and well guarded; yet there had been no signs of guards or patrols. Possibly these were in the houses which lined the street, and certainly they themselves had made the approach safely enough (so far). But Peter did not like it, and liked it even less when he reflected that, apart from the entrance to the station through the centre of the façade, the only way out of the square was along the street, which was particularly narrow at the two points of egress, or (presumably) up one of the staircases and into the huge wooden shanty, which might not prove a very wholesome refuge.

But it was too late to worry about that. Alister, who was leading the replacements (now in one long file) along the east wall of the yard, was already half way to the station façade. When he reached it, he would only have another thirty yards or so to go – along half of the façade itself and then under the fake portcullis and into the Gothic portal. Looking through the rain towards the station (whose pert turrets and dotty battlements reminded him of the silver model of the Depot

Keep in the Mess), and observing Alister as he turned left and started along the façade, Peter breathed a sigh of relief and began to squelch through the mud (not quite a 'Quag' yet, but already glutinous) behind Barry at the rear of the column.

Then two things happened. The late afternoon became night and the rain almost doubled in volume. One moment he could see the façade, could even distinguish turrets and embrasures, and had a clear view of Alister as he walked beneath them; the next moment he could see Barry before him and up to the third man in front of Barry and no further at all. Not to worry. But why has there been no sign of sentries under the portcullis, no sign of anyone to greet us, come to that no sign of life whatever since we arrived in this accursed mud-patch? Do be sensible. This isn't Windsor Castle. Of course there aren't any sentries strutting about in the open, they've all been posted tactically at windows, behind those embrasures . . . out of which they can now see nothing, any more than I can, oh, do get a move on in front.

"Get a shufti on," he rasped at Barry: "pass it down."

Muddle all right, I wanted it, I've got it: nothing but muddle and mud.

"Shufti, shufti," he said.

But Barry, of course, couldn't hear, not unless Peter shouted, and that would be undignified. Anyway, what was he panicking about? They must be within twenty yards of the façade by now, only fifty yards to go in, a thick wall on the right of them, open ground on the left, no one could cross it without the sentries saw them, only of course the sentries couldn't see anything now – *so look left quick.*

Nothing. A wall of water. Look front. Why were there no lights in the windows? Surely *lights* would be visible? What game was Tom playing? Playing possum, playing dead? Someone coming down the line towards him, a huge, menacing figure, striding down like a moving statue . . . Alister, thank God. Alister smiling, waving them on, nothing to fear, Alister receding into the rain now, going up and down the line, no doubt, to keep them moving and reassure them: *there when wanted,* 'that's what it's all about'. Turn left down the façade

. . . look up at the windows, false of course, that's why there wasn't any light out of them, everything easily explained if only a man kept his head.

Under the portcullis and into the porch at last. There was no rain now but even less light than outside. It seemed that some way ahead there was a large inner gate, like a cathedral door. Just in front of Peter in the porch was Barry, and in front of Barry was a queue of figures up to the gate, at which Alister, just recognisable in the torch-light which now and then flicked through the narrow opening, was checking the men through. Over to Peter's left and somewhat to his rear, in a niche in the wall beneath one end of the fake portcullis, a Fusilier was crouching on one knee. A sentry. Not strutting, of course, not out in the open, a proper sentry, crouching in a recess, keeping watch from behind cover as a sentry should.

"An inclement evening, Morrison huzoor," the sentry said.

Peter stood quite still. Barry turned and went to the crouching figure.

"Khan," Barry said.

The figures ahead of Peter shuffled on, soaked, miserable and unnoticing, towards the gate.

"Khan, what are you—?"

"—Don't you know, little Cadet? Get Mortleman here. Make some excuse."

"I'll do that," said Peter.

He walked the twenty yards up the porch to the inner gate, where Alister was admitting the last of the soldiers. On the other side of the gate, visible through the foot-wide gap, was Tom Oake and a Sergeant.

"Good evening, sir," Peter said.

"Peter . . . What's Mortleman doing here?"

"He helped me bring the replacements down. He's going back now."

"I don't understand. Why did you need him?"

"I'll explain later, Tom."

This was the first time he had ever so addressed the Adjutant, who for the moment was too surprised (as he was meant to be) to call for a more ample account. Peter seized Alister by the wrist and swung him away from the gate.

"What the hell?"

"The Khan," whispered Peter. "Come on."

"The Khan?" repeated Alister, loudly and stupidly.

"What was that?" said Tom Oake from behind the gate.

"The car, Tom. The C.O.'s in it, waiting for Mortleman."

"I still don't understand."

"He came to see we got here all right. He's taking Mortleman back."

"But why—"

"—Please don't delay us, Tom, or the road may be flooded." He dragged Alister down the porch.

"Don't forget the password," Tom Oake called after them: " 'The Drum is in Berhampore Station.' "

The inner gate now closed behind them. Peter and Alister reached the portcullis end of the porch and huddled into the recess with Barry and Gilzai Khan.

"What have you done with the real sentry?" Peter asked at once.

"Two of them, huzoor. They're unconscious out there in the yard. You must not blame them when they recover. The rain was very thick."

"Gilzai Khan," said Alister, "what are you doing here?"

"He's leading the riots," said Barry, with a mixture of apprehension and pride. "He hasn't had time to explain properly, but it's all pro-British, in a way. He wants us to stay in India."

"For as long as is necessary," the Khan said, "to prevent the Hindus from slaughtering us Mohammedans – and us from butchering them back."

"But why the riot?" Alister said.

"To make them listen to us in Delhi. They refuse to listen, huzoor."

"Why choose Berhampore?"

"Chance, huzoor. One must start somewhere."

"Peter's known he was here for some time," Barry said.

"You didn't tell us?"

"Yes, why not?" Barry rounded on Peter in accusation, then looked at the Khan as at a man betrayed.

"I suppose he had his reasons," said the Khan lightly.

"He should have told us," Barry huffed.

"But now we know," said Alister to the Khan, "I imagine we ought to arrest you. Beating our sentries about like that. But one can't arrest one's old instructor; it would be like arresting one's housemaster. In any case, I gather your visit is amicable?"

"Yes, Mortleman huzoor. I saw you arrive in the bazaar, and—"

"—What have you done with our guards?" Peter interrupted. "In the bazaar and on the route here?"

"Nothing, huzoor. They don't worry us. They spend most of their time watching the people in the houses. But we are like lice in the woodwork. We come and we go."

"Never mind all that," said Alister: "just what is this visit here in aid of? You saw us get out in the bazaar, you say, and you've followed us here to the station—"

"—I was here before you were, huzoor—"

"—You *came* here to the station. Alone, I hope—"

"—Alone indeed, huzoor—"

"WHY?"

Gilzai Khan gave a sad little grin.

"I have come here . . . to exonerate myself," he said. "You see, some time ago I asked Peter Morrison to keep you, you and the little Strange, away from here when trouble started. Not because there is any real danger – we only wish to gain attention, you understand, not to kill anyone – but because I did not choose to be seen by you in my new role. I am not ashamed of what I am doing, but nevertheless I wished your memories of Gilzai Khan to end with Bangalore. There we were friends, and parted in love and honour. All this, I thought, would be spoiled if I now became for you . . . another wog agitator."

Alister considered this, shivering slightly in the damp.

"And yet you told Peter what you were doing? And you thought he would tell us?"

"I did not mind your knowing, indeed I realised that you must all hear of it sooner or later, but I mind your *seeing*. In the imagination, a rebel leader can be a romantic, even a heroic figure, especially if his cause is good. But when seen in the flesh, screaming and mouthing and spitting and clawing – for that is what leaders of riots must do, my brothers – such a person is without appeal to gentlemen like yourselves. You might say . . . that I did not wish to lose face before you, for in doing so I should lose face in my own eyes too. After all, it is a disgraceful thing to embarrass one's friends.

"But here you are, despite my request, and soon the rioting will be renewed, and so soon you must see me, capering about like a moon-man, throwing stones and exhorting the scum of the Moslem quarters. . . . No, my brothers, I cannot endure that it should be so. And yet it must be so, it seems. So I have come to make the only amends I can." He reached behind him and brought out a long thin object with what looked, in the darkness, like a ball of silver at one end of it. "The sword you gave me when I left you all. It is the dearest gift that I have ever had, and I have kept it bright and sharp for love of you. Now I must give it you back."

"But *why*?" Barry said. "We don't think any the worse of you."

"Don't you?" said Peter. "It was you that said, only the other day, that the very thought of riots made you sick."

"Alister said that."

"And you agreed with him."

"I said I didn't want any part in helping to put riots down. It made me sick to think of pointing a rifle at unarmed civilians. But to *be* a rebel, to fight for something you think worthwhile – there's nothing wrong in that."

"Nevertheless, huzoor, to see the rebel Gilzai Khan leading his rioters will make you truly sick. When you see me, frothing at the lips and calling with arms upraised upon Allah in whom you know I do not believe, *it will make you sick*. There is no time for more talk. Take back this sword."

Holding it parallel to the ground with his two hands, he passed the sword to Barry.

"What difference will that make?" Alister said.

"It is a kind of resignation. Just as I resigned the King Emperor's commission before I could undertake such work as this, so I am now resigning my claim to your friendship. Because I am now unworthy."

Gilzai Khan rose to his feet.

"But you are not unworthy," Barry said desperately. "I don't say it's what I would have wished for you, and I'm afraid it may lead to a lot of trouble, but that doesn't mean I don't want you for a friend any more."

"Right," said Alister. "One doesn't disown a friend just because he makes an ass of himself."

"I am not making an ass of myself, Mortleman huzoor. What I am doing must be done."

"Then why are you unworthy?"

"Because by my acts I am lowering myself in your eyes – and in mine. I cannot explain any more. You will understand when you see me leading my rabble . . . myself a part of it."

Now or never, Peter thought. It hadn't come about at all as he had envisaged, and the presence of Barry and Alister was a factor unforeseen, but nevertheless a variant of his plan could now be set in train. Some attempt, at any rate, could be – must be – made. As for Barry and Alister, if he watched them carefully, they might be less of a nuisance than he had feared. They might even, just conceivably, serve his ends, if only as witnesses. Very well, Peter thought, bracing himself : do as you would be done by and tell no lies.

"I disguised myself in the uniform of one of those sentries," Gilzai Khan was saying, "and left my poor rags over him in exchange. Please see that he is not out of pocket." He passed some coins to Alister. "The rifles of both men are safe in here" – he pointed to the back of the recess – "and I do not think that either will take much harm from his experience, beyond a nasty headache. Indeed, it may teach them to be more alert for the future."

He waved his hand at them, palm outwards, in a limp movement to and fro across his chest, and stepped out into the rain, which was now slackening a little.

"I suppose he's got to take that uniform with him," Barry said reluctantly.

Peter looked quickly into Barry's rumpled face, and was at once made glad by what he saw there. *Of course*; but how could he use it?

"Gilzai Khan," Peter said.

The Khan turned.

"Those rifles," said Peter: "did you think they were loaded when you assaulted our sentries?"

"I thought they might be, huzoor. Later I found they were not."

"No. Because no ammunition has been issued. But you didn't know that. And anyhow, the bayonets were fixed?"

"Yes, huzoor."

"So you had to surprise two men, with fixed bayonets, who for all you knew might have shot you. Quite an undertaking, even for a man of your experience?"

"There was darkness and rain, huzoor. You saw what rain. And they were nearly twenty yards apart."

"Even so. . . . How did you do it?"

"From behind. With a garotte. First one, then the other." Barry shuddered.

"With a garotte? You might have killed them."

"No, huzoor. I know how long to apply the garotte in order to make a man faint without killing him."

"And then what?" Peter said. "They've been unconscious a very long time."

"A powder, huzoor, down the throat. I have no more time for these questions."

"All this trouble just to return a sword? There were a hundred ways you could have done it. You could have slipped it into the porch in the rain. You could have sent it through the post, come to that."

"I wished, very much, to try to explain."

"Let him go, Peter," Alister said. "What are you trying to prove?"

"I've proved it. In order to satisfy his personal pride, his honour I suppose he would call it, Gilzai Khan has endangered the lives of two Fusiliers. Not only has he strangled them and filled them with drugs, he's left them lying in the mud – drowning in it for all he knows – and exposed to torrential rain. Before you leave, Gilzai Khan, you're going to take us to those sentries, and we're going to make sure they're all right."

The Khan shrugged.

"Very well. But please be quick."

So far, so good, Peter thought. Tell no lies and do as you would be done by. I'm not deceiving him or being false to him; I'm merely displaying a proper concern for the Regiment's soldiers – which the Khan of all people will understand.

The little procession set off through the 'Quag' (as now indeed it was). First the Khan, moving quickly and neatly in the Fusilier sentry's jungle green; then Peter, clumsily tramping; Alister likewise; and Barry bringing up in the rear, still holding the Khan's sheathed sword. The two sentries were in fact at the west end of the façade, propped up against it in a sitting position, and to some degree sheltered by the corner which the façade made with the side wall. One was naked, except for socks and underpants, but as the Khan had said, his own clothes (linen breeches and a long shirt) had been thrown over the man as covering. Both soldiers were sleeping quietly.

"There you are," said the Khan.

Peter bent down to examine their throats. The rain had almost stopped now, and the moon was giving a little light through the cloud . . . enough to enable Peter to see that the weals made by the garotte were not serious. They were not even raw.

"Right," said Peter. "Take off that uniform so that we can dress this poor fellow properly. And put these things back on yourself."

He picked up the breeches and the shirt and passed them to the Khan. Barry nodded fiercely in approval.

"I have no time. I've paid for the soldier's clothes—"

"—That's right," said Alister, jingling the coins in his pocket; "forty rupees and the odd anna—"

"—And now I must go. I have a council to attend and I am already late. Good-bye, gentlemen; stay well."

The Khan dropped his clothes and turned. Barry swallowed and scowled. Peter drew his pistol and blocked the Khan's way.

"Gilzai Khan. You are wilfully impersonating a soldier of His Majesty. Pick up those clothes and change."

"Don't be silly, Peter," said Alister.

"He's not being silly," Barry said, earnest and excited. "That's a Fusilier uniform, and Gilzai Khan has no business to wear it. He's going to use it to come spying or something. He can have his own clothes back now, and he hasn't got the slightest excuse."

"Don't be childish, Barrikins."

"He's no right to a Fusilier uniform," Barry said. "*My brothers died in that uniform.* He'll use it to make fun of us to the mob – it's the sort of thing he has to do, he said so himself."

"Do you grudge me a uniform, little Cadet?"

"I won't have Fusilier dress on a rebel," babbled Barry.

"You approved of me as a rebel just now."

"Not in that uniform. You can't sneak round with a filthy garotte wearing that badge in your hat."

The Khan made to pass Peter. Peter cocked his pistol. Alister laughed.

"No use trying that old trick on Gil' Khan," he said: "there's no ammunition been issued."

The statement was true; let it pass. Peter said nothing, but lowered the pistol and looked apologetically at Barry. Now let it work.

"Off you go, Gil' Khan," said Alister, "or you may really embarrass us. If anyone could see us now . . ."

"Take off that uniform first," howled Barry. "My brothers died in that uniform, and you're only an Indian, you're not even in the Army any more, not even the Indian Army, you're just a dirty wog."

For a moment Gilzai Khan faltered and seemed about to turn. Then he shrugged slightly and moved on.

"Stop," wailed Barry.

The Khan walked on. Barry ran up behind him. He drew

the Khan's sword from its sheath and thrust crazily at the Khan's hips. From where Peter stood, the steel strip seemed to stop and buckle, then somehow to straighten after all and to be sliding back into its hilt like a toy or a weapon used on stage. But the Khan slumped to the ground, and when Barry released the sword hilt it wagged on the partly buried blade.

Barry, Peter and Alister stood over the fallen body. The Khan bared his teeth and grinned up at them.

"Morrison huzoor," he said, "I wish you the long and successful career which your ingenuity deserves." He gasped slightly. "Oh Strange huzoor," he said, "oh my little Cadet, why should I not wear your brothers' uniform? We were brothers, you and I, were we not? I only wished to wear, for just a little time, the same badge as you."

"Khan. Oh khan my khan my khan."

And Barry bent to kiss the grinning face, and was too late, for the lips now grinned in death.

REPORT of a SPECIAL ENQUIRY
held at BERHAMPORE (PUNJAB)
on June 20, 1946
By Order of His Excellency the
VICEROY OF INDIA

Subject of Enquiry: The Death by Stabbing of the Moslem agitator, Gilzai Khan, formerly Captain in the 43rd Khaipur Light Infantry.

Members of the Board: The Investigating Officers appointed by H.E. the Viceroy were Lieutenant-Colonel Glastonbury and Captain Detterling, both of the 49th Earl Hamilton's Light Dragoons but presently serving on the Military Staff of H.E. the Viceroy.

Report: Colonel Glastonbury and Captain Detterling, having examined the three Officers of the Wessex Fusiliers who were present at Gilzai Khan's death and also a Medical Witness, and having taken their depositions on oath, have established to their entire satisfaction the following sequence of events :

1 At approximately 1800 hours, on June 18, 1946, at Berhampore Station, Second Lieutenants P. Morrison, B. Strange and A. Mortleman were conducting a draft of Fusiliers into the station hall through the main entrance.

2 Just as they had completed their duties in this respect, they discovered and apprehended (Captain) Gilzai Khan, who was disguised as a Fusilier sentry and lurking, under cover of darkness, in an alcove by the main entrance.

3 All three Officers had known Gilzai Khan for some weeks between January and March of this year, as they had been instructed by him, during the said period, at the Officers' Training School at Bangalore. They therefore recognised him at once.

4 Knowing that Gilzai Khan no longer had any connexion with the Armed Forces of the Crown, the three Officers warned him that he was under arrest. They then searched the alcove and removed from Gilzai Khan's possession two rifles, unloaded but with bayonets fixed, which he had taken from two unconscious sentries (see below), and one sheathed sword, his own personal weapon.

5 2/Lt Mortleman then challenged Gilzai Khan to explain his presence and his dress. Gilzai Khan then admitted that he was the leader of the Moslem rioters in Berhampore (a fact which has subsequently been confirmed by the Special Branch) and had been observing the arrival of the draft of Fusiliers at the station. He further admitted that he had garotted two Fusilier sentries, the uniform of one of whom he was now wearing as disguise.

6 The three Officers then ordered Gilzai Khan to take them immediately to the sentries. These had been left lying in the thick mud some thirty yards from the station entrance. They were still unconscious and had been visibly marked by the garotte. One of them was naked.

7 2/Lt Morrison now ordered Gilzai Khan to remove the uniform which he was wearing, in order that it might be put back on to the naked and seriously exposed sentry who was its rightful owner.

8 Gilzai Khan refused. 2/Lt Morrison threatened him with his empty revolver (no ammunition had been issued to British personnel) but Gilzai Khan was not deceived by the bluff and now attempted to escape.

9 2/Lt Strange, who had been given charge of Gilzai Khan's sword, drew it from its scabbard and tried to detain Gilzai Khan by threatening a pass at his body.

10 Gilzai Khan ignored the threat and was pierced, in the ensuing confusion, between hip-bone and rib-cage at his left rear. Gilzai Khan was dead within a minute.

11 *Expert Statement by Lt. Col. Glastonbury*, British Army Sabre Champion (1938) and selected member of the British Fencing Team for the 1940 Olympic Games:

i) If any thrust delivered from the level and the direction recorded is to prove lethal, the swordsman must pierce part of a very small target area.

ii) The evidence of 2/Lt Strange and his two colleagues makes it plain beyond doubt that he was not aiming at this area, or indeed at any particular area, of Gilzai Khan's body. He was merely making a clumsy general effort to stop a fast-moving man in the dark.

iii) That the thrust went home where it did, and deeply enough to prove fatal, must therefore be deemed the purest chance.

"There we are," said Colonel Glastonbury, looking up from the text which he had been reading aloud to Peter: "no difficulties there, I think."

He took up his pen and poised it over the bottom of the last page.

"No difficulties at all," said Peter; "unless they show it to Major Murphy and ask for his opinion."

"They'll have to be very persistent to get one," said Captain Detterling. "Murphy's dead."

"One of those accidents which Viceroy's Gallopers are heir to," Glastonbury said : "a bomb in his engine."

"Had his transfer come through?" asked Peter stupidly. "To Lord Curzon's Horse?"

"No."

"Pity. He'd have liked that. You might at least have done that for him before he was killed."

"My dear fellow, you speak as though I were somehow responsible for his death."

"Who was?"

"Messengers who carry bad news," said Detterling, "are never popular. It was Major Murphy's job to carry very bad news, far and wide, to all sorts and conditions of people. One of them was a certain Maharajah – Dharaparam, as it happens – in whom H.E.'s Government had rather a pressing interest. . . ."

"Dharaparam used to come to our cricket matches at Bangalore. He wouldn't have killed a fly, let alone Murphy."

"But he had loyal servants who might have been more energetic. Mind you, we can't prove anything. Nor, where Murphy is concerned, do we want to. You see," said Giles Glastonbury, "we quite like a quick turnover in this particular appointment."

"I do see," said Peter. "No names, no pack drill?"

"That's about it. . . ."

Glastonbury signed the report at last and handed the pen to Detterling, who signed in his turn. Glastonbury then piled all the sheets together and worked carefully at them with his two middle fingers until they were absolutely flush.

"You'd better show this to your two chums," he said, rapping the neat pile. "You'll all three have to countersign it. And then you'd better spruce yourselves up and get out your best uniforms."

Peter gave him a puzzled look.

"In order that there should be general recognition," Glastonbury said, "of your timely action in apprehending the rebel leader, and of your steady performance of duty in the very difficult circumstances thereafter, you are each to receive a scroll of commendation from the Viceroy. I shall have to telephone Delhi for final confirmation first, but I've no doubt . . . none at all, Morrison . . . that it will be forthcoming. The scrolls will be publicly presented to you by myself at a parade of your Battalion – such of it, that is, as is still fit to be mustered. We do not intend to make much noise by the presentation : just enough to make it absolutely clear to everybody concerned that your honourable and resourceful behaviour was in no way compromised by the death of Gilzai Khan, any attributable blame for which is solely his own."

Peter stood quite still, looking at the sheaf of paper which Glastonbury was now holding out to him.

"Don't stand there like an imbecile," Glastonbury said. "Take this Report off to Strange and Mortleman, and tell them to get their servants busy on their kit. I'm now going to telephone Delhi to assure them that everything's *thik hai*" – he rose from his seat and stretched languorously – "and then I shall arrange with your C.O. for the presentation parade to take place this afternoon."

"God, I feel horrible," Barry said, after Alister and he had read the Report of the Enquiry.

"It wasn't your fault," said Alister. "Glastonbury's made that clear enough. It was an accident."

"That's all whitewashing. Because they're glad he's dead and the riots have fizzled out."

"Not whitewashing," Peter said. "They're just . . . putting it all in the correct official perspective, so that no one can be got at later on."

"Same thing. Whitewashing."

"Look, Barrikins," said Alister: "the one thing they've established beyond any doubt at all is that we were not responsible for the Khan's death. There *is* nothing to whitewash."

"They're glad he's dead. So they don't care whether we're responsible or not, but they want it to look good on paper. Then no one can make trouble for Delhi or the Government in the House of Commons. Those scrolls they're going to give us – they're about as genuine as a three-pound note."

"That just isn't true," Peter said. "We're being commended for what we did *before* the Khan was killed. They're saying to us that we did exactly what we should have done in very tricky conditions, and it's not our fault that Gil' Khan got killed at the end of it."

"But all the same they're jolly pleased he's dead. Don't tell me that these . . . commendations . . . haven't got something to do with their satisfaction at his death. Some of that satisfaction has got into their feelings about us."

"Even if that's true," said Alister, "we're not to blame for it. Why can't you just accept the facts? The Khan's death was an accident. You were quite right to try and stop him when he was escaping, but you didn't mean to kill him, and you couldn't have killed him even if you had meant to – had it not been for a chance of one in a thousand."

"How can you know what I did mean or didn't?"

"All right," said Alister crossly : "do you want me to go and tell Glastonbury that you meant to kill the Khan after all and ought to be charged with murder?"

Barry bit his lip till the blood came.

"It's not as simple as that," he said; "and I don't suppose I could have meant to, not really. But what makes me feel so rotten is all this pretence, all this business of scrolls and parades and speeches. Whatever you say, it's a kind of celebration. Why can't they just shut up and leave it at that?"

"Because," said Peter, "they've got to put their message over, for their sake and for ours – particularly yours. They're not celebrating the Khan's death; they're disowning it. What they're saying is this : we grant that a lot of good has come of this death, which has therefore been very convenient for us, *but*, they're saying, we insist that no one in the Army, near or far, was responsible for it. They're commending us in order to assure everyone that we were absolutely above-board all through and *didn't* kill Gilzai Khan."

"Except that we did. Or at least I did."

"Not *culpably*. That's the point they want to make."

"Then they're protesting too much," Barry said. "Why can't they just keep quiet?"

"Because they want to create an atmosphere of normality, of routine. You can't do that by keeping quiet. Normality requires that people who behaved as we did—"

"—As they like to think we did—"

"—*That people who capture rebel leaders* should be mildly commended for their services. So that's just what is being done. A small parade, nothing out of the way, but just noticeable and probably recorded in two lines at the bottom of a column in the *Telegraph*. A small parade, I say, and three scrolls of fake parchment, and a few words from the Viceroy's representative. Just what everyone would expect after a decent sort of show. Entirely suitable – and therefore entirely forgettable. That's what they want, Barry, and that's how it will turn out: the whole thing will be forgotten by most people within ten days."

"Not by me, it won't," Barry said.

". . . And furthermore," said Colonel Glastonbury to the assembled Battalion (of which about half, in the event, had been fit for parade), "I know that His Excellency would wish me to add this: that another reason why the conduct of these Officers is felt to be truly commendable is that it was based upon consideration, upon good manners. Consideration for their own soldiers, consideration for their opponent – even though they were bound to restrain him. Gentlemen of the Wessex Fusiliers, next to duty it is courtesy that we are rewarding this afternoon."

Alister, Barry and Peter stepped forward, in reverse order of seniority, to receive their handshakes and their scrolls. As Glastonbury handed his to Peter, it started to rain again, and under cover of this Captain Detterling (who was a yard behind

Glastonbury and a yard to his right) just perceptibly winked. Only for a split second, and his face, both before and after, was as heavy and blank as a tomb : but during that split second the serene surface of things was rent by Detterling's wink, and through the crack which opened the devil smiled out at Peter in joyless amusement at the joke.

Nobody else much smiled that afternoon, except Colonel Brockworthy, who was pleased that the disagreeable duties connected with the riot were now over, and that credit (albeit of a kind he himself valued little if at all) seemed somehow to have accrued to the Regiment. Most officers, being wet through and somewhat puzzled by the whole affair, simply looked cross and slunk off to change as soon as possible. Even the three who had just been distinguished seemed to think that modesty (or discretion) required them to stay out of the way; so that very soon after the parade was over only Glastonbury, Detterling, Colonel Brockworthy and Thomas Oake were left in the Mess. After a very long silence, Tom Oake looked into his whisky and said :

"Too many lies. There's something fishy in all this."

"They rather like the smell in Delhi," said Detterling lightly. "I'd remember that if I were you. Anyway, what lies?"

"About Mortleman, for example. He shouldn't have been there."

"That was all explained," said Glastonbury : "Mortleman and Strange came to be with their men."

"I wasn't told at the time that Strange was there at all. And as for Mortleman, Morrison said he was going straight back – in the C.O.'s car, of all things."

"I expect," said Detterling, "that Morrison had a lot to think about. His immediate concern, remember, was to fetch Mortleman to help guard Gilzai Khan. He had no time to lose, so he probably told you the first thing that came into his head."

"He could just as well have told me the truth and fetched *me* to Gilzai Khan. That's what he should have done."

"That," said Glastonbury, "is a tricky area, I admit, but it's covered by the Old Chums Act."

"Old Chums Act?"

"Gilzai Khan had been their commander and their friend. They wanted to sort it all out themselves if they could."

"Their duty was nonetheless plain. And there are a lot of other things which don't add up. What do you say, sir?" he said to his C.O.

Colonel Brockworthy pondered.

"I say," he said at last, "that when you have bloody things like riot duty there's no good in stirring up trouble afterwards. Riot duty isn't proper soldiering; you must expect peculiar things to happen – and then do your best to forget about 'em. They don't really count."

"A very sensible attitude," said Glastonbury. "Of course there are a few inconsistencies here. There always are on these occasions. But if," he said to Tom Oake, "you had anything of importance to raise, you should have done so before the presentation parade."

"How could I? You never even called me as witness at your Enquiry."

"Because you couldn't possibly have had anything relevant to say, my dear fellow. You were stuck behind that gate the whole time."

Tom Oake took a swig at his drink.

"Then allow me to say something that is relevant now, Colonel Glastonbury. When you telephoned Delhi before luncheon . . . to ask them to confirm that you could hand out those bits of cardboard . . . you didn't get through. The wires have been down for the last twelve hours. And yet you went ahead with the presentation."

"During the Monsoons," said Colonel Glastonbury, very patiently, "telephone wires are coming down all the time. This being so, a man of foresight always obtains provisional instructions, in case. Mine were quite clear. I was to use my judgment in the matter – a judgment in which those about the Viceroy were sufficiently confident to advise His Excellency to sign those scrolls before I left. I was given permission, in case of losing contact with Delhi, to award them or withhold them, as I saw fit."

"So much the worse for you," snarled Oake, "if your judgment turns out to have been at fault."

"Come, come, Oake," said the C.O.

"So much the worse for nobody," Detterling said. "The whole thing's over, man. Don't you know what those scrolls mean? They mean that the Viceroy, and therefore the King Emperor whom he represents, considers that those three boys behaved in a praiseworthy and honourable fashion. The *King* has said that this is so, and if the King says it, it is so. If the King ennobles a man, that man is noble, no matter what the shifts which procured him his patent. If the King has honoured three of your Officers, then they are honourable, and it ill becomes you, who carry the King's commission, to say else."

"I suppose that's true," said the C.O. wearily; "in the context," he added, and looked at Tom Oake guiltily, as though he were somehow letting down the Regiment by using such a sophisticated phrase.

"You'll excuse me, sir," said Tom to Brockworthy alone, and walked stiffly out.

"The poor fellow can't understand," said Detterling, "that this is the only way of making a hopeless situation at all tolerable."

"I don't quite follow," the C.O. said.

"We are soon to leave India," Glastonbury told him, "in circumstances of confusion and disrepute. It's a bad thing, Colonel, and it entails every kind of treachery and deceit, daily and at all levels. The formula which we have devised, and used successfully here, ensures that at least *some* semblance of order and of honour is retained."

"There has been deceit here?" said the bewildered Brockworthy.

"I'm not saying that. I'm saying that if there had been, then here as elsewhere our formula would guarantee ... an impression of seemliness."

"I see," said the C.O. at long last. "Correct me if I am wrong, but I don't think this formula of yours is altogether new."

"Far from it. We have merely adapted it to the time and the place. We use it to save face, Colonel, to keep things ticking over . . . and to protect men who can't really help what they do."

"My three Officers?"

"One of them, perhaps," said Captain Detterling, and shrugged. "Never mind which. For whichever it may or may not be, he's not to blame. He's not so much a fraud as a victim – a victim of the Necessity of the times through which we are passing."

"All that's a bit beyond me," the C.O. said. "But mum's the word, if I hear you right. I'll see you to say good-bye before you go back to Delhi. But just now I think I've got this diarrhoea coming on."

Colonel Brockworthy wandered lugubriously out. Colonel Glastonbury faced Captain Detterling.

"Promising fellow, Morrison," said Glastonbury. "I'm glad he's had a pat on the back."

"It couldn't happen to a more suitable chap. Just where it's wanted. From now on the upper class is going to need all the heroes it can get."

"Or fabricate. Not that we've quite made a hero of Morrison."

"No," conceded Detterling, "and a good job we haven't. We don't want to overdo it. But a Viceroy's commendation is the sort of thing that can tip the scales heavily in a man's favour, if it's used in the right way, and so it could help him a lot later on."

"In what?"

"Oh, I don't know. But he's the kind of man who might become prominent in something. Those other two will never get anywhere, they've not got the right stuff in them – not enough shit. But Peter Morrison – he's full of it."

"I thought Morrison was quite decent," Glastonbury said, "as people go."

"Oh, he likes to do the right thing . . . to be seen to do the right thing, and even to believe it himself, if he possibly can. But he's got a lot of shit in his tanks – else he'd never have come through all this in one piece."

"I suppose you're right," said Glastonbury. "But I'm not sure we want chaps like him becoming prominent. I mean, could you trust in him, knowing what you know? If you met him in the City, say, or in Parliament?"

"*Vanitas vanitatum*," said Captain Detterling, "*omnia vanitas*. I don't trust in anybody, myself. But at least Peter Morrison knows what to wear and what noises to make, which is something to be thankful for, I suppose."